Sweet Nothings

AND OTHER CONFECTIONS

Sula Sullivan

Content/Trigger Warning

At its core, *Sweet Nothings and Other Confections* is a cozy, sweet, and lighthearted novel. Still, it does touch on serious topics such as food neutrality/eating habits and agoraphobia, as well as including vivid descriptions of anxiety and chronic illness. There are also brief mentions of blood. Take care of yourself, dear reader.

This is a work of fiction. Names, characters, places, and incidents either are the product of the author's imagination or are used fictitiously. Any resemblance to actual persons, living or dead, events, or locales is entirely coincidental.

First ebook edition June 2023

Cover by Alenna Rucoba

ISBN 979-8-9860244-7-9 (Paperback)

Eating is so intimate. It's very sensual.
When you invite someone to sit at your table, and you want to cook for them, you're inviting a person into your life.
-Maya Angelou

To the one who nourishes my soul

.

Part One

A Lesson in Jumping from the Pan to the Fire

*L*ucille Waters forgot to whisper. "I'm offended that the cooks don't simply poison us. The rats at least get high-quality arsenic," she said loudly.

A stifled laugh rippled through the dining hall, echoing endlessly as the sound bounced from floor to ceiling in the large chamber. Lucille clamped her hand over her mouth, but it was too late. The clicks of the headmistress's heels were already reverberating through the cold stone room as she was making her way over to the "undignified" disturbance. The headmistress was a short, severe-looking woman who was never seen without her black heels on. Her hair was radiating around her head in a perfectly shaped afro, bobbing slightly as she strode across the floor. Both her hair and heels accomplished their intended effect of adding height and giving her more presence. A presence that Lucille wished was anywhere but here.

Lucille shot a glance at her dear friend Kenna, who looked almost as horrified as Lucille. She took one more glance at her food (meat and potatoes that had been boiled and brined for so long that they had lost all sense of color) before she felt herself being dragged up by her ear.

"Excuse me, stop accosting me! I have not finished my dinner! Have you no decorum? No decency?" Lucille shrieked in an attempt to lessen the pain stabbing through her ear.

"I'll have oatmeal brought to your room," the headmistress replied as she shooed Lucille towards the doors at the far end of the hall.

Fantastic: she had talked her way out of brined potatoes and into brined oatmeal.

Lucille quickly made her way from the dining hall and up the stairs to her room. As she got to her door, she saw that her oatmeal was already waiting for her on an ornate gold platter as if it were a delicacy prepared for the Queen.

Lucille picked up the tray and balanced it on her hip as she opened her door. The room that she and Kenna shared was modest, containing only a set of beds, desks, and a single shared armoire. As future teachers and governesses, they were expected to live simply and put the teaching of their charges above all else. She crossed the room and sat dejectedly at her desk, balancing her weight carefully as the construction of their chairs left much to be desired.

Lucille stared at the gelatinous blob of grains quivering in its tin bowl. With a shudder, she tried to dip into it with her spoon, but it promptly bounced back.

As Lucille started to place her bowl on her desk, the door to her room creaked open.

"Don't worry, I haven't finished it yet," she said, not bothering to turn around.

"Thank goodness, we'll toss it," Kenna said with a giggle. "I have a bit of food for you if you're interested," Kenna added slyly.

Lucille twirled around. "How'd you manage that?"

"The staff is dealing with a small kitchen fire."

"How fortuitous."

"Quite," Kenna said with a smirk. "I swiped your mail before it was sorted too."

"Oh, where is it?"

"In my under pocket, but first, you need to eat." Kenna held out a bundle tied with a red and white striped handkerchief.

"Oh, this smells like heaven."

"Bread." Kenna wiggled her fingers dramatically. "And bacon."

Lucille took a few bites of the bread and then hesitated. "Did you eat?"

Kenna nodded and pulled a bruised apple from her pocket. "I swiped this too."

Kenna's resourcefulness never ceased to amaze Lucille. Both girls look similar in their averageness: medium brown skin, medium build, and their dark kinky hair was almost always braided down in straight backs. The only difference was that Kenna was always eager to flash a smile and wiggle her ears playfully. Lucille was always serious; more often than not, her face was contorted into some pensive expression.

Their room was so small that Lucille had to tuck her legs under herself on the bed before Kenna could crawl under the frame to put the apple in her secret hiding place.

The sun was doing its very best to push its way through the hazy window into their room. Lucille groaned, struggling to shake off the last bits of sleepiness as she and Kenna began packing their goods for selling at the market. It was absurdly early, but it was one of the few ways they could make money. Neither girl had bothered lighting a tallow candle and instead moved in the shadowy semi-darkness. The cheap candles always made the room smell of mutton, and they hopefully would not be in the room long. Lucille shivered, wrapping her thin woolen cloak around her shoulders. In its past life, it had been a large throw, but one of the other girls had refashioned it into a garment.

"Is this all that we need?" Kenna said, pointing to the jars lined up on the scratched dresser. Lucille watched her point to each jar and silently mouth the numbers.

"I believe so," Lucille said, then she wrapped up the last few tins that were sitting out, carefully tucking them in holey hand-kerchiefs and putting them in her wicker basket. Neither girl was fond of gardening nor mixing tinctures, balms, salves, or oils. It was messy hot work, but they made fair wages.

"Thank you for assisting me," Lucille said as she did every Saturday. She was certain there were a thousand other things Kenna would prefer to do than wake up at dawn and tend to Lucille's stall.

"Oh, stop," Kenna said, waving her hand. "I really haven't got anything else to do." She batted her eyes dramatically. "Perhaps I will catch the eye of a handsome clergyman."

"You can have the one my parents have their eye on," Lucille responded.

"Is he handsome?" Kenna said, pretending to swoon.

"Hardly," Lucille said.

"Rich?"

Lucille shook her head from side to side. "Apparently not."

Kenna tied her shawl. "You may keep him, my dear."

To Lucille's surprise, the market hadn't filled up yet. The cold must have discouraged those with warm beds from staying in them. Linking their arms together, Lucille and Kenna navigated through the nearly empty cobblestone streets and found their favorite tea cart easily.

"Kenna, Lucille," Stevie said, already pouring tea from the large cans.

In addition to being a world-class gossip, she also only charged them for half a mug each.

"We'll take three ham sandwiches and two boiled eggs," Lucille said, passing over the notes. She added, "Keep the rest," although it was unnecessary as they had the same routine every week.

They nibbled on their food as they walked to their stall. It seemed as if they had just finished arranging their wares when the throngs of crowds came swarming towards them. Apparently, everyone in the city had woken up at the same time.

"Was there anything interesting in the post?" Kenna asked as she made change for a customer.

"Not particularly," Lucille said, pushing some jars forward to fill the empty spaces. "I believe we need to make more rosehip oil for next week."

"Hmm," Kenna said, eyeing her warily.

"Do you have the butter with the sand?" A woman asked, peering over the table to the empty baskets.

"It's a walnut and salt exfoliator," Kenna said sweetly. "I saved a tin for you."

Once the woman had left with her purchase, Kenna turned back towards Lucille. "Are you certain there's no news? That was an awful lot of notes for—"

"I need a tincture for dry elbows." A gentleman interrupted.

"Alright, roll up your sleeve," Lucille said. She looked at the scales that covered the man's inner elbow. "This balm is what you need." Another rush was coming, she realized, looking at the crowd forming outside the stall. Thank goodness.

When there was finally a lull, Kenna looked as if she might say something more about the letters.

"I'll return the mugs to Stevie. She'll need them for the fishermen. Would you like another?"

"No, I-" Kenna started but Lucille was already halfway down the alley and didn't bother turning back to see what she was going to say.

Lucille took a long time walking towards Stevie's cart. The letters had been a struggle to read, and she did not want to speak their contents out loud, or it would be true. She had been rejected from nearly all the art schools she had applied to, save for the one that was hopelessly expensive. Her parent's letters were the usual creative mix of berating and cold. However, this last batch of letters was more direct than any of the previous sets. Her mother's bold, sweeping script clearly outlined that her options were to marry a clergyman or become a lady's companion for their Aunt Matilda, who lived on the continent. As if it had been an afterthought, another option had been squeezed in: becoming a governess. In the three years she had been studying at Brittlebone, it had never occurred to Lucille that she would actually become a governess. She had always imagined the Brittlebone School for Professional Ladies as more of a threat, a cheap place to stay, and a steppingstone to whatever her true destiny was. Now, each day it seemed more and more likely that the school would serve a more literal purpose in her life. She had trained to be a governess, and now it seemed as though she would become a governess. The best she could hope for was a decent post.

"Lucille!" Stevie yelled.

Lucille spun around. "Oh, I forgot myself," she called back; she had overshot Stevie's cart by several feet.

"Here are your mugs."

"Are you alright, dear?" Stevie said. Lucille could tell she was searching her face.

"Ah yes, I was simply lost in thought."

"Mmm," Stevie said, but it sounded as if she did not believe her. "Well, if you need to lay your burdens down, have a chat with Kenna or me."

Lucille nodded.

"Here," Stevie said, taking the mugs out of her hands and filling them with cocoa. "Alright, take this. It'll make you feel better."

Lucille nodded, scrunching her nose and breathing in the rich chocolate smell. "Thank you so much."

Lucille awoke to Kenna swatting her face. "Up, up, up." She blinked several times; it took her eyes several moments to adjust. How early was it? They didn't have a stall at the market this Sunday. Or did they?

"Come, we're going to church," Kenna said.

"Which church?" Lucille asked groggily. She sat up and stretched.

"Mulvaney Square."

"There's no chapel at Mulvaney Square." Lucille yawned and swung her legs over the side of the bed.

"Is there not? We'll say a prayer and pass a nun or two. Practically a full service." Kenna said with a shrug.

"The square is so far." Lucille groaned. "And we must clean." Luckily, their bare little room hardly took any time to clean. Lucille wiped down their trunks and straightened their few knickknacks while Kenna turned down the beds and swept up the floor. Despite Kenna being terribly excited, Lucille took the time to do her makeup. It was not in regulation for the Brittlebone dress code, so she could only apply it on the weekends. She applied rouge to her cheeks and nose with a heavy hand.

"You want a swipe of this miraculous Mahogany Powder?" Kenna asked.

"Just a bit," Lucille said. She did want to try it, but she knew it was terribly expensive.

"Fabulous, you look fabulous! Now let us go!" Kenna said playfully, stomping her foot.

Lucille pretended to cough. "You're kicking up dust since you did such a poor job sweeping."

"Shall we hire a carriage?" Kenna said once they were outside.

"Mmhm, I think we'll be fine to walk," Lucille answered, peering up into the white clouds. It was a rather dreary, damp day. Thick humidity that hung in the air but there were no rain drops yet.

Kenna nodded, rearranging her thin cloak around her shoulders. Unlike most of the girls who attended their school, Kenna and Lucille did not receive even a minor allowance. While the school provided the barest of necessities, any of their other wants or needs had to be eked out of the small proceeds they gained from selling herbal remedies. Lucille hummed as she walked, looking at the various shops as they walked. She avoided looking at Kenna, but by the time they had reached Mulvaney Square, she was running out of songs to hum.

"Now that your little concert is over, would you like to tell me what the letters told you? I would have read them myself, but you burned them."

"I did not; I hid them in-" Lucille clamped her gloved hand over her mouth. "Oh, Kenna, you tricky fox."

Kenna giggled. "You'll tell me after we get a treat or two."

There were several fancy carts hawking their wares, but they would wait until they made it to the less fashionable part of town. Lucille tried to think of something to distract the conversation. "Ah, I believe The Pebble and Fig has new signage."

"Do you wager it's made of solid gold?" Kenna said, wiggling her eyebrows.

The Pebble and Fig was the most exclusive confectionery shop in the entire city. Even its sign was elaborate, it featured a brightly painted fig next to a gemstone. The body of the sign was covered in elaborate scroll work and the sign was attached to the building with a brass pole and gold chains. While they had never actually gone in, she and Kenna admired the sweets through the windows. The shop windows were painted with simple sketches of the desserts one could purchase inside. Lucille and Kenna stopped for a moment to watch the waiters dart out of the shop to deliver sweets to the ornate gilded carriages of the city's wealthiest and most famous residents.

"Do you think we'll ever be able to afford treats and a seat?" Kenna asked.

"Perhaps, or we shall be so wealthy we won't be bothered to enter the shop," Lucille said, swishing her cloak dramatically. "We will wait in our carriage and have them send a translocation attendant."

"Yes!" Kenna said, playing along. "We are far too fancy to have our ices melt!"

They sat on a bench and watched the fashionable ladies walk by as the carriages slowly rolled through the crowded square.

"Would you like to speak on what your parents wrote?" Kenna asked, scooting a little closer.

"I was promised a refreshment," Lucille said, trying to keep her tone even.

"Oh! Oh!" Kenna said, clutching at her arm. Lucille followed her gaze. One of the non-magical attendants was weaving through the crowds with a massive tray full of jellies that were quivering violently. Lucille breathed a sigh of relief when he reached the row of carriages he was delivering to.

"Let us go before we witness a tragedy," Lucille said. They made their way through the courtyard until the streets became narrow, the buildings less grand, and the faces in the crowd more familiar. Lucille felt less embarrassed in her simple dress. This part of the city was loud in its vibrancy, the happy yells and laughs roaring in her ears, a sharp contrast to the soft buzzing of Mulvaney Square.

"Shall we start with flat beans?" Kenna asked, nodding towards one of their favorite kiosks.

"Mhmm, yes," Lucille said. Flat beans were a simple dish, but Lucille was fond of the fried mashed fava bean patties. They paid the vendor, and then Lucille tucked into the treat, which was served on a warm roll. The patty was crispy on the outside, and she practically moaned when the crunchy outer skin cracked, and she bit into the soft insides.

"Would you like some sauce?" Kenna asked, holding up the little dish.

"Mmmh," Lucille said, her mouth full. She savored another bite full of potato, garlic, onion, and cumin.

"Slow down," Kenna said, dipping hers in the sauce.

After they returned the dish, they walked a ways. "Oooh," Kenna said, running her hands through a display of hanging waist beads. The strings of colorful glass beads sparkled even though there were precious few rays of sunshine breaking through the clouds and into the crowded market.

"These are lovely," Kenna said wistfully.

"I have woven options." The artisan said, his voice tinged with pity.

"Let us see those," Kenna said before Lucille could protest.

21

The artisan pulled out a tray of daintily woven bracelets; each had a small bead sewn onto the threads.

"Oh, these are darling," Lucille said, forgetting the unspoken rule of not revealing your excitement to the seller.

"They're two jingles a piece." The man said.

"And those?" Kenna said, pointing to another tray full of knotted cord bracelets. At the center of each one was a ring, and the cord was attached on either side, making a continuous loop.

"Ah, this is stunning, a work of art," Kenna said.

Lucille eyed her with surprise; Kenna was even more streetwise than herself.

"These are five jingles." The man said evenly.

Lucille and Kenna exchanged glances. "Are they stolen?"

The artisan chuckled and held up a bracelet. "No, if you look closely, they're made of imperfect signet rings purchased at a discount."

"Off the dead?" Kenna said flatly.

"Uh, well. Not always." The man said, his demeanor finally cracking.

"Alright, we'll take this one," Kenna said, holding up a bracelet with a gold band and a dark brown cord. "I'll give you two jingles."

"Four." He replied firmly.

"Three, and we tell all the girls at school where we got it."

"Deal," The man said.

As they walked away, Lucille giggled.

"Here," Kenna said, slipping it onto Lucille's hand and up her wrist. She tugged on the knot. "Perfection."

"Oh no, I don't need this." Lucille protested.

"You do; you need some goodness," Kenna said as she began dragging Lucille back towards the food stands.

Lucille examined her new bracelet; it had a delicate "F" engraved on it and a small starburst that contained a diamond chip at its center.

"Let's get some fried plantains and–" Kenna spun around. "Hmm, stuffed pastries. We'll take them back to the square."

Lucille was more excited about the stuffed pastries than the fried plantains. The school served plantains at least thrice a week, and although the ones purchased at the market were more flavorful, she was still often tired of the dish. This time, Lucille ate her snack very slowly. The triangular pocket was full of tuna, raw egg, herbs, and olives. The soft filling perfectly contrasted the pastry's flaky yet crispy skin. Hers had been fried a touch too long, but she was still grateful.

"Now that I've bribed you, will you discuss what your parents wrote?" Kenna asked, lowering her voice as they reentered Mulvaney Square.

"The usual. Upon graduation, I must marry or find gainful employment." Lucille said slowly.

"What of your art?" Kenna said hopefully.

Instead of answering, Lucille just shook her head ever so slightly. "Mhmhm."

"Oooh," Kenna said, wrapping her arm around Lucille's shoulder and giving her a gentle squeeze. "I am so very sorry. But we'll find a way."

"Let us not sulk," Lucille said. "Do you see that woman's bonnet? I believe those are the loveliest feathers I've ever seen."

"It's getting late," Kenna said wistfully. It seemed as if their people-watching and chatting lasted only a few moments, but in truth, it had been hours, and it was going to be dark soon.

"Yes." Lucille sighed.

The crowd was beginning to thin. "We haven't got much left, but we could get some eel jelly for dinner."

"Ah, I assure you that would be better than whatever sludge they're serving in the hall," Lucille said.

They made their way back towards Brittlebone, passing the little boy on the counter, flapping broadsheets.

"I'll give you a coin if you give me the highlights," Lucille said teasingly.

"The Fondants have purchased more real estate in the city. Word is they'll be in the city full time. One of the Carson daughters was seen unattended, taking the air with a strange gentleman. A certain rake was seen at the Broken Tusk gambling den and is reported to have lost a great deal of money…" The boy took a deep breath. "And lastly, the engagement of Paula Elizabethson and Laura Word has been broken. No word at which party is at fault."

"Thank you," Lucille said with mock solemnity. "Here ya go." She said, tossing him the coin.

"Ooh, do you think we'll get a glimpse of the handsome Lord Fondant?" Kenna asked.

"I think not," Lucille said, laughing. "You're so dramatic. Have you seen anyone in their family out and about?"

"Well, no," Kenna said, thinking it over. "But we're not exactly out and about in society. You know Artemis?"

Kenna thought for a moment, then a vague picture of a short girl with a small button nose and fluffy curls formed in her mind. "The first year, who does the pretty lace?"

"Yes, her father is the clergyman in the village where the Fondants live. Their country estate is Sugarlump Manor."

Lucille stopped to adjust her slipper. "Where is that? I haven't had a geography lesson in years."

"Is it outside of Albertson?"

"Alright," Lucille said, peering down the street at the cluster of people that signified the eel jelly stall.

"Artemis says she's never seen any of them."

"Odd," Lucille said simply, her mind wandering to the stack of rejections hidden in the false bottom of her desk drawer.

"You know what that means?"

"Uh-huh." She responded absentmindedly.

"They must be magical, with the power of invisibility."

"Hmm. Perhaps they are simply private, or they stay in the city without making announcements."

"Ah, you are so clever!" Kenna said. "You will make a high society lady one day."

"You before me, my dear," Lucille said.

"Nah." she said as they stopped at the edge of the throng of people. "I believe my chance at love has passed."

"Miss Hopeless Romantic has given up on love?"

Before Kenna could respond, the eel jelly lady called out. "If you're not payin' or returnin' ya dishes, move!" The crowd began to shuffle away, and Kenna pushed her way to the front, dragging Lucille behind her.

"Two jelly eel and a pint of pea soup." She said cheerfully. The seller had a big smile and an even bigger bosom. "Coming right up." She said, ladling the food into the dishes. Behind her, her husband and daughter scrubbed up cups and spoons.

"Tell the family we say hello," Lucille said, depositing the coins in her hand. Just as quickly as they landed in the eel jelly lady's palm, they disappeared.

After they received their food, they took a step back, and the girls peered into the cups. "I swear it used to be a coin for all this," Lucille said.

"Agreed," Kenna said as they tucked into the food. They ate in silence, scooping the salty, gelatinous mixture into their mouths. This stall had the best by far; chopped eels in fish stock seemed like a simple enough dish, but the herbs and spices she used were otherworldly. Once or twice, they had even bought from another seller to compare. They returned to their own seller since the eel jelly was hotter, and they got more pieces.

"You wanna lick the pea soup bowl?" Kenna said, holding it out.

"No, it's your turn."

Kenna slurped the rest of the liquid from the cup and then gathered up their dishware to return.

"Let us hurry. It's nearly curfew."

Another slow, gray and depressing week had nearly gone by when Lucille had what was either a brilliant or terrible idea. She would need Kenna's help deciding so after their advanced penmanship lesson, Lucille dragged Kenna to their room.

"I have a plan!" Lucille said loudly.

"Shhh," Kenna said, glancing towards the door. "Hush now, or everyone will have a plan. What is it?"

Lucille took a deep breath. "I have decided to apply to more master artists and schools."

"How wonderful," Kenna said, clapping her hands softly.

"But this requires more time..."

"Hmm?" Kenna said, her face awash with confusion. "Well, yes, I hadn't thought of that. You'll need a posting by graduation which is only a few months' time…and your parents want an answer now…."

"Yes, and they shall have it. We will give them one. We will tell them I am betrothed to Lord Fondant."

"Oh, won't they find that odd?" Kenna said, any excitement she had shone was clearly waning. Lucille held up her hand. "I can explain."

Lucille sat down on her bed which groaned under her weight. "We hardly speak. They sent me off to this godforsaken school where I only have one companion."

"You say only as if I am not delightful!" Kenna said in mock indignation.

"You are of course, what I mean to say is that they know nothing of me, nor do they care. Now, I must write carefully so it sounds believable," Lucille said, gathering her writing utensils from her case. She flipped over some of her class notes and began to write her first draft.

"Dearest Father and Mother, I fear…." Lucille said carefully.

"Regret." Kenna said, sighing and sitting beside her.

"I regret to inform-" Lucille said, nodding.

"Wait, no. Let us sound more persuasive. Sound confident. Excited." Kenna said slowly.

"Of course. How does this sound? 'Dearest Father and Mother, I am excited to tell you of my engagement to Lord Fondant. While our courtship was unconventional due to Lord Fondant's reclusive nature."

"Reclusive nature or reclusivity?

"Is reclusivity a word?"

"It sounds as if it should be."

"I hope your hands are not idle, ladies." The school Marm popped her head in the doorway.

"Of course not; we are writing to our families and discussing grammatics," Kenna said with a smile.

"Lovely." the marm said, disappearing.

Lucille tried to focus on her lessons over the next few weeks but it was terribly difficult. Out of the classroom window, a tree was bending concerningly in the wind.

"Miss Waters!" Mrs. Anderson's baritone rang out. She was a short, slight woman with a nasally voice and a face that was quick to pucker, especially in Lucille's direction.

Lucille dragged her eyes away from the window. "Yes, ma'am."

"We are discussing the best way to disseminate information to a pupil."

"Clear instruction followed by demonstration and allowing them to present it back to you?" Lucille said carefully.

"Yes!" Mrs. Anderson said, barely bothering to hide her surprise.

Her deskmate, Cathleen, whispered. "Obviously, you know nothing of how to be a proper pupil."

"Clearly, you know nothing of shutting your stupid face, you blowzabella." Lucille hissed back a little too loudly.

"Miss Waters, proper language!" Mrs. Anderson said desperately, trying to contain a laugh.

"My apologies to the class, Mrs. Anderson," Lucille said quickly.

"What of my apology?" Cathleen said with a tone of indignation.

"You are wholly undeserving; consider yourself fortunate that was all I said."

Cathleen glared at her. "Lucille, where did this sudden boldness appear? I am unaccustomed to you showing even an inkling of personality. You're too busy cowering behind your little wife."

"You're too dense to even form a proper insult. If you would like me to pass along your regards to Kenna, you could have asked. Being a scrub is not the way to go about courting someone."

"Lucille! Cathleen! That is enough," Mrs. Anderson said. "Lucille, why don't you take some air?"

Lucille gathered up her supplies. "Gladly."

"Why am I not allowed to take air?" Cathleen whined.

The class, who had, up until this point, managed to keep their wits together, burst into an uproar of laughter.

"You could take air if you simply closed your mouth and inhaled through your nose," Lucille said as she walked out of the door.

She stopped by her room to set down her primer, pin up her skirt and tie on an apron. Then she made her way to the garden. Lucille took her time clipping the herbs she needed for this week's batch of balms and butters. They were only allowed to use the kitchen one night a week, so she tried to do as much preparation ahead of time.

When she returned to the room with her basket apron full of herbs, Kenna was sitting on the bed, an unfolded letter in her lap. She sat down in the chair and began tying the herbs in bundles. Lucille had made it through two before Lucille spoke.

"You've certainly done yourself in this time. I fear we've been too creative." Kenna said in a horrified whisper.

The realization dawned on Lucille. "You opened my letter!"

"Well, yes,"

"And read it?" Lucille said, putting down the bundle she was knotting.

"No, I opened it and used it as a fan!" Kenna said, rolling her eyes. "Your parents seem rather skeptical but wish to make his acquaintance."

"Oh, my goddesses. They want to make his acquaintance?"

"Are you surprised?"

"They've never shown any interest in my life thus far."

"You never gave them a reason to believe you'd provide them with a windfall."

"Oooh, they want to hobnob. This won't do." Lucille said. "They're on a tour. Perhaps I'll be lucky, and you can orchestrate a heartbreak."

Kenna winced. "That won't do. They have already planned a detour."

"Oh," Lucille said with a sigh.

"Chin up; we'll figure it out. We always do." Kenna said.

"Here's what we'll do," Kenna said after a moment.

"Dry the herbs?"

"No," Kenna said, grabbing Lucille's wrist. "We'll send them this!"

"Huh?" Lucille asked.

"Your bracelet, made from the signet."

"Oh, they'll pawn it in an instant," Lucille said, a brief flicker of concern running through her.

"Perfect, so that they won't examine it too closely," Kenna said with a clap. "We'll get you another."

Kenna reached past her to take a bundle of rosemary, and she began to bind it.

Lucille lay in bed, stomach grumbling, debating on whether to dip into their stash of dried meats and crackers. In the hazy almost sleep, an idea began to form in her mind. Perhaps, I could go to Albertson, I've been once before. I was young, but a village is a village. I could convince old Lord Fondant to help me. Gentlemen are required to help ladies. What is the worst that could happen? She could always come back and be in the same spot as before.

"Ken, Ken…" Lucille hissed into the darkness.

"Yes, I'm starving as well," Kenna said softly, her voice husky with sleep.

"No, well yes, no, I'm hungry as well. I need your help getting to the station." Lucille whispered. She waited for a barrage of questions, but there was none.

"I wish to go to Albertson. To speak with Lord Fondant."

"Oh."

"What is it?" Lucille asked.

"Oh, nothing," Kenna said. "I thought you were rushing off to the art academy to convince them, but this sounds like a much more striking adventure."

"Based on my feedback, I believe this is a more worthwhile endeavor." It took Lucille a few more moments to realize that if Kenna knew about the art academy rejections, she had been reading her mail.

"You read my letters!" Lucille exclaimed loudly.

"Shhh," Kenna said softly, but it was too late. The sound of heavy boots thumped down the hallway. After a moment, the door creaked open, and a lantern was thrust into the room. Lucille closed her eyes and went limp. Across the small room, Kenna snored very convincingly. After the door closed and the footsteps faded away, she heard her friend's mattress shift ever so slightly.

"Do you have the fare for the coach? I'll send for a ticket," Kenna said simply.

"I have a bit."

"Alright, I'll put what I have with what you have, and you should be able to get you there." Kenna said.

"Thank you, Kenna. I appreciate your help."

"Oh, shut up. Don't get sentimental." She said, tossing a pillow at her.

"I'm keeping this," Lucille said, putting the thin pillow on top of her nearly flat one.

"It'll take a day or so, but I'll post a letter saying I'm your sick aunt, and I sent for you and included a ticket."

"Brilliant." Kenna grumbled.

"Why do I feel as though you've lived a thousand secret lives," Lucille said, propping herself up on her elbow.

"Go to sleep, Lucille."

The next morning, Lucille resisted the urge to pack her things, but she pre-sorted everything, even making a list of things to leave behind so it seemed as if her packing was impromptu.

"Miss Waters." Mrs. Anderson said, appearing in the doorway, her nasally voice was uncharacteristically high.

"Yes, Mrs. Anderson?" Lucille said, placing her pencil down.

"Darling." Mrs. Anderson said, pulling her into a hug. "Your auntie Neisha is gravely ill. Don't panic, but she sent for you."

Lucille hugged her back, unsure how the gesture worked. Mrs. Anderson pulled away, and after a second, Lucille did as well.

"Oh, are you in shock?" Mrs. Anderson said, cupping her face.

"Uh, yes, I love my auntie." Lucille tried to remember the name Mrs. Anderson had just said.

"I'll send Kenna to pack your items. Speechless?" Mrs. Anderson said.

Lucille nodded and then slumped dramatically into the chair. Was this hair-brained scheme really going to work?

The answer to that was a resounding yes. In less than half an hour she was sitting at the station, with hopefully everything she owned in small packages beside her. Luckily, if Kenna had forgotten something, it couldn't have been anything of value as Lucille didn't own any such items. Lucille spun her bracelet around her wrist.

A carriage rolled to a stop in front of the platform "Coach to Albertson!" The driver called out.

Now, or now, she thought to herself. Uncertainty must certainly be better than the past.

The countryside slid past her like a green stroke of oil paint. The bunches of trees and scrub were sliding and blending into each other. If she stared too long, it made her dizzy. To her shock, the carriage was completely empty save for herself. But most of the high society folks were already in town for the season, and she imagined if one lived in Albertson, they were already there. She sketched absentmindedly in her book and tried to think of what she would say to Lord Fondant. She would have to be convincing. There was no other option. After a great long while, the carriage came to a jolting stop. After a moment, there was a thump on the roof. She swung the door open. Lucille took a step off the carriage and promptly fell flat on her face.

"You alright?" The driver called down to her.

"Yes, yes." She said hurriedly as most of the injury had occurred to her pride. She shook herself off. "Which way to Sugar Lump Manor?"

"Straight down the lane, through the square, and keep going straight. No turns."

As she made her way through the nearly deserted town. After what seemed like an hour of walking she reached a large, perfectly symmetrical manor. The stucco was a warm brown color, and the trim was pure white. She used a candy-shaped golden knocker to bang on the door several times.

After a long while, the door opened. An attendant eyed her suspiciously. "Please leave; we are not receiving guests."

"I am here to see the lord of the manor," Lucille said firmly.

"Ma'am, I am certain you have the wrong estate." The attendant went to close the door, but Lucille jammed her foot in.

"I have traveled a long way, and I am certain that I am exactly where I am meant to be." Lucille stepped forward, using her bag as a battering ram of sorts. Once she had shoved herself inside, she realized she was indeed at the right home. The ornate wallpaper was a beautiful swirling motif of lollies and macaroons. A series of gold handrails dotted the wall, breaking up the pattern.

A gentleman was descending the stairs; his shirt was partially undone, but not to the point of indecency. His cravat hung loosely around his neck, secured with the loosest of knots as it covered most of the exposed skin. He was shorter than average with garish yellow hair, brown walnut skin, and a slightly off-kilter gait. Lord Fondant was terribly handsome, and while perhaps a few years older than Lucille, he was certainly not an old man. *Never mind that,* she thought to herself. *I must be convincing.*

"My apologies, Lord Fondant. We simply must speak!" Lucille called out. But before she could continue, the attendant stepped in front of her; arms splayed wide to shield Lucille from view as if his flailing arms would make her disappear.

Lucille peered over the attendant's shoulder. Lord Fondant stood there bemused. She watched as he flicked his wrist, and then she heard the door slam behind her. She turned around. No one was near the door.

"Can you see ghosts?" Lord Fondant asked playfully. He stopped at the landing and twirled about.

"No? No, I cannot," Lucille said, a bit confused; she went to move past the attendant, but he blocked her again.

"Oh, Perry. Let the lady be, she's obviously confused. Perhaps dehydrated from travel." Lord Fondant said, his low baritone voice having a melodic tone she was not expecting.

Begrudgingly. Perry moved out of the way, but he scowled and only took a few tiny steps as if ready to lunge forward and contain her at any moment.

"I am not confused, sir," Lucille said, trying to regain her composure.

"I believe you are."

"I am certain I am not," she said firmly.

"Would you bet your life on it?" Lord Fondant said, smiling and baring a dizzying number of sharp teeth. Two of his front teeth were elongated, like fangs, and subtly protruded just enough to be noticeable when he smiled or spoke. Despite each tooth looking razor-sharp and frightening, Lucille noticed they were all pristine, gleaming like polished ivory.

"Oh," Lucille said; the sight made her queasy, but she steadied herself. "I would." She set her chin in a determined line, rolling her shoulder back and inhaling deeply.

Lord Fondant giggled and then bit his full bottom lip as he smiled. He made a delicate motion with his finger as if swirling his fingertips around the rim of a wine glass. She heard a whizzing sound and instinctively looked up. A large crystal chandelier was falling towards her, and although she wanted to move, she was stuck to the marble floor with a mixture of fear and shock. She glanced towards Lord Fondant, who, after a moment, held his hand up. She felt the pendant of the chandelier graze the top of her hair. She would not be deterred. She took another step towards him. "Please, we must speak."

All around her, the smaller chandeliers that had been strung up at the ceiling around the larger ones were lowered to the ground blocking her path. She squeezed in between two of them, thankful that none of them were lit.

"You do not understand," Lucille said forcefully. "I have no time for your parlor tricks."

"Alright then?" Lord Fondant said, sliding down the banister until he landed on the floor in front of her. "Out with it, you trespasser."

"I am in a desperate circumstance. I told my family we were to be wed. I was under the impression that you were near death and that your family's candy empire is run by a number of nephews. I was informed by a young woman who I attend school with that you are a recluse who never receives company, and I thought perhaps you would be dead by the time my ruse was discovered..."

"I do not believe I am unwell," Lord Fondant said, patting himself dramatically. "Perry, do I look unwell?"

"No, you look quite well," Perry said, glaring at Lucille.

"Of course," Lucille said in a tone she hoped was endearing. "As I said, I took some creative liberties based on the rumors I heard whilst at school."

"Oh, so you are a liar and a trespasser? Aren't you a bit old for school?" Lord Fondant said, cocking an eyebrow.

"Hmph," Lucille said, a bit offended. "I am. I was in training to be a governess."

"And now you're in training to be a liar and a trespasser; and a poor one at that." Lord Fondant said with a smirk.

"No, well, yes. My family lives abroad on the continent, and they shall travel here in a few months' time," Lucille said quickly. "They are taking a brief detour from their sightseeing of Monarch's Field. There won't be any trouble."

"At the risk of boring myself with my own repetition, you are mistaken. Your friend is mistaken, and the next time you lie, I would suggest you do a bit more research." Lord Fondant said, and with a flick of his wrist, the front door flew open.

"No," Lucille said firmly. "You do not understand."

"Despite your prattling, you have not explained anything." Lord Fondant raised his hand, and she felt a pressure on either side of her arms as if she was suddenly being held by invisible hands.

He made a motion like pushing, and she grabbed onto the banister. "No! I'm begging you; you just have to pretend to be my husband for a couple of weeks, three at the most. I am quite useful and pleasant."

He laughed, and the pushing sensation stopped. "Lord Fondant is dead."

"Are you a charlatan?" Lucille said, almost relieved, perhaps this gentleman would be more likely to help her if he was also pretending to be something he was not.

"I am Lady Fiona Fondant, Lord Fondant was my uncle. And I do not need a wife even for a theatrical performance."

Lucille felt her shoulders drop.

Lady Fondant turned her back on Lucille, but then she turned around slowly as if suddenly realizing something.

"But I am in need of an apprentice, and if that apprentice's family visits and coincidentally they are confused and believe we are married, I could be persuaded not to correct them."

Lucille unclasped her hands from the banister and clapped. "Thank you! I am in need of employment as well." It was a strange turn of events, but she was not one to look a gift horse in the mouth.

Lady Fondant smirked. "The payment is food, board, and my discretion."

"We shall negotiate." Lucille nodded curtly and tugged at her Spencer, which had risen up. She was careful not to tug too hard as the jacket was quite threadbare.

"Perry, take our guest's bag to the jam room."

Perry nodded begrudgingly and carried her small bag up the stairs.

Fiona

$\mathcal{F}$iona raced up the stairs to her room and excitedly flung herself onto her massive bed. Her manservant, Marty, stood there arranging her massive collection of neck scarves. She ignored Marty's groans of protest and moved a pile of silk scarves off the bed so she could stretch more comfortably. Then she excitedly relayed the last few minutes' events to Marty as he folded and organized her cravats.

"Forgive me, I heard but did not comprehend," Marty said, rubbing his temple. Marty was a tall, well-built fellow with a shiny round head and a pleasant, albeit nervous demeanor. His deep brown skin almost always glistened with sweat; today was no exception. Despite him and Perry being nearly identical twins, Marty was decidedly more pleasant.

Fiona repeated herself. "There's a woman here who wants me to pretend to be her fiancé, so I agreed, but only if she is my apprentice."

"Absurd. What was your reasoning here? I seem to lose the trail of logic." Marty dabbed at his forehead with a handkerchief.

"Perhaps I'm being altruistic?" Fiona said, grinning.

Marty wiggled his eyebrows. "Is she pretty?"

"Stunning, looks like she has a head cold but the prettiest woman I've seen; prettier than Bree."

Fiona noticed Marty grimace at the mention of her ex-fiancé.

"The true measure is if she is as vain as Bree?" Marty responded.

"I'm uncertain; however, from the looks of it, she's poor as a church mouse," Fiona said. "How do I look?"

"Like a rake," Marty said, patting her shoulder.

"Delightful." Fiona groaned.

"Did you check to see if the gelatin had set?" Marty asked, returning to folding the massive piles of silk cravats that lay on every available surface of the room.

"Oh, no," Fiona said sheepishly. "I got a bit sidetracked."

"And let me guess, we will not be finishing organizing the cravats," Marty said.

"We will. Just not now." Fiona said, clapping Marty on the shoulder. "I have a guest to attend to."

"Are you sure this-" Marty hesitated before saying, "Is an endeavor you feel up to?"

Fiona's brow furrowed, the lines on her forehead deepening. She pondered the question for a long moment, her mind grappling with her current state of health. Although the last vestiges of her exhausting bout of illness still clung to her, she was eager to make a friend and have a distraction from work. She smiled to herself, weariness momentarily forgotten as a sense of excitement washed over her. With a determined expression, she pushed herself upright and clasped her hands together. Then she remembered Marty was still waiting for a response.

"I am quite certain," Fiona said cheerily.

Marty nodded, his expression one of approval mixed with only a trace of the lingering concern he undoubtedly was trying to hide. "Lady Fondant, perhaps this is not the best time."

"If you have to ask, it normally is," Fiona said with a smirk.

"The leeches-" Marty started, but Fiona cut him off.

"Guzzle, Swig and Nip." Fiona said, motioning to the large jar where the leeches lived. She had acquired them from a quack doctor a few months ago. While they didn't serve a medicinal purpose, she found their thick pudgy bodies amusing and watching the water ripple soothing. When she had time, she also enjoyed decorating the habitat with moss and twigs.

"Must be fed," Marty said, wrinkling his broad nose.

"Yes, I will attend to that, but I believe we've left our guest long enough," Fiona said.

Fiona took a deep breath and then made her way downstairs, Marty following closely behind her. They passed Perry on the landing where he stood glaring at Lucille, who, for her part, was standing in the foyer looking everywhere but at them.

"How did she get in?" Perry said with a harsh whisper.

Fiona hesitated for a moment. She hadn't considered how Lucille had made it past the front gate. The protection field should have kept her out.

"Perhaps the lady is where she needs to be," Marty said with a little shrug.

"Perhaps," Fiona said.

"Or perhaps we should send her on her way." Perry said.

"You said I needed a friend," Fiona said with a shrug.

"You know this is not what I meant, ma'am," Marty said.

"Besides, when do you listen to us?" Perry hissed.

She ignored him and made her way down the stairs. "Allow me to show you about Sugar Lump Manor," Fiona said, motioning to the wing off of the foyer. Fiona hadn't hosted anyone since inheriting the manor, but she was excited to show it to someone. Even if that someone was a random annoying intruder, albeit a gorgeous one. Sugar Lump Manor hadn't been in their family terribly long; they had purchased it from a much more established family. Over the years, though, they had made it their own. Candy motifs were intertwined throughout the decor. Even the door handles and knobs were shaped like biscuits or macaroons. In place of traditional portraits were paintings of various family members either displaying or creating their favorite dishes. The early evening light shined through the hard-candy stained glass windows. They cast a rainbow of colors across the pair as they walked. She watched the lights bounce and glimmer across Lucille's brown skin. Fiona noticed they also caused Lucille's large brass hoops to shine like gold.

They passed a gingerbread servant on the third floor. Fiona watched with amusement as Lucille did a double take, remembering her very own first time encountering them. When Fiona had inherited Sugar Lump Manor, she had quickly grown accustomed to seeing the gingerbread men in their fuchsia waistcoats and yellow breeches. In addition to traditional floral embroidery, the uniforms were also adorned with intricate details, such as buttons, collars, and cuffs, which were made from icing. Despite their delicious appearance, Perry had warned her sternly that the gingerbread servants were not to be consumed. Not only were they stale, but it would also be in poor taste. Fiona wasn't sure if this pun was intentional, but she understood the sentiment. She treated each one kindly and addressed them each by name. Often they ignored her, but they were terribly busy, she would watch them sometimes as they would carry out their duties with precision and care, never faltering in their tasks. They would clean and polish the floors, dust the furniture, and attend to her needs, often before she voiced them. Despite their apparent lack of emotion, she had on occasion seen that the gingerbread servants would often make little jokes or puns to each other. When the weather was reasonable, they would play on the lawn, and when it was cold or rainy, as it often was, they played cards and charades.

"They're lovely really." Fiona said, relaying to Lucille the basics of the cookie staff.

"I am certain they are." Lucille said, still staring at the gingerbread man walking away from them.

When they reached the second parlor, Fiona paused. "I would pay a fortune for your thoughts" Fiona said to Lucille. While she waited for an answer, she appraised her new guest. Lucille's dress was carefully mended and there was not a wrinkle on the entire ensemble. While the material of Lucille's dress was not terribly fashionable, the cut was in the latest style. Fiona wondered if Lucille had it resewn from an older piece. The frilly square neckline drew attention to her décolletage which was modest. While her bust was small, the thin fabric stretched at her ample hips and clung to her soft belly. She, like most people, was taller than Fiona but not curiously tall.

"I would accept it." Lucille quipped. "Your home is delightful."

Other than being beautiful, the most notable thing about Lucille was the excited energy she exuded. Fiona could tell Lucille was taking great care not to speak too loudly or quickly or to move too sharply. Throughout the tour, Lucille had reached out as though she was going to touch something, but she never did; instead, she just dropped her hands to her sides and straightened the skirt of her dress. Fiona smiled at her broadly.

"Do you have any questions?" Fiona asked.

"Do your-" then Lucille stopped. "I beg your pardon. I forgot myself for a moment."

"Please ask." Fiona said.

"Do your teeth get in the way of-"

"Kissing?" Fiona asked.

"Oh no, eating."

Before they could carry on with the current direction of conversation, Lucille began to spin around in a small circle, her arms out wide, head back, eyes to the mural on the ceiling. After a moment she stopped so abruptly Fiona was afraid she was going to topple over. Instead, she wobbled and then steadied herself. "I am so sorry, it's so open here." She said breathlessly.

"Don't apologize, what good is a home if you can't spin in it? Was your school small?" Fiona asked.

She chewed on her thick bottom lip. "Yes and no, it's complicated. It was not lovely like this. And our quarters were tight."

Fiona was more pleased with this answer than she cared to admit. She had expected Lucille to have experienced elegant, historical homes brimming with luxurious history. While Sugar Lump Manor was full of wonders and quite spacious, it lacked the authenticity and old-school charm that ancestral manors typically held. It had only been in their family for a few generations, purchased on the sheer luck of another family's misfortunes. Her grandfather had been awarded a title by the King before he had any property, save for the shop in Mulvaney Square. Fiona wanted to explain this, but instead, she nodded sympathetically and guided Lucille to the greenhouses. She opened the door to the closest one and motioned for Lucille to step in.

Lucille

$\mathcal{F}$rom the outside, the greenhouse was modest, and Lucille had been unable to see inside as the frosted windowpanes distorted her view of the contents. However, once she was inside, she realized the greenhouse was cavernous. It seemed to stretch on nearly endlessly. In the distance, she thought she could make out a wall, but she could not be certain. She looked up, and instead of a ceiling and a view of the sky through the glass, as she expected, she had an unobstructed view of clouds and sunbeams filtered in. It was not too cold or too hot, and curiously the floors were a springy dirt mixture of some kind.

"What is this place?" Lucille said half to herself.

"It is a greenhouse, or perhaps in the city you all call it a hothouse?"

"I am uncertain what one would call it as I have never experienced it." Lucille said, spinning around.

"We grow nearly everything." Fiona said, allowing Lucille to wander through the rows. "Do you grow plants?"

"I grow herbs for my tinctures." Lucille said, peering at the plants. "What is this?" The plant was fibrous and reminded her vaguely of cactus but there were no spines. Perhaps it was another sort of succulent. The smell of vanilla wafted up to her nose.

"It's a vanilla extract plant," Fiona said.

"That's an oxymoron…you must have a vanilla plant to extract the essence." Lucille said, peering down at the plant.

"Oh no." Fiona said, "This is a special plant."

Fiona bent down and pulled out her swinging knife. She nicked the stem and sap oozed out. "You'll find the garden is full of wonders like this."

"I'll have to explore it more." Lucille said, eyes still wide.

Fiona nodded. "Pick as much as you'd like. Have you eaten?"

"Oh, no." Lucille said, dusting herself off.

"Come let us make our way to the dining room." Fiona said, taking her hand lightly and helping her up.

Lucille stopped in the middle of the hallway as they re-entered the manor and stared down at the floor. "This mosaic, what is it made of?"

"Licorice lozenges."

"Oh." Lucille in a mystified tone as they continued walking.

As Fiona and Lucille entered the formal dining area, the dining room tables slid themselves out and stamped their legs excitedly like horses clambering in a carriage line.

"Did they just move?" Lucille said, jumping back.

"Yes." Fiona said, taking her seat at the head of the table. The seat to her left wiggled playfully.

Lucille sat down, staring at the chairs warily. After a moment she dragged her eyes away and watched as she stared down at the place settings. Lucille picked up a fork gingerly and held it up to the light twisting it around.

Fiona

$\mathcal{A}$s Lucille picked up the fork, Fiona suddenly felt embarrassed that each handle of the silverware was thick and angled.

"Do you require different silverware? This is more comfortable for my hands and most people find them more ergonomic." Fiona asked. Marty stepped forward from his spot next to the door.

"Oh no, they're beautiful." Lucille said, patting them gently. She smiled at Marty and gave him a little wave. "I'm quite alright." Marty nodded curtly and went back to his post.

Fiona watched as Lucille twisted around to see the dishes as they were placed on the table.

"Venison, parsnips, sausages." Fiona motioned to the first platter.

"Venison, parsnips, sausages." Lucille whispered.

"Meat pies, ragouts, creamed potatoes." Fiona said, pointing to each dish in turn.

This time Lucille didn't say it out loud but Fiona watched her lips move. "Meat pies, ragouts, creamed potatoes." She mouthed soundlessly.

"Excuse me for a moment, I must check on dessert." Fiona said.

"This soon?" Lucille frowned.

"I eat all the courses at once. The soup must have been delayed; I'll check on it." Fiona said.

She popped into the hallway. Marty and Perry were standing off to the side.

"She keeps repeating the food, is that a society norm?" Fiona whispered softly.

They shook their heads in unison. "I believe she's in awe. The professional schools are quite sparse." Marty said.

"Yes, the one we went to served us gruel." Perry said, his face twisting into a grimace.

"Oh." Fiona said. She swiped her hand across her face and sighed deeply.

"Ma'am?" Marty said hesitantly.

"Are you nervous?" Perry said.

"A bit." Fiona sighed.

She waited until the attendant with the soup entered, and then she followed closely behind him.

"The soup has to be carried slowly up the stairs from the lower kitchen where the meals are prepared." Fiona said, taking her seat.

Lucille nodded. "Versus the confection kitchens."

"Yes." Fiona said, serving Lucille a generous helping of each item. "You'll see the rest of them tomorrow."

Lucille gasped "There are more kitchens? I saw at least two."

"Yes, ma'am" Fiona selected the glass with the prettiest whipped syllabub and set it beside Lucille's plate and then slid over a small dish of apple compote.

Lucille took a sip of the soup. "Oh, this is quite good!"

"Have you never had white soup before?" Fiona said, a bit confused.

"Yes, of course, at a ball or two, but I don't get invited often, and at the school, the food is horrid, which is just as well since there isn't much of it." Lucille finished the small bowl quickly and then began to tuck into the venison. Fiona liked the way Lucille ate, she took quick little bites, and every so often, she sighed contentedly.

"Here, take a second helping." Fiona said, ladling her more soup.

"Oh, I couldn't impose," Lucille said, covering her face with her hand.

"You're not imposing. You're nourishing yourself." Fiona said with a smile. She started to eat apple compote: the jammy-like substance was one of her favorites. She wrinkled her nose; too much pepper in this one.

"Is something wrong?" Lucille asked mid-bite.

"The compote has too much spice." Fiona paused and took a spoonful of the whipped syllabub, which was supposed to be a zesty mousse, but it was thick and didn't have enough citrus notes. "And the syllabub needs more flavor."

Lucille put down her fork and tried the compote. "Mmmhmm, this is amazing. I would love to taste what perfect tastes like if this is not it."

Fiona felt embarrassed by her critique. "Are you used to servants flitting about?" She asked to change the subject.

"No."

"Not even at dinner?"

"No." Lucille looked at her, a bit perplexed "We serve ourselves and whoever is near. If you're a person of note, the footman stands at your chair, but they do not, what is the word you used, flit? They don't flit or flutter about."

"That's what we do in the country, I was curious how it's done in the city."

"It's the same. Have you never been?"

"Not since I was a child."

As they ate, Fiona listened to Lucille talk about her art which, curiously, she did not attend school for.

"I am woefully uneducated in the art, but I do love gouache," Fiona said hesitantly. "It's so vibrant. Do you work in gouache?"

Lucille nearly choked on a parsnip. "Oh goodness no," she said when she recovered. She coughed once more and continued. "I don't believe I could afford to touch a pan of gouache. Not to mention the cold pressed paper or sable brushes."

"Hmm," Fiona said as she swiped up the last pools of butter sauce with a piece of nearly raw venison.

"I half expect your deer to come back to life and come bounding across the table, it is so fresh." Lucille said playfully.

"I like my meat very rare, bloody if possible," Fiona said. She debated about elaborating further, but then she decided against it. "Shall we have tea?" Fiona asked, motioning to the empty dishes.

"Oh. Have we really gone through all of this?" Lucille said, embarrassed.

"It wasn't very much." Fiona said, shrugging. "We can have more sent up, cold meats and bread would be fastest, but we can have whatever you would like prepared."

"No, no." Lucille said quickly, standing up. "Tea, let us take tea."

Fiona guided Lucille to her personal parlor. The entire room was plush and soft. She had everything custom dyed a rich shade of emerald green, and all the molding and furniture was a rich mahogany brown. Velvet fabric lined the walls, there were several layers of rugs, the furniture was tufted and overfilled, and, best of all, the ceiling was draped with billowing scarves.

"You must despise the color green." Lucille giggled.

"Yes, I loathe it and mahogany." Fiona said, giggling.

"What is this?" Lucille asked; she motioned to the beautiful, gilded frame the teapot sat on.

"Oh, it's a pot tipper, the teapot is strapped in, and there's a hinge, so it's easier, and it flips up and supports the pot.

"How charming." Lucille said. "I imagine your tea is just as divine as your food selection."

"I will let you be the judge, but I grow my own herbs for tea, so judge well." Fiona said with a smirk.

Fiona picked up her teacup, placed it gently under the tipper, and began to put a sugar cube into the bottom. Her teacup was similar to the rest of the set, with pink and yellow roses against a field of pearlescent white. The only difference was that hers had two swirling handles instead of one.

"How curious." Lucille said, leaning forward. "Does your cup have two handles?"

"Yes." Fiona said, adding a bit of sugar to Lucille's.

"Mine does not." Lucille said. She struggled to hide her confusion, she blinked a few times as if that would trigger some sort of comprehension and when that failed, she twirled the teacup around in her hands.

"No, it does not." Fiona said, bemused. She handed Lucille the teacup with one handle, and as the steam rose from the delicate porcelain teacup, Lucille took a deep breath, clearly savoring the warm, comforting aroma of freshly brewed tea. Fiona took a tentative sip of her own drink, her eyes closing in delight as the perfect balance of peppery and sweet flavors hit her tongue.

Lucille turned towards her, she smiled warmly, gratitude and appreciation shining in her eyes. Her dark eyes had the depth and complexity of a cup of black tea, and they were just as soothing. "This is perfect," Lucille said softly. "Thank you so much for taking the time to make this for me."

Fiona smiled back. "It was my pleasure," she said. "I got the sense that you needed to be refreshed, and what better way to do that than with a perfect cup of tea?"

Fiona snapped her fingers. "I've forgotten," Fiona said. "Would you like milk?"

"Will you judge me?" Lucille whispered conspiratorially.

"No," Fiona said in an equally soft whisper. She poured a bit of milk into Lucille's cup.

Lucille nodded, taking another sip. "You have a real talent for tea blends," she said, her voice filled with admiration. "I don't think I've ever had a cup of tea this wonderful before."

Fiona shrugged, a modest smile on her lips. "It's all about taking the time to get it just right," they said. "And seeing the pleasure it brings to someone such as yourself makes it all worth it."

There was a scratching at the door frame. "Here, Bon Bon." Fiona said, patting her leg. Her chocolate tortoise scuttled towards her. As he crawled through the room, the chocolate turtle's shell gleamed in the firelight, its rich brown color and smooth texture would have been enticing if Fiona didn't love him so much. His body was solid and sturdy, made entirely of the finest quality chocolate, and his legs and head were formed from creamy caramel. His eyes were made of bright and shiny candy, and his expression was one of quiet determination. He moved with a slow and steady gait, his chocolate legs plodding along the rug as he curiously surveyed the world around him. When he finally neared, Fiona picked up the turtle and rubbed its shell gently.

"Oh, you have a pet, is he..." Lucille said. "Is he made of chocolate?"

"Yes, among other materials. He came with the manor but he's terribly old and nearly blind." Fiona said. "Would you like to hold him?"

"Of course." Lucille said, to Fiona's delight the turtle curled up in Lucille's lap and quickly fell asleep. Lucille rubbed the turtle's shell and head as it snored gently.

After they had several cups of tea and Lucille was yawning, Fiona realized she should offer to take Lucille to her room. "Let's put Bon Bon down and I'll show you to your room." Fiona said.

She noted the care with which Lucille placed Bon Bon on the floor. "This isn't too close to the fire, is it? I don't want him to melt."

"That's perfect," Fiona said.

"This way," Fiona said, leading her into the foyer.

"These columns are beautiful." Lucille said, gently touching one as she walked past it. "Wait!" Lucille said, turning around. Fiona watched as Lucille pushed her hand into the column and marveled as her hand left an indent that bounced back out.

"Marshmallow marble." Fiona said laughing. "You can eat it but then we'd have to patch it."

"Can I eat this?" Lucille said tapping the railing.

"No, that's wood." Fiona said. "You can lick the wallpaper; it tastes like whatever is depicted."

"I'll have to try it later." Lucille said, then she added nervously, "I'm quite tired."

"Come," Fiona said, taking her hand and leading her up the stairs to her room.

"Your room is the jam suite." Fiona said.

Fiona pushed the door and motioned for Lucille to enter. She hoped her new visitor liked the room: it was one of her favorites. It was decorated in rich red and pink jewel tones. They had worked hard to carry a strawberry motif throughout, down to the embroidered strawberries on the mesh of the bed canopy.

"I'll have the housekeeper hang thicker bed curtains to keep the draft out."

Lucille was spinning again, looking up at a section of the ceiling which was solid and held both a vine chandelier and mural of the countryside.

"I love it." Lucille whispered.

"Fantastic." Fiona said, her joints were beginning to ache. "I'll leave you, the washroom has water on tap and champagne."

Lucille giggled. "How charming."

"Good night." Fiona said, nodding curtly.

"To you as well." Lucille said, still looking about.

In the safety of her rooms, Fiona undressed and drew a bath. She sank back into the water and let the exhaustion and nausea roll through her body. Water splashed over the edges of the tub but she couldn't muster the energy to care. As she shifted, the water lapped over her sore muscles and swollen joints.

"Fiona?" Marty asked from the other side of the door.

"I'm fine, leave me." Immediately she was embarrassed by how gruff she sounded.

Fiona stretched her arm out away from her body. She looked at the tender, scabbing skin at the bend of her elbow. Was it worse?

The next morning, Fiona penned a brief note and had Marty deliver it, then Fiona waited in her private parlor.

"Hello," Lucille said shyly. She was clothed simply but her blue dress complemented her brown skin and her thick hair was braided in neat rows. Fiona noticed she had swooped her baby hairs down on her forehead and they curled around her hairline like calligraphy.

"Good morning." Fiona said. "Sit, sit. I thought you might want to take the day to rest. I have books and tea."

Lucille sat on the sofa farthest away from her. She draped a crochet blanket over her lap. "What a lovely set up."

Fiona opened her book and pretended to read. She noticed out of the corner of her eye that Lucille hadn't chosen a book. Before she could ask why, Lucille shuddered ever so slightly.

"Are you uncomfortable?" Fiona asked.

"There is a draft. I'll be alright."

"Is a draft a euphemism?" Fiona asked, her eyebrows raising inquiringly.

"No." Lucille said quickly. "I'm fine."

"You don't have to dismiss your own feelings. The world will do that readily enough." Fiona said. "We'll add more kindling to the fire."

The fire poker and tongs unhooked themselves from the stand and wriggled to the fire. Once a new log was placed and the fire was roaring, they hopped back into place.

"They're quite useful." Lucille "It would be fabulous if there was a set for every room but that could get crowded. As I imagine they all like to move about in the summer."

Fiona nodded and eyed Lucille who was staring at the fire as she continued to talk about the fire tools.

"Forgive if I'm being forward." Fiona said, leaning towards Lucille as if to mirror her words.

"Why do I have the sneaking suspicion you're always forward?" Lucille said with a smile still avoiding eye contact.

"You can relax, the furniture is solidly built." The sofa wiggled in agreement.

"I am quite relaxed." Lucille said, still sitting very rigidly.

Fiona spread her legs, relaxed her body and slumped down, sagging into the cushions. "Have you tried this position?"

Lucille giggled. "I would have a sore back."

"As I do," Fiona said sitting more upright. "Show me how you relax."

Lucile hesitated but then she slipped her shoes off and tucked her legs up under her. She leaned on the arm of the sofa. "When permitted, I sit like this."

"Wonderful." Fiona said. "Would you like to come sit by me?"

"Yes…" Lucille said slowly, she rose and came to sit on the far end of the sofa Fiona was on.

"Are you comfortable?"

"Quite, this is a much better view." Lucille said sweetly.

"Of?" Fiona said, her voice tinged with confusion.

"The fire." Lucille said, her voice soft and low, almost a murmur.

Fiona heard Lucille's stomach growl.

"Would you like something to eat?" Fiona asked.

"Uh yes please." Lucille said.

"What would you like?" Fiona asked evenly, trying not to make Lucille more anxious.

"Cold meat, bread…" Lucille said hesitantly.

Fiona nodded and flicked her wrist; the bell on the wall jingled, and after a moment, Perry appeared.

"We're hungry. Could you please send us some cold meat, eggs, bread, honey cake, and brioche?" Fiona thought for a moment. "Do we have oysters?"

"Yes." Perry grunted.

"Then oysters as well please. Thank you." Fiona nodded.

Fiona watched Lucille's lips part in surprise as the trays of food were set down before them. A twinkle of amber light caught the dark brown of Lucille's eyes and Fiona watched as they gleamed with excitement.

To Fiona's delight, her uninvited guest was an early riser and had found her way to the kitchen with no issue. Her joy, however, was short lived when she realized the King's order of chocolates was due in less than a month. Fiona shook her hands in front of herself. She was always full of energy, but this was not the happy energy that normally filled her. Instead, she was a bit wary and anxious. She surveyed the chocolates that littered the tables. These chocolates were only a test batch, but she did not care for their design.

"Where shall we begin?" Lucille said, clapping her hands.

Fiona looked at Lucille appraisingly. She was used to working with Marty, Perry, and the gingerbread men who knew better than to interrupt. She returned her gaze to the chocolates and then after a long while she said, "Perhaps a proper introduction?" Fiona said not looking at Lucille. Instead, she was looking at a series of nearly identical gold plates topped with chocolate shells.

"I am Lucille Waters," Lucille said cheerfully.

"Alright? I know that."

"Was that not what you meant by introduction?" Lucille said, her voice still full of cheer.

Fiona drug her eyes away from the chocolate shells. "Not at all, I wanted to give you a brief lesson on chocolates."

Lucille hopped from foot to foot excitedly. "Shall I take notes?"

"You will learn the techniques. Take as many notes as you like." Fiona said.

"Are the recipes secret?" she said in a hushed voice. "Shall I guard them?"

"No, they're nearly useless without the proper technique." Fiona said with a smirk.

"I see. My apologies for asking too many questions."

"No need to apologize." Fiona hesitated. "What do you know of confections?"

"Virtually nothing."

Fiona sighed.

"I am a fast learner," Lucille said quickly.

"And a liar," Fiona said with a smile.

Lucille rolled her eyes. "How long will you hold that against me?"

"First impressions rarely change."

"Well. You nearly killed me!"

"That's rich. You trespassed."

"It was necessary."

Fiona walked around the table examining the chocolates once more.

"You have yet to explain why. Just allusions. You mentioned you did not care for your school and wanted to study art."

"Well, yes, as you know, my parents sent me to a vocational school to become a governess. I would like to become a painter and have been studying in secret. I am hoping to secure an apprenticeship-"

Fiona cut her off. "You succeeded on that front."

Lucille pursed her lips, her dark eyes flashing with annoyance, then continued "I have yet to make it into an art institution or find an artist to study with. When I heard that you, or rather who I thought was you, Lord Fondant, was a recluse, I thought I could postpone my parents' need to find me a posting by claiming I was engaged. Once I found an artistic position, I could then convince them that Lord Fondant broke off the engagement and that I would be pursuing art."

"Hmmm." Fiona thought this over. "Have you been to one of our shops?"

"No. Of course not."

"What do you mean?"

"It's too high! And exclusive."

"That was not my doing." Fiona said quickly. She wanted to tell Lucille that eventually she wanted to have stalls or carts or perhaps salespeople who sold their wares from carts. *Will she find me patronizing?* Fiona wondered.

Lucille shrugged. "It's not necessarily a bad thing; I made peace with my position a long time ago."

"Except for your occupation."

"That is different; I am not attempting to rise above my station. I am trying to simply follow my passions."

Fiona looked up to meet her in her eyes. "There is no reason for you not to do both."

"While we're asking questions, where is Lord Fondant?"

"He's dead."

"Did you kill him?"

Fiona laughed. "No, he passed of old age. He was either eighty or eighty-one."

"Oh. Why was no announcement made?"

"Eh, it's bad for business. The Fondant family benefits from its mystique. Perhaps too much."

"Do you truly have secret passageways under your shops? I saw the magical waiters who-" Lucille made a snapping motion with her fingers. "Poof and reappear. But there's so few of those and the other attendants move nearly as fast."

"I've never been." Fiona said with a shrug.

"What?" Lucille said. "Would it not be simpler for you to write the recipes and teach the shop assistants how to create them? It seems a long process for you to create the recipe, send it to them for study and for them to approve and you send word what is wrong or what is correct. I imagine if it is a complex recipe this back and forth could last months, even with servers who can magically transport themself."

"I cannot leave," Fiona said flatly, putting down the chocolate she was inspecting.

"Why not? Are you cursed."

"No. It makes me terribly anxious. I turn into a blubbering mess. Before I left my parent's estate to come here, I had only been into our village two times in the last twenty-odd years."

"Then it was very brave of you to do so."

"It's alright. You may laugh." Fiona said, glancing away. When she looked up, Lucille's gaze was holding hers.

"The situation is not humorous," Lucille murmured.

"You are not upset?" Fiona sounded relieved but then she added. "Then you'll not try to make me go?"

"Goodness no, if you don't like taking a turn round the park, why would I try to force you into a carriage?"

"Oh," Fiona said flatly, not answering.

"Perhaps we'll go for a walk to your village, and when you're ready, we can explore more. In the meantime, we'll make do just as you have been."

After explaining the basics of the chocolates and what to look for, Fiona gave Lucille a piece to eat. "You'll notice our chocolate is not as bitter as what is currently in fashion." Fiona watched her eat, vaguely uneasy as to how much she enjoyed watching Lucille taste the chocolates.

"Why do you do your makeup like that?" Fiona said appraisingly, trying to distract herself. Lucille's cheeks were heavily rouged, the pink color extending up towards her ears with a swipe across the tip of her nose. The shade of pink glowed off her warm brown skin. It wasn't exactly that Fiona did not like it, she just found it a bit odd. When Lucille had first arrived, Fiona had thought her face was flushed from the frigid air. But after seeing her in the light again today, she quickly realized Lucille probably always looked this way.

"I am an artist! It is self-expression."

"You look as though you have a head cold."

"I am inspired by the cold weather. The frost, the chill. Winter is my favorite season."

Fiona frowned, pondering it over. "I was under the impression that women appreciate a natural look."

"It is natural. It's an interpretation of how one looks when one has been out in the elements." Lucille snapped "I have no more than a dab of rouge and a bit of lip salve on the whole of my face. Besides, they are both made of vegetables. What could be more natural than that?"

"Did the chemist tell you this?" Fiona said with a snort.

"My apologies for not having a maid to mix my paints and lotions," Lucille said, stabbing a potato so hard with her fork that Fiona was shocked the plate did not crack.

Fiona reached across the table and swiped her pointer finger across Lucille's brow. Fiona looked down and rubbed her finger against her thumb aggressively. Nothing was there. Fiona licked her finger and repeated what she had just done, this time rubbing a bit harder against Lucille's eyebrow.

Fiona held up her finger to Lucille.

"Bare."

"Obviously," Lucille said, rolling her eyes. "You shabbaroon. And you, ma'am, could use some moisture if you would like to fix your dull tone naturally; I have a hydrating salve. There's nothing to be done for this attitude, I fear." She scoffed.

"I did not mean to offend you." Fiona said. "Have you considered that if we are to be friends, you'll have to be less sensitive?"

"Have you ever considered, just for a moment, that you should not say every thought that pops into your mind.?"

"I do not," Fiona said, clearly offended.

"I shudder to imagine the inner workings of your mind if what you say is filtered."

"From my impression, you speak what is on your mind half the time before you've even fully formed the thought." Fiona said.

"My thoughts aren't nearly half as cruel as yours." Lucille snapped.

Fiona shrugged. "I'll make more of an effort to say the good thoughts as well."

"Come again?" Lucille said.

"You make it seem as though I only speak negatively, so I will make more of an effort to remind you of the things I appreciate."

"No." Lucille said. "You flirt enough. That would make me uncomfortable."

"Is there no winning with you? If I'm rude, then you're upset. If I'm complimentary, you're upset."

"Oh hush, forget I spoke. This is silly, as if we're going round and round."

"Well, Miss Waters, with you as my partner, I would gladly dance in circles for the rest of my days," Fiona said.

Lucille waved her hand dismissively. "What is next?"

"Lemon drops," Fiona said with a sigh. "You add citric acid to boiling water."

"Alright." Lucille walked over to the tap.

Lucille's tongue peeked out through her front teeth as she concentrated. Fiona took note of this. It was endearing. This was a simple recipe but Fiona appreciated that she had only had to tell her the measurements and steps once and she was carefully following each step.

"What is your dream?" Fiona asked.

"You're horrid at small talk," Lucille said with a giggle. "What is yours?"

"Hmm, I think my dream would be to create a notable confection. And yours?"

"I would like for a suitor to give me flowers."

"You need more elaborate dreams. What about art school?"

"My art career is a goal. It's obtainable."

Fiona nibbled on a piece of chocolate. "I am confused, becoming an artist with very little training and no prospects is more attainable than someone showing you a kindness?"

Lucille laughed hollowly. "Well, when you phrase it thusly…"

"I did not mean…"

"If our lesson can wait, I would like to go write to my friend…"

"Of course." Fiona nodded watching her walk away.

Lucille

Lucille resisted the urge to stomp up the stairs and instead took careful steps to her room. Once she was alone, she took a deep breath trying to stifle the strange mix of annoyance, fear and excitement that was gurling inside her. While Fiona left a lot to be desired in the way of conversation, it was a better turn of fortune than the school. The food was warm, well flavored, and seemingly endless. It also helped that there was so much space. Even in her room there was a bowl of fruit, enough fruit it seemed to stock the entire market, completely unblemished and shining brightly just for her. To think she would be enjoying this beautiful estate that smelled like sugar, almonds, and vanilla for the foreseeable future. Unlike Brittlebone's cold gray atmosphere, every room in Sugar Lump Manor was cast in a warm orange glow. In place of candles, the manor used sconces that were illuminated by orange stones. She would examine those later. For now, she simply relished in the softness of it all. Quietly she removed her slippers and softly hopped across the plush carpet in her stocking-ed feet. Lucille stamped her feet gently and then threw herself onto the bed, landing face down and screaming into the pillow.

After collecting herself she sat down at the dark wood desk that was etched with strawberry vines and their small round flowers. She picked up the first pencil stub she found in the drawer and began to write her letter when suddenly the pencil crumbled in her fingers. She shrieked and then examined it closely. It was cake. She picked up another pencil and bit into it. Also cake.

She stood up and walked down the stairs. She expected to see a servant walk past but she couldn't find one.

"Hmm." She said, making her way down the stairs.

Perry and Marty stood on the landing looking at a large pile of crumbs and a pile of clothes.

"Gingie ate Ginger," Perry said, "I need to find a broom."

"I believe that's Gin," Marty said, looking down at the crumbs.

"Aw, guess we must make more," Perry replied.

"Excuse me?" Lucille said aghast. "I thought they came with the manor."

"The gingerbread servants? They bake themselves in batches." Marty said as the servant handed him a broom and dustpan.

"And they eat each other?" Lucille asked. She had just grown accustomed to the statue-like attendants with their pebbled skin and brown sugar aroma but now she was concerned.

"Occasionally if they add too much spice. Sometimes they run off." Fiona said, making her way up the stairs. She was dressed in a fine matching ensemble, the lapels of her jacket and her vest were both embroidered with swirling vines of glittering thread. Each vine was heavy with glass bead berries.

"I attempted to write to my friend and my pencils were all cake." Lucille announced to no one in particular.

Marty laughed. "If you check the second door there are real pencils. No cake."

Lucille made her way back upstairs. She was suddenly very tired, she closed her eyes and drifted off into a restless sleep. It seemed as if she had only been sleeping for a few moments when her eyes fluttered open. There was a glowing orb above her face. *How odd,* she thought to herself before her exhaustion tugged her back to sleep.

When she awoke again, there were three piles of neat, butcher paper wrapped packages on the nightstand beside her. She had forgotten to draw the bed curtains, so she had a clear view of the large room. Similarly wrapped articles covered both the desk and bench. On the wall opposite the windows, an easel was propped up. On the floor was a large wooden book with a heavy looking golden clasp. Beside them were several pre-stretched canvases. She hesitated for almost a moment, surely this must have been a dream. *If it is, open them before you are disturbed,* she thought to herself. One by one she opened the packages, revealing a somewhat odd mishmash of art supplies. There were gouaches, pencils, watercolor blocks, and a variety of papers. To her shock there were even white and black paints in tubes. One package had linseed and walnut oil, another had turpentine. Lucille checked through all the open packages, there were no more oil paints or tempera. Charcoal and pastels were also conspicuously absent. Still, she was happier than she had ever been. She traced the watercolor blocks with her fingertips, gently as if they would turn to dream dust if she was too rough. She neatly folded up the wrapping paper and string. And then she dressed for the day, her fingers trembling as she tried to pull the drawstrings of her dress. There was a gentle knock on the door. "Miss Waters, Lady Fiona has requested your presence in the kitchen with the green door."

"Alright, thank you." Lucille called back. She hesitated, should she ask for directions? No, that would be silly. She would be able to find it, it was a massive estate but it couldn't be that huge. She wandered to the floor above hers into a hallway lined with built-in bookshelves, each one filled with golden spined books. In some areas, the windows extended all the way to the ceilings.

"Miss Waters?" Fiona's voice boomed out, echoing down the hall. "Are you lost?"

Lucille turned around sheepishly, "Hopelessly."

"Allow me to bestow upon you some hope." Fiona motioned to a green door that Lucille was certain had not been there a moment prior.

"Is this yet another kitchen?" Lucille asked, certain she had never seen this door.

"I dunno, is it?" Fiona said with a giggle, opening it. Lucille followed closely behind her, worried that if the door closed behind Fiona, she would not be able to find it. This kitchen was simple with an exposed stone fireplace, roughhewn wood table, and clay pots.

"This is the best kitchen for what we need, there's at least one hundred kitchens at Sugar Lump Manor, they appear as they're needed."

"But the other rooms stay put?" Lucille asked, worried at the idea of losing her room and it never coming back.

"For the most part," Fiona said with a shrug. "Relax, my little sack of flour. The other rooms should be where they are. Now, let us begin. We're making biscuits." *Sack of flour? She says it like a pet name but sounds more like an insult,* Lucille wondered.

"I wanted to thank you for the art supplies," Lucille said awkwardly, fiddling with the hem of her apron.

"You're welcome. Those were the only items I could find in the surrounding three villages. If you provide me with a list, I will order more." Fiona said.

"Thank you," Lucille said again.

"As I said, you are welcome. You're quite the silly scraper!" Fiona said, arranging a series of small seasoning bottles into a line.

"Why do you call me names?" Lucille said, not being able to contain her confusion any longer.

"They're pet names," Fiona said as if it should have been clear.

"Most pet names are sweet, like a honey bun or sugar plum," Lucille said. "Or the actual confections."

"The ingredients and tools make the confectioner." Fiona. "You should take the compliment."

"Well, I can't argue with you there," Lucille said with a giggle.

"I thought you could argue anything."

Lucille shrugged. "I'll try to be more agreeable."

"I like it. Thus far, I like everything about you, almond paste, don't change on my account." Fiona said with a wink.

Lucille listened intently as Fiona described the cookies they were going to make. Apparently, the important component was a hard candy shell. She carefully rolled the dough and then placed them in the oven. "And now we wait," Fiona said.

Lucille watched as Fiona sat with her legs spread wide, her arm slung into her lap. Through the slit at the bottom of her fitted pants, Lucille could see her bare ankle. While Lucille was not acquainted with many gentlemen, Fiona's posture reminded her of the few she knew.

"Is everything alright?" Fiona asked.

"Yes," Lucille said.

"If you have a question, it's best to ask. An unanswered question is like a bad fish, it will give you indigestion." Fiona said with a smirk.

"You're a woman…"

"That's not a question," Fiona said, still smirking.

"But you dress and act as a man does." Lucille continued.

"Is that a question?" Fiona said.

"You don't match what…I expect…of a woman." Lucille said, clamping her hand over her mouth when she finished. Was that terribly rude?

"I believe the word you're looking for is nonconforming," Fiona said. "Did you have a question?"

"No, I mean…well, is there anything I should know?" Lucille asked.

Fiona shook her head. "No."

Fiona

$\mathcal{A}$fter their awkward cookie lesson, Fiona spent the next few days avoiding her guest, which proved to be unexpectedly easy. If Lucille was about, Fiona didn't see her. On the fourth day, however, her luck came to an end. Fiona was making her way to her parlor when the door to her favorite kitchen appeared on the wall to her left. It was a solid oak door with a gold brass knocker that resembled a macaroon. She turned the cut crystal handle and pushed the door open, half expecting it to be empty or for Marty or Perry to be sitting there baking a cake to resemble a household object. Instead, her new house guest stood there in a green dress that had been mended so many times it looked more like a patchwork quilt than a garment.

"Ah, Miss Waters. You're practicing your baking."

"Oh, there you are. I'm frothing egg whites for your hair." Then she said, holding up a bottle of cream rum, "We'll rinse with rum."

"Were you expecting me?"

"No, I was going to find you once I was done but it's as if the house knew." Lucille said excitedly.

"You wanted to find me to douse me in egg and rum?"

"Yes! And a bit of rose water. Your hair is so dry, it needs some care." Lucille said sweetly.

Fiona was about to tell her that was ridiculous, but she looked so excited, her brown eyes glittering, she could not say no. "Alright, do what you must."

Fiona cringed as Lucille plopped the foamy mixture onto her head but it wasn't terrible.

"When do you rinse it?" Fiona said, careful not to move her head too much as a bit of the mixture was already dribbling down her neck.

"Half hour, possibly an hour."

"What am I supposed to do for an hour?"

"Perhaps it could be half an hour, depending on how the mixture is working." Lucille said, smiling coyly. "And normally, friends chat." she added in a matter-of-fact tone.

"You'll stay?" Fiona said, perking up.

"Yes," Lucille said. "What would you like to discuss?"

"What do you speak about with your friends?"

"You asked a question in response to my question," Lucille said. "Mostly, we talk about suitors, classmates, gardening, or our markets. We people watch."

"People watch?"

"Yes, we go to the city and watch the rich people. Imagine their lives, critique their fashion." Lucille stopped. "Well, when it's described as such, it seems horrid."

"No, I've just never been. I don't like to leave my estate. I hadn't realized it was a pasttime."

Lucille gave a sheepish shrug. "What do you do for enjoyment?"

"I read." Fiona tried to think of something else she liked but nothing came to mind.

"Would you like me to read to you?" Lucille asked. "So you don't get the pages wet?"

"If you wouldn't mind."

"I would love to; in fact, I have had an entire course on this matter."

"Reading?"

"Reading aloud." Lucille corrected.

Fiona did not know what the story was about, the names of the characters, or even what time period it was set. Instead, she bathed in the sweet airy tone of Lucille's voice. Fiona let herself ease into it, soak it all up and float in the sound of her words.

Once Lucille had rinsed Fiona's hair and finger coiled it, she excused herself.

Calm down, Lucille said to herself as she made her way to the drawing room Marty had told her she was free to use. The walls were adorned with ornate lollipop-printed wallpaper, which was punctuated with richly painted panels and regal-looking portraits. The floors beneath her feet were covered with plush carpets, with only the perimeter of the room showing the finely polished wood beneath. She knew Fiona preferred her own parlor, but Lucille thoroughly enjoyed this drawing room. The mahogany furniture was heavy, and the furniture was arranged in a horseshoe, and Lucille liked to imagine a room full of close friends discussing everything from philosophy to music and the latest gossip. She curled up in the armchair and pulled out her sketching pad.

There was a knock on the door. "Come in." Lucille said not bothering to check who it was.

"Miss Waters, nuncheon." Marty said, sitting the tray down and nodding curtly before exciting.

"Thank you," she said as he exited.

Then she began to eat the crusty homemade bread Marty had brought her. It was still warm from the oven and slathered with hot creamy butter. She bit down, enjoying the crunch that gave way to a fluffy light interior. Beside the bread on the tray was a comforting spiced cider swirling with cinnamon, nutmeg, and cloves. Once she finished the bread and half of the cider, she uncovered the last dish. It was a savory hand pie filled with tender chunks of meat with diced vegetables, herbs, and a savory gravy. A touch of honey brought out the natural sweetness of the carrots, parsnips, and turnips.

A young lady could get used to this, she thought to herself. But a nagging voice replied: But you should not.

Whatever concerns Lucille had that her lessons with Fiona would be as dull and monotonous as lessons at Brittlebone, they were quickly assuaged. Fiona was a funny teacher, quick witted and an engaging storyteller. While Lucille wasn't particularly fascinated by lime drops, making them with Fiona was proving to be a pleasant way to spend the early afternoon. Besides, the rain that erratically beat down on the glass ceiling created a playful soundtrack to their endeavors. Lucille watched Fiona carefully, taking notes in her small book about her techniques. The proper way to zest and squeeze the lime and so on and so forth. She watched as Fiona ladled the mixture into the molds, and then moved on to the next. After a moment, Lucille realized the second set of molds were too close to the edge. Fiona must have realized the same thing as she went to scoot the mold back, but her other hand had already tipped the ladle. Lucille called out a moment too late and watched in horror as Fiona poured the ladle full of hot sugar water onto her hand.

"Oh, Lady Fondant!" Lucille rushed over and began to dab at her hand. Then she thought better of it and wet a cool, clean rag and wrapped it around Fiona's hand. "Are you alright?"

Before she could answer Lucille cradled Fiona's hand in her arms and kissed her on the forehead. "You must be in so much pain." She gave Fiona's hand a gentle squeeze and positioned it so Fiona could lay her head down.

"Is this alright?" Lucille asked.

"Wonderful," Fiona said, sighing and closing her eyes.

"You're not hurt at all!"

"No?"

Lucille unwrapped the rag from Fiona's hand. The skin was damp but unbroken, no discoloration or boil.

"Are you a demon? A spirit? A vampire? A witch?" Lucille asked, taking a step back.

"I don't know if there's an equivalent in your culture. I believe it's beyond your comprehension."

"Understood." Lucille nodded, shaking her head so she wouldn't cry.

There was a gentle knock on Lucille's door. "Come in." she called out.

It was Fiona, carrying a large book. She sat up a little bit straighter in the bed. "Hello, I was just sketching." Lucille adjusted her knotted silk scarf, she cursed herself silently for tying her hair up so soon. She probably looked like an egg. Fiona stood there shifting her weight back and forth. Lucille wasn't sure what to say so she began to gather up her loose pages. "Did you need something?" she asked finally.

"I would like to show you a family heirloom."

Lucille nodded, then glanced around the room. There was a seat at the vanity, a bench, a trunk and then the bed. Fiona climbed up on the bed and sat near the foot. "This book is a history of my family and our practices."

Lucille nodded. Her family didn't have such a thing and if they had, someone would have pawned it by now.

"Where my family comes from is called Esha. Have you heard of it? Unlike the Monarch's field or the continent, Esha is huge. My family comes from the eastern region." Fiona said.

"The continent is huge," Lucille said. She had seen this new, mostly unexplored land on maps.

"Mhmm not like Esha, in my native tongue we call our homeland 'The land of infinite mothers.' It is a magical place, powerful, ancient and sacred. I will show you on a map one day." Fiona said. "I've never been but it is much larger. I've visited the dream world."

"Oh." Lucille was not sure what else to say.

"My grandmother was a vessel for a spirit, well no. A demigod of sorts, a force of nature…I'm not sure of the word. We call them the Sher, or they call us the Sher," Fiona said slowly.

"You are a Sher, this type of magical being?"

"Yes."

Fiona opened the book. "This is very personal to me."

"I won't touch it." Lucille said, going to sit closer so she could see the illustrated page better.

"You can," Fiona said, passing it to her.

A Sher is a supernatural entity that acts as a conduit between the three realms… Lucille pondered this for a moment, she had always thought there were beings who existed that could travel between realms but she hadn't considered one could travel from this world to the underworld and all the way to the heavens. She continued to read but the words were complicated and foreign.

"What does this mean for you?" Lucille said finally. Perhaps Fiona could help her make sense of all this.

"Uh, not very much. I'm not dangerous. You've seen my abilities to move materials with my mind, but I am not a strong Sher like my grandmother. There's degrees. I have some vampire-like tendencies. I crave blood as I'm anemic."

"Do you need a donor?" Lucille asked. "I have plenty of blood. Once I had to bleed with leeches, that was quite the ordeal but afterwards they were thick and plump and…" She trailed off realizing she was talking too much.

"No, but I appreciate your eagerness," Fiona said, smiling.

Lucille shrank away embarrassed.

"No, please don't shrink away or apologize for being thoughtful and kind." Fiona reached over and patted her hand.

"Go on," Lucille said. "I'm sure there's more."

"I have abilities to control things with my mind; here and there, I shift…."

Lucille clapped her hands excitedly. "Into an animal?"

"No, sorry to disappoint." Fiona said. "I transform into a light."

"You, a ray of sunshine?" Lucille laughed.

"An orb of light, a ball."

"I know what an orb is." Lucille said, rolling her eyes "You said vampiric earlier…"

"I'm anemic and crave blood. I can go in the sunlight."

"Are you immortal?" Lucille whispered.

Fiona leaned in, "Not quite."

"Can you transform for me?"

"I'm too tired now, but soon," Fiona said, closing the book. "I need to be getting to bed."

"Thank you," Lucille said.

Lucille awoke to a knock on her door. She rolled over and stretched. For a moment she considered pulling off her ruffled silk bonnet and unwrapping her braids. Before she could decide, the person called out through the door, "Miss Waters, Lady Fondant asked for you to join her for tea."

"Thank you, Marty," Lucille called out loudly.

"Perry, Ma'am but you're most welcome." he said gruffly.

Wonderful, Lucille thought. Another reason for the man to hate me. She looked at her meager selection of dresses, a couple of which were already stained from her confection lessons. "Oh, well, this will have to do." She tugged on a yellow dress, even with the drawstring cinched as tightly as she could manage, the neckline was still loose as it had been stretched from several previous owners. She tucked in her best fichu; the neck scarf only had a few snags on it and they were mostly hidden in her bosom. Lucille looked at her reflection for a long while, crossing the scarf off and over, to and fro, until she liked the way it was tucked into the neckline. She only had one pair of hollow brass hoops that were etched to look like vines. Those would have to do, she clasped them on her ears. Then she carefully made her way through the large house to Lady Fondant's private parlor. Her fingers absentmindedly trailed the gold rails that periodically lined the walls.

"Ah, there you are, Miss Waters," Fiona said as she entered giving her a warm smile. Lucille could have been imagining it, but she thought she saw a faintly eager look flash in her eyes.

"My apologies for being late. I was dressing," Lucille said nervously, fiddling with the end of one of her braids.

"Of course," Fiona said motioning to the seat beside her.

"You did not have to wait for me..." Lucille said, slipping into the chair. It scooted itself forward.

"During your time here, you'll take tea with me." Fiona said, then as if she thought better of it, she said, "That's not an instruction, it is a request."

"Alright," Lucille said, picking up her teacup to disguise her trembling hands.

"I sent for more dresses. You can have some made as well but the village modiste is very busy this time of year."

Lucille choked on her tea. "Ah, I don't...." She tried to think of something that was not a lie.

"I noticed that you've been getting dirty during our lessons. I've also sent for detachable sleeves and aprons."

"Thank you." She said softly, staring into her teacup. She needed new clothes; she had needed them for the last three years. *Accept the gift,* she thought to herself. *I can repay her kindness later.*

Lucille traced the pattern of the tablecloth and chewed on her tongue absentmindedly. She wondered if the swirls were purposely designed to resemble piped icing. They sat in silence for several minutes, but it was an easy soft silence that wrapped them lightly like a knit shawl. Lucille stole a glance at Fiona's face, such a charming profile, tense with concentration as she read a letter of some sort.

Fiona finished her tea with a large swig. "Miss Waters, if you're done we should get to our lesson."

As they walked down the hall, Lucille noticed the gold railings that were on the walls. Each one was slightly different, some swirled into feather motifs and others into craggy branches. "What are these railings for?" Lucille asked as she tugged at the nearest one. It was firmly affixed to the wall.

"To hold on to." Fiona looked at her curiously. "If I'm tired or unwell."

"Isn't that what your..." She hesitated. "Your walking stick is for?" Lucille asked.

"There are days when I start off not needing my cane, and then I need support," Fiona said. She held up her hands as if to remind Lucille that the cane was gone.

"Oh, I hadn't realized."

Fiona nodded. Lucille felt foolish for asking but Fiona's eyes were gentle, and a bemused smile curved on her lips.

"I didn't mean to pry," Lucille said sheepishly.

"Ask as many questions as you'd like," Fiona said.

"Do you not like to leave because of your condition?"

Fiona laughed, it was a delightful sound, musical, low and throaty just like her voice. "No, no. Being physically sick in this instance doesn't have anything to do with my myriad of mental struggles. Unrelated, as is my difficult disposition and good looks."

Lucille smiled despite herself. The kitchen they arrived at was grand but narrow, it was how she imagined the kitchens in the fashionable townhomes of Mulvaney Square to be arranged. Fiona seemed preoccupied with getting the materials ready for the lesson, so Lucille took the opportunity to stare at her. Hopefully this need to be constantly studying her every feature and movement would soon subside. Lucille doubted it but it was a hope.

Despite not wearing a cravat, Fiona's shirt was half undone. She wore a gold chain which, while large and thick, did not cover much skin. *Was she even wearing a pair of stays? Surely she must be wearing something.* Lucille wondered if it was cool or if it had been warmed by Fiona's skin. Fiona was generally very cool, so it was probably cool to the touch. Would it leave indents if they embraced?

"You like this one?" Fiona said, holding the chain up with her thumb. So much for her being preoccupied.

"Mhmm," Lucille said, not knowing what to say.

"Come here, take a better look," Fiona said; the smile she gave her was so sweet, and her eyes so inviting; the moment was as intimate as Lucille imagined kissing to be.

Lucille leaned over. On certain links there were embedded gemstones scattered across certain links.

"It has a secret message. Each gemstone means a letter."

"I've seen similar items…" Lucille trailed off, not wanting to say she'd only seen them at the market.

"Would you do me a favor?" Fiona interrupted, not waiting for a response. Instead, she guided Lucille's hand to her throat. "Can you undo the clasp?"

Lucille didn't trust herself to speak so she simply nodded. She twisted the chain around so the clasp was in the front and then she undid it, when it fell to her hands it was even heavier than she had expected and it was indeed warmed by Fiona's skin.

"Wear it for me," Fiona said. Lucille blinked several times, she just stood there with the glittering chain in her hands, her dizzied senses not registering what she should do or say.

"What does it say?" Lucille said finally, hoping to buy more time before she answered. She tried to sort through the mix of feelings that suddenly surged. Was this a cruel joke?

Fiona smirked. "You'll have to decode that yourself, my little spy."

"Put it on." Fiona prodded. There was a frustrating hint of dominance in her tone which aroused Lucille more than she would care to admit. She twisted her arms behind her and clasped the chain on.

"If you like gold chains, I have a rope twist as well," Fiona said, not bothering to hide her roving gaze as it slid down Lucille's body and then back up to her eyes.

"Is it similar to the hairstyle?" Lucille said, trying to picture how such a piece would look.

"Yes, the chains are intertwined. It would complement you."

"How so?" Lucille wanted to take note of which metal tones and gemstones were complementary. In case, one day she could afford them.

"It brings attention to your face," Fiona said as if it were obvious.

Fiona

$\mathcal{T}$he next day, Fiona set about explaining to Lucille how to infuse shortbread with various flavors. She started with lavender, Earl Grey and blackberry as the flavors complimented each other well. In that way, if the measurements were not precise, the dessert would still taste reasonably fine. Lucille was a timid baker; she was slowly adding in the loose Earl Grey tea leaves and lavender bits into the flour and sugar mixture. Fiona had to stand on tip toes to watch over her shoulder, between every tablespoon, Lucille would look at her notes, then at the measuring spoon and then back at her notes as if she were terrified of making a mistake.

Fiona brushed her hand across Lucille's back. She was going to tell her to calm down, but Lucille flinched away from her so hard she knocked into the kitchen counter. Fiona took a step back quickly, knocking into a rack of copper pans that banged together loudly. Lucille turned to face Fiona, her expression tense. She smiled but there was no warmth; it was moreso a wince of pained awkwardness trying desparately to put the gesture behind them.

"You're a jumpy one," Fiona said.

Lucille shrugged. Fiona wasn't sure if it was supposed to appear to be an aloof gesture, but she resembled a wooden peg doll.

"If we are to be engaged, you may want to control your skittering," Fiona said playfully.

"I'm just not used to it is all. Besides, how proper is it for fiancées to touch?" Lucille said, returning to her mixing.

Fiona frowned. "When I was engaged there was a good deal of grace afforded to my fiancée and me. Within reason of course."

"Afforded, past tense?" Lucille asked.

"Yes, her name was Bree. Well, I'm sure her name still is Bree, but she is no longer my fiancée. When we were engaged, we were appropriately affectionate." Fiona said, explaining quickly.

Lucille managed a tight, tentative smile. Fiona could tell she wanted to ask questions, but she did not, instead she said, "Alright. Touch me where you think appropriate." Her voice raised an octave as she took a step back and spread her arms and legs out.

"Oh?" Fiona said, trying to control her face.

"Yes! Best to get it over with," Lucille said.

Fiona placed her hand on her shoulder. Then her side, near her hips. Then she squeezed Lucille's hand.

Then Fiona kissed her forehead, she leaned up and whispered in Lucille's ear. "Is it your turn?"

Lucille cleared her throat. "Uh? No. My family won't expect me to be…affectionate."

"The conservative sort?" Fiona asked.

"Not hardly, they're the cold sort."

The barley water at the hearth began to boil. Fiona added the perfect amount of sugar and then carefully mixed in the cream of tartar. Fiona could feel Lucille's eyes on her as she sat the metal tin down.

"What does this do?" Fiona asked, pointing to the tin. She had told Lucille the content's earlier and was curious if she would remember.

"It keeps the candy from becoming too brittle," Lucille said confidently.

Fiona clapped softly. "Now, pour them into the mold."

"Now what?" Lucille asked once the metal toy-shaped molds were filled.

"We wait and have tea." Fiona said.

"A great deal of your confectionary process seems to involve tea," Lucille said, wiping her hands.

"You're a fast learner." Fiona said with a smile.

Part Two

Recipes for Love and Disaster

Lucille

*F*iona rolled her neck, and Lucille noticed her cravat glittered with something. At first Lucille thought it was a brooch, but then she realized it was a clasp or ring of some sort because the tails of the cravat were tucked into it.

"You're staring Miss Waters, careful eyes like yours are dangerous."

"Excuse me?" Lucille said blinking several times, one again stupefied by Fiona's flirtatiousness.

"Your eyes, they're dark and warm, decadent even. They remind me of chocolate moonstones. Looks like that will get you in trouble."

"What confection is that?" Lucille asked.

"It's a gemstone," Fiona said, tilting her head to the side slightly.

"Oh?"

"Why were you looking at me?" Fiona asked. The question was more of a challenge.

"Your brooch? Is it a brooch?" Lucille said, pointing to Fiona's neck.

"Oh no, it's a neck ring. Well, not a proper one. I have so many rings, I can hardly wear them as I'm always baking, or my fingers are swollen. I will try to find other uses for them." Fiona said.

"What a lovely problem to have," Lucille said mockingly.

"That it is," Fiona said; if she had picked up on Lucille's sarcasm, she did not acknowledge it. "Would you like to see a chocolate moonstone? The one I have is very modest, but you're welcome to it."

"I-" Lucille started, before she could answer Fiona took her hand and guided her through the halls and up the stairs. "What of our tea?"

"It'll be there," Fiona said; Lucille could tell she was excited from how quickly she was going up the stairs. Lucille jogged up the stairs behind her, careful not to trip on her slippers as the silk was separating from the sole.

"What room is this?" Lucille asked.

"My sitting room. As you know I prefer my parlor which is also my study. I don't use this room terribly often. My jewelry collection doesn't fit in my dressing room." Fiona seemed embarrassed to be explaining all of this."

She opened a box and dug around. "You know, my family isn't some old dynasty. My great grandfather came to Monarch's Field to become a chef and he stumbled into confections. My apologies if all of this seems excessive. I'm just proud."

"Don't apologize on my account. You should enjoy the things afforded to you." Lucille said softly.

"Ah, here it is." Fiona held the necklace out to her.

The colorful necklace consisted of gold filigree and several gemstones, each one square cut in its own setting, surrounded by a frame of floral, in between the square cut gems were dangling coral teardrop pendants.

"This is small?" Lucille said.

"The chocolate moonstone is," Fiona said.

Lucille looked at the necklace more closely. Indeed, one of the gems was a rich brown.

"I could not accept such an item," Lucille said finally.

"Please, it hardly gets any use. You may take all that you would like."

"No, really."

"Well, you should wear something. My fiancé would never walk around unadorned."

"Did your former fiancé wear these?" Lucille said motioning to the jewelry box.

"No, she had her own jewelry."

"But of course."

"Some of it was paste and steel cut," Fiona said weakly.

"But of course," Lucille said again.

Later, in the safety of her room, she pondered her good fortune. She had gone from having no jewels to two beautiful pieces. Fiona, for all her bravado, really seemed quite sweet. And terribly handsome. Lucille lay back and thought of Fiona's playful frisk earlier. She wondered what Fiona's firm hands would feel like skimming her curves in a more sensual manner. Every inch of her body craved Fiona's calloused hands. Lucille clenched her thighs together tightly and grasped at the bedsheets thinking of Fiona's touch. Before she could get too lost in her reverie, the door flew open. She drew her legs up, recoiling back towards the headboard.

"Lucille? Are you alright?" Fiona stood there in the doorway.

"Uh, yes, you scared me," Lucille rearranged her blanket, aware of the sheerness of the threadbare night dress. "I startle easily."

Fiona laughed and dropped her cane; she curled her hands into claws. And stalked toward the bed dramatically.

"Arrrgh, I've come to devour you." In an instant, Fiona's fluttering fingers danced across Lucille's ribs. She squealed and then snorted.

"Don't you laugh." Fiona teased. "I'm a scary monster."

Lucille's thoughts spun; the playful lightness of the moment whirled around her.

"Goodness, you're cold," Lucille said once she regained her breath.

"Oh, I'm sorry." Fiona rubbed her hands together.

"No, no, it's quite alright," Lucille said quickly. "It's stuffy in here. The coolness was refreshing,"

"What were you thinking of? You seemed lost in thought and jumpy." Fiona asked, perching on the edge of the bed.

"I am used to those who knock," Lucille said, cocking a brow.

"Ah, noted," Fiona said. "I haven't had guests in a long time. But what were you thinking of?"

"Nothing really."

"Well, I have this for you," Fiona said, producing a small leather book. "For your jewelry decoding."

Lucille reached her hand out but instead of handing it to her, Fiona leaned forward and kissed her palm. She flashed a devilish smirk. Lucille gasped, surprised at how eagerly her body responded to the simple gesture. Fiona handed her the small book and Lucille was thankful for the distraction. She flipped through it gingerly. The illustrations were clearly hand painted and it was organized like an encyclopedia. Each stone or crystal had its own paragraph. When she looked at the inside cover, she realized in pen it was marked with a short note "To L, Regards, -F."

Before Lucille could respond and express her gratitude, Fiona spoke again.

"Your room is so cold. The servants must not remember you are here. It's not often we have a change of routine," Fiona crossed the room to the now smoldering fire. "Ah, it's practically out."

Fiona dug around in the trunk at the foot of Lucille's bed and produced a thick knitted blanket. She draped it across Lucille's shoulders.

"This blanket is quite thick, thank you."

"I'll light a fire so you can sleep in the warmth." Fiona said.

"Oh, please no, don't trouble yourself," Lucille said, quickly clutching at the blanket around her shoulders, she had completely forgotten she was in her nightdress.

"It's quite alright, the wood is here, let me see." Fiona patted the ornate mantle "Ah yes, the tinder box."

Lucille watched as Fiona fumbled with the small silver kit. She wanted to offer to help as she'd done it hundreds of times, but she was awkwardly clutching her blanket up to her chin with one hand, the other draped across her shoulders.

"That is that," Fiona said once the fire was blazing. She wiped her hands. "Well, I'll be going now. Good night." Lucille watched as she stiffly bent down to pick up her cane.

"Lady Fondant..." Lucille called out just before the door closed.

"Yes?" Fiona said, peeking her head back in.

"What is it you needed?" Lucille asked. Surely, Fiona hadn't stopped in just to give her a book.

"Needed?" Fiona asked. "To give you the book, but more importantly, I came to say goodnight. I was lost in the sums for the shop and realized you'd already gone to bed."

"Oh, of course. Well goodnight."

"Goodnight."

Lucille didn't go to sleep. Instead she brought out the gold chain necklace. It was cool under her fingertips. She laid it out in the scarf she had it wrapped in. The first gemstone was a light green.

She flipped through the book. It looked like a Peridot. She continued on, the next crystal was purple, Amethyst. She continued looking from the stones to the book.

Peridot, Amethyst, Sapphire, Sunstone, Iolite, Opal, Natrolite. *Passion.*

Had Fiona commissioned this for herself? Was this an heirloom? She had been expecting it to say adore, regards or perhaps dearest. She wrapped the chain back in the scarf and placed it next to the other necklace that Fiona had given to her.

Dinner at Sugar Lump Manor reminded Lucille of the banquets her and Kenna read about in their novels. The food was plentiful, the linen elegant, and the tablescape shone with ornate dishware and mirrors to catch the light. The only element that was not traditional was the gingerbread attendants who delivered the dishes. Their livery was made of supple velvet fabric and trimmed with white piping that resembled icing.

"Thank you," Lucille said and moved to the side so the attendant could place the dish in front of her.

"Have you had an artichoke?" Fiona said. The radiance of her smile warmed Lucille from across the table.

"No…" Lucille said, wondering where Fiona was going.

"They're delicious, much like brussels sprouts." Fiona said, the smile still curled on her lips.

Lucille eyed the bulbous cabbage skeptically. It looked as if it was stuffed with a sandy mixture of some kind.

"It is delicious, I assure you. They're not eaten often because the outer leaves are tough and require a great deal of trimming and preparation beyond cooking." Fiona said. Fiona placed one on Lucille's plate and then one her own.

"Perhaps they are inedible or poisonous? This sounds unnatural," Lucille said, giving it a tentative poke with her fork.

Fiona smiled. "What is worthwhile is often difficult."

"I am uncertain of how one would eat this…artichoke," Lucille said.

"Let us make a lesson of it," Fiona said.

"Do you make confections of it?"

"No," Fiona said, the side of her mouth quirked upward as if she was trying to stifle a smile. "I am not that creative. Here, tear off a leaf and scoop up the filling with it and scrape."

"It seems rather inconvenient. A bit fortified for veg." Once she had consumed all the stuffing and looked at the piles of discarded leaves that littered the table, there was only a hairy piece remaining.

"I call it the armadillo of vegetables," Fiona smirked. "This is the choke," She motioned to the spiky fibrous part that was now exposed.

"Was the rest the art?" Lucille asked.

Fiona chuckled. "Now scrape that off."

Lucille scraped at the fibers with her spoon, mimicking Fiona's actions until she was left with a fleshy thick saucer shaped piece. "Now what?"

"Eat the heart," Fiona said, her tone suddenly serious.

"The heart?"

"The center, trust me, it is heavenly," Fiona said; she scooped the heart up on her fork and guided it towards Lucille's mouth.

"Ah, it is divine," Lucille said.

"Lesson complete."

She swallowed hard, trying to manage a response. "This was not about veg," Lucille said finally.

Once dinner was finished, Lucille made her way back to her room, thinking of what sketches she would work on for her portfolio. As she made her way down the hallway, she noticed one of the ornate gold frames was askew. She went to gently tilt it back into place and her fingers left an indent. She pressed harder and it crumbled.

"Sponge!" She cried out.

Somewhere nearby she heard a giggle. She turned around to find Perry nearly doubled over, the normally glum-faced man's features were contorted in laughter. She broke off another piece of the painting and half-heartedly tossed it at him. "You sir, are the worst!" Then she flounced away dramatically.

Fiona

 t took very little time for Fiona to realize Lucille was not only brilliant, but absurdly creative. She picked most things up after one explanation. Cheesecake, however, did not seem to be most things. Fiona took a bite of the blackberry and sage biscuits they had made and waited for the next onslaught of questions.

"Cheesecake, what cheese do you need?" Lucille asked, scribbling away in her little notebook.

"Cheese? No cheese!" Fiona said, her voice involuntarily slipped into a groan. She enjoyed Lucille's company, but she had so many silly questions.

"Then what?" Lucille asked, propping her elbows up on the table, clearly unperturbed.

Fiona finished arranging the decorative elements before answering, "Egg, custard...almonds. It's on the paper, my little spoon."

"And?" Lucille said expectantly.

"Uh, lemon, sugar, flour water, almonds." Fiona said.

Lucille groaned. "You said almonds. I did not even observe what you did. You moved too quickly."

Fiona shrugged. "There's a lot of almonds."

"Alright, what of the cheese?" Lucille

"I said no cheese!" Fiona said she tried to get her annoyance under control. "Here, you sit and I'll finish decorating this. It's a very important recipe."

"I hardly did anything," Lucille said, pouting. "What are you doing now?"

"Sugar paste decorations," Fiona said, motioning to the ball of dough she was forming.

"I can sculpt, let me. I hardly did anything."

Fiona dabbed a bit of flour from the counter onto Lucille's nose and then swiped some more on each of her cheeks.

"There, it is much more believable. You look like gingerbread dough dusted with flour."

Lucille laughed and twisted her face into a grimace, pretending to gag. "You are the only person I shall allow to compare my countenance to a food item. Once I had a suitor compare my skin to the 'most supple bitter chocolate'. Who would think of such a thing, write it, read it and then mail it?"

"Someone lovestruck by your beauty," Fiona said. "Although, there are a number of other ways I would describe your beauty. I can understand why one's mind might automatically think of consumables."

Fiona watched as Lucille's mouth opened and then closed quickly. She did this motion twice in rapid succession as if gasping for air.

"My apologies," Fiona said, returning to shaping her sugar paste duck.

"No, no need. I am very flattered..." Lucille said, her voice trailing off into silence.

"But?"

"That was all. My sentence was complete." Lucille said with a curt nod. She hesitated slightly and Fiona wondered who she was trying to convince.

"I'll finish this, let it set up, and then we'll go read and..."

"Have tea?" Lucille finished.

"Or cocoa," Fiona said sheepishly.

"Would you like a piece of taffy?" Lucille asked, pointing to the small bowl of the candies on the table.

"No, why?"

"You're chewing on your lip so hard. I'm concerned about it," Lucille said with a mischievous wink.

Was I? Fiona released her bottom lip from where it was rolled under her two front teeth.

Lucille

 he fire in Fiona's private parlor always seemed to be the perfect temperature. She watched as Bon Bon settled into a soft spot under the side table. Lucille wasn't certain where the turtle lived but it seemed as though this was Bon Bon's favorite room. The tea Fiona had chosen was slightly bitter with citrus notes. They discussed the sculptures they had created, what had gone properly, what areas could have improvement and then Lucille settled into her romance novel. Fiona laid on her back on the settee and clasped her hands behind her head, seemingly lost in thought. Lucille wondered for a moment what she was thinking about but then returned to her book. Fiona was always thinking of some grand idea or improvement to a recipe. After a long while, Fiona yawned, stiffened her legs and then gave them both a thorough shake.

"I'm tired. Would you like for me to walk you up?" Fiona asked,

"No, thank you," Lucille said, holding up her book. "I'll stay up a bit longer to finish this section."

As Fiona walked by, she leaned down and pressed a soft kiss to each of Lucille's eyelids. Then she briefly brushed her lips against Lucille's. It was so subtle and fast that Lucille half wondered if she imagined it, but the tingling of her lips told her she had not.

Fiona straightened, yawned again, and half whispered. "Good night then."

Lucille looked up at her. Fiona's eyes were almost closed, and she looked exhausted. "Good night."

Lucille lingered for a long while with her book closed. The fire went out, but she didn't bother stoking it. She brushed her fingertips across her lips, thinking of Fiona and the faint taste of vanilla. Lucille desperately wanted more of her. More of what, she wasn't precisely sure of. *You can't stay here all night,* she thought, willing herself to stand up. Then she twisted the amber stones in their sconces so they went dark and then she made her way upstairs to her room. The heavy wooden armoire was open, and she immediately saw it was full of a rainbow array of gowns. She noticed her old dresses were still there, mixed in among the new garments. The dresser drawers were staggered open and equally as full of clothing. Both the vanity and nightstands were covered in neatly arranged boxes, each one open, with the lids propped open to incline the boxes to look like a shop display. She looked down and realized the entire perimeter of the room was lined with slippers and boots. It gave Lucille an odd sense of satisfaction that Fiona had added a rather large box of face products. And from the looks of it, expensive ones. She picked up a gold circular tin. It took a bit of force to pop it open, but it revealed itself to be filled with a paper disc of foundation. There was a matching gold pot of rouge and a tin of colored lip pomade. When she held the lip pomade up to the light, she realized it was engraved with a delicate LF. She picked up another compact. It too had an LF. As did the hand mirror. *Curious,* Lucille thought to herself. Fiona was taking this ruse very far. But Lucille did not give herself too much time to dwell on it because she was too excited by the variety of dresses. It was so late: she knew she should go to bed but instead she tried on each piece in turn until she unceremoniously fell asleep admidst her new collection.

Lucille was regretting her decision to spend half the night playing dress up. She yawned widely and her eyes fluttered closed for a moment.

"Miss Waters!" Fiona said.

Lucille felt her catch her wrist and stop her from pouring anymore sugar water into the mold. Her mind jolted back to consciousness. She was supposed to be making confections not nodding off.

"Too much?" Lucille said, placing it down.

"Yes. Making confections is very precise. Not so free spirited like art." Fiona explained.

Lucille shook her head. "Not for myself." She was tired but not too tired to argue about her views on art.

Fiona frowned. "Would you like to be more creative with the recipes? Or with the decorating."

"Oh no, I'm sorry, that's not at all what I meant," Lucille said with a yawn.

"I misunderstood."

"It's alright. I did not explain well." Lucille said.

"Explain it to me; I'm listening," Fiona said, peering up into her eyes.

"I like art because I can control the world around me and manipulate reality. When I draw something, I'm showing my perception to the viewer and presenting my own viewpoint and in that way it's about control."

"I see." Fiona said. "I believe it's similar to my confections. I enjoy the control of making them but also the connection with people without engaging with them."

"I have a difficult time connecting with others," Lucille said, fiddling with the handle of the pitcher.

"Even in your big school full of people?"

"Especially there. Some of the girls were very kind but the staff was horrid."

"You went to an all-girls school?" Fiona smirked, "That sounds quite fun."

"It was more nunnery than brothel," Lucille said.

"Ah, perhaps being educated at home wasn't terrible."

"How does one court if you did not leave your estate?"

"Society would visit during the country season," Fiona explained. Then she added, "Do you have many suitors?"

"None. I had one my first season and attended a few smaller events, nothing with The Ton, but after that, no."

"Why?"

"My looks. I believe in myself and my personality." Lucille said simply.

"Your beauty is intimidating, but I find your personality to be quite approachable," Fiona said.

"Ah," Lucille said, tapping the mold casually, with an ease she most certainly did not feel.

"Why do I feel that your lack of suitors does not simply come down to a lack of social engagements?" Fiona said, her piercing gaze unwavering.

"It's hard to trust people and know what's real. Take for instance, this situ-" Lucille hesitated, choosing her words carefully.

"You can trust me," Fiona said.

"Well-"

"I'm sorry; go on," Fiona said gently.

"Sometimes in this situation, I forget you're just pitying me and I'm not a real apprentice or a fiancé. It's all very sad. What's real is sad."

"I don't pity you. I adore you already. You're the friend I hold dearest to my heart. My care for you is real. My regard." Fiona said quickly; her voice, while still deep, was higher than Lucille was used to.

"I am uncertain if I trust it."

Instead of responding with anger, Fiona gave her a warm, reassuring smile. "My trust in you is steadfast and concrete. I have faith enough for both of us."

"I appreciate that," Lucille said.

"I'm sorry I can't give you...what is conventional." Fiona, reached out, grazing her face with a featherlight touch. The mere brush of contact made her warm. Fiona wrapped her arms around Lucille and she melted into the embrace, a sigh of pleasure escaping her.

"You've been exceedingly generous." Lucille breathed out.

Too quickly, Fiona pulled back slightly, only separating them a few inches but it felt too far for Lucille. "Is what I have to offer enough?" Fiona said her face awash with concern. She was searching Lucille's face.

"What are you offering?" Lucille said hesitantly.

"I'll sponsor your art applications, your tuition, whatever it is you need."

Lucille laughed mirthlessly. "Thank you."

She was upset with herself for feeling so ungrateful, but she couldn't get the hurt aching feeling to subside. Fiona did not seem to notice she was upset, so Lucille tried to muster as much false cheer as she could.

"You're most welcome," Fiona said, returning to the molds.

Lucille followed Perry's instructions to meet Fiona in the library right after breakfast. When she walked through the large oak doors, she was shocked by how average the library looked. Perhaps average was not the correct word, it was large with seemingly endless rows of shelves and lush burgundy carpets. In the center of the room was an oak table nearly as large as a banquet table from Brittlebone. Still on either side there was enough space for smaller tables, armchairs and their ottomans. She had the nearly uncontrollable urge to climb on one of the steel rolling ladders and slide down the length of the shelves. However, it didn't have the obvious candy motifs and bright colors that adorned most of the house. It was also bare of the ornate draping, detailed scrollwork and murals she had become accustomed to seeing at Sugar Lump Manor.

"Good morning, Miss Waters!" Fiona called out. Lucille waved; she had been so in awe by the cavernous library that she hadn't seen her sitting at the table.

"I didn't see you there," Lucille said, hurrying over. She wondered if she should mention her new dress, but then she thought better of it. Fiona had them delivered, so obviously, she knew what they looked like.

"Oh, your new dresses have arrived. That blue is fetching on you." Fiona said standing.

"Can you read minds?"

"No," Fiona said with a frown. "Are you alright?"

"Yes, yes," Lucille said, smoothing the net fabric of her skirt, her fingertips skimming the bumps of the embroidered blueberries.

Fiona leaned in and whispered. "Were you thinking of something scandalous?"

"Yes," Lucille said, leaning in slightly. "I would like to ride on the rolling ladders."

"Your wish is my command, my lady." Fiona held her arm out and motioned to the nearest ladder. Lucille climbed up, far past where it was high enough so that her skirt did not catch in the mechanism.

"Hold on tight," Fiona said from somewhere below her.

She looked down and watched as Fiona twirled her pointer finger and then made a sharp pointing motion. Before she could respond the ladder went hurtling down the rail with astonishing force. A breeze heavy with the smell of old paper and cardamom hit her full force and after a moment she jerked to a stop, breathless. She was glad she did not let go, for after only a moment she was hurtling backwards. She yelped and closed her eyes tightly. Even after she came to full stop, she clenched the sides of the ladder tightly. Lucille tried to will herself down, but her clenched fists would not respond, even though the iron was digging into her palms and she was dizzy from the speed.

Suddenly, she felt a warmth on her back, and Fiona's familiar scent of toasted vanilla and almond surrounded her. "I'm sorry,"

Fiona said gently into her ear. "We'll climb down one step at a time, and if you fall, I'll break your landing."

Lucille giggled and opened her eyes. Together they made their way down the ladder.

"I'm sorry," Lucille said breathlessly. "I did not expect it to be that invigorating."

"The fault is mine, let us rest for a moment before starting our lesson."

"Yes, lovely·idea." Lucille reached for the ornate porcelain pitcher that sat at the middle of the table surrounded by glasses. A big glass of water would be perfect.

"Miss Wa-" Fiona said as Lucille picked up the pitcher. It crumbled in Lucille's hand, leaving her holding the handle which seemed to be made entirely out of sugar paste. From where the handle had broken off, Lucille could see cake peeking through.

"Oh, Perry when I get my hands on him-" Lucille said with a frown.

"I believe this is Marty's work," Fiona said with a grin. Lucille let the sugar paste handle fall to the table and sat down.

"Shall I call for refreshment?" Fiona asked, sitting beside her.

"No, no we've already wasted time." Lucille peered at the leaflets strewn about the table, brushing cake crumbs off of one. "What's all this?"

"Flavorings and pairings. An important part of confection. We will study and discuss them. I thought it would be a nice change of pace from you burning things."

"Thank you kindly for that," Lucille said dryly.

The flavors weren't overly hard to memorize, there were herbal ones like earl grey, rose, and lavender, ones based on veg such as cucumber, eggplant, asparagus, and celery. A more refined palette craved savory or complex tastes and for those they offered parmesan cheese, anise seed, tarragon, and ginger. The pairings though, she struggled with. She rarely had more than one course in a meal, let alone multiple options for dessert.

"Toasted muffins are best served with…" Fiona prompted helpfully.

"Tea?" Lucille said weakly.

"Yes," Fiona said, slamming the table excitedly.

"It is hopeless, every confection can be served with tea. I'll never remember the important pairings."

"You mustn't be so hard on yourself. Here let us do an easy one to get your confidence up." Fiona said, patting her hand. "What confection would you suggest for a lady who wishes to imbibe."

"Oh, whip syllabub made with Rhine wine."

"Precisely," Fiona said.

Lucille could certainly use one of the refreshing treats now, it was easy enough to make. She knew how to whip the frothy cream and exactly how much wine to add to the bottom of the glass.

"I'm bored of this. Shall we make our way to the kitchen? I'll make the syllabub and you can question me about burnt almond and port."

Fiona laughed. "Sounds like a wonderful plan."

Lucille studied Fiona carefully and watched her as she moved about the kitchen expertly gathering ingredients for the syllabub. Lucille had noticed that some days Fiona had a slight limp and a bounce to her gait, but it seemed more pronounced today than it had the last few days. After a moment it dawned on Lucille that Fiona wasn't using her walking stick today.

"Do you require assistance?" Lucille said not wishing to bother her but also wanting to be useful.

"No, I have my cane if I need support." Fiona said pointing to a wall where the delicately carved wooden stick rested. "And there's always a stool if I need to rest."

"Alright." Lucille said, attaching her apron to her dress with straight pins.

Fiona stopped for a moment, arms full. "Thank you for asking before taking over."

"I wouldn't dream of it," Lucille said.

"Will you teach me how to make ices?"

"No. Anyone with money can make a decent ice. It's so tedious." She pointed a finger towards a large tub with a crank, "if I want to punish you, I'll have you make a few."

"Oh," Lucille said quietly. She had always assumed there was a great deal of skill involved in ices, but it made sense now that it was simply a matter of time, molds and the means to keep them cold.

"I'm sorry; I didn't mean to make light of your financial hardship," Fiona said quietly.

"It is fine, I find your humor reassuring. It's more palatable than pity." Lucille said. "I used to sit outside your family's shop with my friend Kenna."

"Have you had any of the confections? I would love your thoughts," Fiona said.

"No, but I watch your attendants; the magical ones are my favorite," Lucille said. She snapped her fingers. "They're here." She snapped her fingers. "Then they're gone."

Fiona nodded. "They're hard to find. Those who can project themselves farther get better paying posts so we are restricted to the ones who can only manage short distances."

"I did not realize there was so much to manage," Lucille said.

"Rub these lemon peels with the sugarloaf to get the essence," Fiona said, handing Lucille the cone of sugar.

"Is it that simple?" Lucille asked.

"No," Fiona said with a giggle. "This is a very involved process."

Fiona

By the time they had finished the syllabub it was the awkward time of evening where it was too late to start a new task but too early to go to bed so instead, they settled onto the sofa under the guise of reading. Fiona had quickly realized that Lucille was not used to such long hours. More often than not she'd take a nap midway through the evening. Sometimes in the middle of speaking she would be curled up like a cat, or like tonight, she'd mold her body into Fiona's almost using her as a blanket. While fully awake, Lucille was a bit standoffish and unaffectionate, when she grew tired it seemed as though she didn't have enough energy to be tense or anxious. Fiona inhaled the shea butter and citrus smell of Lucille, and wrapped her arms even tighter. Fiona enjoyed being able to stare at Lucille without making her uncomfortable. Lucille was taller than Fiona with wide hips and a soft stomach accentuated by gentle rolls that Fiona loved. Her braids splayed out in all different directions snaking across her shoulders and back. Lucille was easy and soft when she slept. She spread and sprawled. After thirty minutes or so she began to stir.

"Am I hurting you?" Lucille mumbled.

"No, this is perfect. Are you asleep?" Fiona said.

"Yes," Lucille said groggily.

"I have a question or a hypothetical inquiry."

"I may have an answer or a theory." Lucille said.

"If you weren't a charlatan-" Fiona was cut off.

"Creative storyteller-" Lucille said.

"Right, if you weren't lying-" Fiona started but was interrupted once again.

"Lady Fondant!" Lucille said in mock annoyance.

"Shhh, if this was not all make believe…could you love me, all variables being the same except for the circumstances?" Fiona asked.

"Yes," Lucille said; Fiona was a bit taken aback by how quickly she responded. "Although nothing can be all the same and completely different."

She heard Lucille's stomach growl.

"Here, finish this…" Fiona put a soft-boiled egg on Lucille's lips. Lucille nibbled and wrinkled her nose. Then she took another small bite.

"Do you not care for boiled eggs?" Fiona asked.

"They are not my favorite, but I eat them quite often."

Fiona put the half-eaten egg on the tray. "Don't be ridiculous, if you're not enjoying the food don't eat it. You've been eating these for weeks."

"Yes, and I eat them at home; I don't want to waste-"

Fiona tore a scone in half and smeared it with clotted cream and a swipe of strawberry jam. She pressed it to Lucille's lips. "Mhmm," Lucille said. Fiona felt the tip of Lucille's tongue on her fingertips. A glob of jam oozed onto Lucille's thick bottom lip. Fiona pushed it into Lucille's mouth.

"Thank you," Lucille closed her eyes and let out another throaty moan.

Fiona looked down at her, she was clearly unaware of how suggestive and enticing she looked.

"Lady Fondant, you must transform for me."

"What?" Fiona said.

"Into a sunburst. You said you would, I was dreaming of it."

"Orb." Fiona corrected, trying to stall for time.

"Orbital sunburst, yes. Do it." Lucille said, sitting up.

"Alright, but when I tell you I'm shifting back you have to close your eyes."

"Why?" Lucille asked.

"My clothes don't transform with me."

"Oh, of course." Lucille said hurriedly, almost as if she hadn't even considered the idea.

Fiona stood up and concentrated, a tingling warm sensation began to radiate through her body. She took a deep breath, closing her eyes, she felt her clothes, her weight, everything solid, fading away. She could feel herself floating and she saw Lucille staring at her, eyes wide, the light glowing in her dark eyes, mouth slack. Fiona took a deep breath and then bounced around the room as quickly as she could. Lucille clapped excitedly.

"Alright, close your eyes."

Lucille did as she was instructed, and Fiona watched as she covered her face with her hands like an excited child. She sighed and focused on shifting back into her human form until she felt herself being stretched and tugged. Once the transformation was complete, she shrugged on her wrapping stays, long shirt and britches. Not bothering with her stockings.

"You can look now," Fiona said, trying not to look disheveled.

Lucille

*I*t was difficult not to act too excited about seeing Fiona transform and so instead of blurting out all her questions she simply thanked her and got out a book to read. Fiona followed her lead and sat down beside her with her own book. The room was quiet, save for the crackling of the logs in the fireplace and the soft rustle of the pages turning. As Lucille read, she could feel her eyes growing heavy, and soon she succumbed to the warmth of the fire and drifted off into a peaceful sleep. Vaguely she could feel the nubby silk of Fiona's pants and the soft jutting of her kneecap against her cheek.

She was awoken by the sound of an urgently ringing bell. She sat up in bed, her heart racing; she looked around, patting the sofa for Fiona and listening intently for a clue as to what was happening. Once her eyes adjusted to the darkness, she was confident the room was empty. After a few moments, she heard the sound again, the bells followed by a soft rustling, like someone shuffling quickly into the hallway.

With a trembling hand, Lucille reached for the lantern on the side table and twisted the amber stone in its cradle until it glowed. As she slid open the pocket door and made her way down the hallway, the manor felt colder, the shadows darker. But there was no one there. She swung the lantern about but only succeeded in casting eerie shadows on the walls.

Lucille shuddered, unsure if to return to the parlor or make her way to Fiona's room or her own. She stood there frozen until the lantern became heavy in her hand, and then she sat it down. Staring at it like a moth stuck in the orbit of a flame.

"Miss Waters, Lady Fondant is unwell and has been taken to bed. We did not mean to alarm you." Perry called out. He took another few steps towards her and picked up the lantern. "Lady Fondant needed assistance making her way to her rooms."

"Did she try to rouse me?" Lucille asked as she followed him down the hall.

"I believe not, ma'am; Marty found her partially to her room. I believe she did not want to disturb you."

"Oh, I see. Of course." Lucille said, still shaken. They walked the rest of the way to her room in an uneasy silence. She did not bother changing into night clothes. She picked up a book and began to read, waiting for the dawn to break and the safety of daylight to return and bring word of Fiona's condition.

Fiona

The next morning, Fiona watched as Lucille worked her way through a candied orange peel recipe. Lucille yawned and Fiona heard the now familiar sound of Lucille's stomach growling.

"Are you hungry?" Fiona asked.

"Famished."

"Did you eat breakfast?"

Lucille shook her head. "No one called me down."

"Miss Waters!" Fiona said exasperated. "You are supposed to take all meals and tea even if you're not called down."

"Alright," Lucille said, frowning. "I understand now."

"I'm sorry, in the mornings I take time for myself and occasionally lose track of time. Let us take a break for food and then we'll work on cut rock."

"I am terribly excited," Lucille said, "For cut rock and also for you to tell me what happened to you last night."

"I was unwell." Fiona said tugging on the fabric bell pull.

"And now you are well." Lucille stated as they sat there waiting for their food to arrive.

"Yes." Fiona said simply then she changed the subject quickly. "Have you considered finding a wealthy match?"

"No." Lucille said. "I don't possess the charms or looks to negate my poor fortune. Nor do I have connections."

Fiona hesitated; she could give written introductions or host an event. However, that could be successful, and Lucille might get married. Fiona mulled it over for another second before deciding she wanted what was best for Lucille. *No reason to trap two birds in this golden, bejeweled cage,* she thought bitterly. "I can make introductions. I don't mind acting as both your benefactor and guardian."

Lucille looked up to meet her eyes. "No, thank you. I believe marriage would be wonderful, but I prefer a love match. I haven't any money now and am perfectly content to earn my living."

"But not as a governess?"

"It is not my calling," Lucille said simply. "Are confections your calling, or is it simply something you do because your family did it?"

"Yes," Fiona said.

"Which is it?" Lucille asked.

"Both. I also appreciate what my family had to do in order to provide for me." Fiona hesitated. "That too is a blessing and a curse. Sometimes people look at me and see nothing but a bank note."

A gingerbread servant brought in a large tray covered in cold meats, breads, and cuts of fruit. He returned quickly with glasses and a pitcher of orange juice.

"If you're so concerned about others spending your fortune, why are you so free with your favors?" Lucille said, Fiona watched as Lucille fiddled with her wrist, which now jangled with thick gold bracelets that shone brightly when she made the slightest movement. Did Lucille not like her presents?

"Well," Fiona said, taking a swig of orange juice. "I enjoy sharing my wealth when it is deserved."

Lucille's eyes bore into her own, and for a moment, Fiona felt as if she were made of the same candy-colored stained glass as the windows. Fiona tried to clear her face of emotion; sure, she had grown up surrounded by luxury and privilege, but she had always felt a sense of emptiness and longing that no amount of wealth or status could fill. Despite their vastly different upbringings, Fiona sensed Lucille could empathize, but Fiona was too worried about sounding jaded or ridiculous.

"I have done nothing to be deserving of your generosity." Lucille said softly, averting her eyes.

"You're a hard worker, beautiful, charming, funny. You take care of me. You're beautiful, and you smell like shea butter and bergamot."

"I smell like a lime?" Lucille said, looking up quickly.

"Well, yes, no. They're actually oranges." Fiona sighed. That was beside the point. "It was simply the closest I could think of to the smell of you; it's spicy and floral; it's pleasant. I assure you,"

"You also said beautiful twice." Lucille said. "Not that looks are anything more than a stroke of luck. It's like playing whist."

"Well, in that case, you were dealt the best hand; you simply need to strategize."

Lucille sighed. "Despite the circumstances of our meeting, I'm not conniving or opportunistic."

"Did I say you were any of those attributes?" Fiona said.

"Well, no, but you've implied that others have used you,"

"Lucille, if I have something to say to you, I'll say it. You are not other people. Furthermore, you may use me, however you'd like. Thus far, I'm enjoying the experience."

Perry cleared his throat loudly from his spot near the doorway. "My apologies for interrupting but perhaps it is time to proceed to cut rock making."

"Oh yes!" Lucille said, clapping her hands excitedly.

Fiona smiled, the intricate designs of cut rock was one of her favorite things to create as well. She was always amazed at how creative one could be with the tubular hard candy.

"Now, carefully, knock the end off and reveal the design," Fiona said.

Lucille knocked the end of the candy cane with a surprising amount of force and before she had even looked at it closely, Fiona knew from the sound it was ruined.

"You've cracked the entire cane; this is ruined," Fiona said.

"Perhaps we can use it for—"

"No." Fiona snapped.

"I'm sorry. I'm so sorry." Lucille said, her voice thick with tears.

"It's fine. I'll give it to the village children." Fiona said, trying to gentle her tone. Knocking the ends off of cut rock was not easy.

"I'm sorry," Lucille repeated.

"It's alright. I was just surprised is all. The crack doesn't look so bad." Fiona said quickly.

Lucille nodded and upturned her mouth in something that resembled a grimace, but Fiona was sure it was meant to be a smile.

Fiona made a show of popping one into her mouth. "The color and taste are fantastic," Fiona said. "It's alright." She patted Lucille's arm.

"Of course." Lucille wiped at her eyes with the back of her hand. "I'm sorry."

"It is me who should be apologizing. I was simply frustrated."

"Let us forget it," Lucille said, nodding. "I'm tired, and I'll go rest now."

Before Fiona could respond, she had darted out of the room.

"Marty?" Fiona said quietly.

Marty popped his head in the doorway.

"Yes ma'am?"

"How much of that did you hear?"

"All of it, ma'am."

"I-"

"You must be gentler, Lady Fiona. Miss Lucille is not nearly half as brave as she pretends."

"Yes," Fiona said flatly.

"Perhaps you should go see-"

"I already apologized and she said she was tired."

"I assure you she is not tired and you don't need to apologize again. Try a gentle embrace." Marty said helpfully.

"She's skittish."

"Ask first, of course. Don't accost the girl."

"Is that all?"

"Do I need to give you instructions on how to get to her room? What more do you need?" Marty said with a smile.

Fiona shook her head and made her way out of the kitchen.

Lucille

Lucille curled up in the armchair in the corner of the library. She shivered and the armchair crawled slowly towards the fire. "Thank you," she said, giving its scrollwork arm a gentle pat.

"Is there room for two?" Fiona called out.

The chair wiggled slightly.

"Mmh?" Fiona asked.

"Yes of course." Lucille said, her eyes glued to the same spot on the page.

Lucille inhaled deeply as Fiona curled around her. She smelled of citrus and nutmeg. It was a departure from Fiona's usual smell of vanilla and almond but it was nice.

Fiona raised her arm to her nose "Do I smell?"

"No, I ah..." Lucille tried to figure out the best thing to say. "You smell like confections."

"There are worse things to smell like," Fiona said. "Is it complicated?" she asked after a moment.

"Pardon?" Lucille asked.

"Your book, you haven't flipped the page,"

"Oh, I was lost in thought."

"I hope the cut rock isn't vexing you," Fiona said quietly.

"No," Lucille said, flipping the page.

"You're a horrid liar," Fiona said, squeezing her tightly. "I'm sorry."

They sat there in silence until Marty's voice disrupted the stillness. "Lady Fondant, Miss Waters, dinner is ready."

"Bring it here," Fiona said, not bothering to sit up or untangle herself. When they'd finished the fish, mushrooms, and macaroons, Fiona stood up. "I must mind the books. I'll be back. If you can manage to wait up." She said, and with a wink, she was gone.

Fiona

iona closed the thick record book and rubbed her temples. Her eyes were blurry and on a normal night, she'd have gone straight to bed, but she remembered she told Lucille she would check on her. Fiona watched from the doorway as Lucille danced languidly in time to the pianoforte's soft melody. Lucille rolled her hips and moved her shoulders in fluid motions creating curves and swirls with her body. Fiona was lost as to how she managed to move herself in segments in such a way, it seemed wholly unnatural. Goddess-like even. She watched the delicate rotations of her wrist. The music quickened almost matching the thumping of Fiona's own heart. Lucille shook her shoulders, her entire body quivering. She began to shake her hips at such a fast pace Fiona eyes could hardly keep up, Fiona gasped then immediately clamped her hand over her mouth.

Lucille froze, looking at her quickly and then back down at the rug.

"Don't let me stop you. You were doing beautifully…this is very…I'm not used to dances without a partner."

"I'm tired actually."

"Here, have some water," Fiona said, crossing the room to the sideboard.

"My apologies," Lucille said, taking a sip and then placing the glass back down.

"Don't apologize for your dancing, I could sit and watch you for hours."

"I believe I would drop from exhaustion."

"Perhaps I can have a music box created in your honor, the little figurine would quiver, and when you tired, I would wind you up with the key." Fiona said dreamily.

"You flatter me."

"Oh, before I forget…" Fiona said, pulling a letter from her pocket. "I believe this is from your friend."

Lucille practically tore the paper from her hand. "Ooooh my!" She said loudly then stomped her foot.

"Is everything alright?" Fiona asked.

"Yes, yes, yes," Lucille said, spinning around. "Kenna will be traveling to the continent. She's answered a newspaper ad to be a wife, and she says she'll write with details when she's settled."

"That is wonderful, I believe?" Fiona said stupidly. Truthfully it sounded very dangerous and a bit strange.

"If I am gone, you'll forward the letter, won't you? She's my only friend in the entire world."

"Yes, certainly," Fiona said, trying to control her face. Lucille was too excited to notice or care. Lucille gave her the briefest of hugs and then skipped away, wishing her a good night as she passed her on the way to the door.

"I am supposed to beat this for a full hour?" Lucille asked in horror. She looked back at the list, two pounds of sugar, eggs, fine starch…this would take forever.

"Yes, it is to build character. White icing is a staple in the confectionary profession," Fiona said. "It builds both character and muscle. I'll leave you to it."

By the time she had finished the icing, Lucille's arms ached. Marty had taken pity on her and iced the actual cake. She sat and ate some of the coconut balls and melt-in-your-mouth cookies they'd made the day prior. Fiona knocked on the door frame with her cane to announce her entrance.

"Has it set up?" Fiona asked.

"I believe so."

"Tell Marty I appreciate his craftsmanship but next time you should ice the cake."

"My arm was practically about to fall off." Lucille said with exaggerated wince.

"Please cut me a slice if you can manage, and we'll see how you did," Fiona said, peering at the fruitcake with its smooth, even layer of pure white icing. Lucille practically had to saw through it to get a piece.

Lucille took the smallest of bites. "Oh my god. I could chip my tooth on this." Lucille said, she spat the rest of the fruit cake on to the plate. Fiona hadn't touched her slice.

Fiona laughed. "It has to survive the post."

"I imagine mortar would be softer," Lucille said.

"We actually use sugar icing in place of mortar when renovating Sugar Lump manor," Fiona said, tapping the exposed brick wall with her cane.

"What did you use for bricks?"

"Why bricks, of course," Fiona said, looking at her as if she had two heads.

"Are we done?" Lucille sighed.

"The candies we made yesterday have firmed and they must be wrapped."

"By me?" Lucille asked.

"Well us." Fiona said.

Despite her complaints, Lucille was gingerly wrapping the candies and Fiona watched her carefully without looking down at her own hands. Lucille seemed to be blooming under the doting, albeit somewhat nagging, care of Marty. Her pretty face was fuller, and her arms and belly had softened gently, as had her swaying hips. Fiona's eyes lingered over Lucille's small breasts, today contained by the ruffles of her shimmering purple dress.

She seemed to like the dresses they had chosen for her; each color complimented her brown skin more than the next. Fiona's mind wandered to the buttery yellow gingham gown with silk flowers that was her favorite. Why hasn't she worn that one yet?

"You're staring at me," Lucille said, her face scrunching up.

"To have noticed that you must have been staring at me," Fiona said gruffly.

"No, I asked a question; you did not answer, and so I looked up."

"Oh?" Had she been asked a question?

"Are you feeling unwell?" Lucille asked.

"No, I'm fine. I was curious about the yellow gown you have…."

"The one with the beaded vines?" Lucille asked, putting down the piece of candy she had finished wrapping.

"Uh, no, it has the silk flowers?"

"Oh yes, with the check!" Lucille said excitedly. "It is lovely. What brings it to mind?"

"The early morning light hitting your skin, I was imagining how you would look in yellow; it would be quite complementary."

"I'll wear it to dinner," Lucille said casually. "I have a headpiece that matches. Well, you know that." She added with a sheepish giggle.

"Thank you," Fiona said. She was waiting for Lucille to burst forth with something silly or a protest. Instead, Lucille gave her a warm smile and went back to wrapping candies.

After a moment, she looked up. "Don't you think these would look better on pink paper?" Lucille asked.

"I hadn't considered that," Fiona said slowly.

Lucille smirked. "Well, Lady Fondant, you are not the only person who can decide which colors are complimentary."

"I-" Fiona started, but Lucille cut her off.

"I'm teasing; I thought it would be helpful if they were pink. Then everyone would see when someone was eating your candy. All your competitors also use white, I believe," Lucille said.

"That is a fabulous suggestion. I'll send word to the shop to make the switch immediately." Fiona said. "If we're done, we should make our way to dinner."

"Oh, what a clever bowl and the soup is delightful." Lucille carefully picked up the clay bowl which looked remarkably like a tortoise shell. She gently placed the bowl down on the table and took another spoonful. Slurp. Fiona loved how detail-oriented Lucille was, it was endearing how she noticed the simple things and enjoyed trying new foods.

"Oh, I'm sorry," Lucille said, clamping her hand over her mouth in horror.

"You're quite endearing," Fiona said evenly. "I enjoy watching you enjoy yourself." Fiona surveyed the table. There were so many florals she could hardly see the platters and dishes. Clearly, Marty and Perry had taken her instructions a bit too literally.

Lucille looked down into her bowl.

"Is this your favorite dish?" Fiona asked. "I should know these sorts of things to convince your parents."

"Ah." Lucille laughed. "You could tell them anything. Please do in fact. Something absurd."

"Alright," Fiona said with a nod. "But tell me, I would love to know."

"Oh? Probably Saucer Fritters."

"Sausage fritters?"

"Saucer, what you place a teacup on. It's street food. They're potato patties, cooked in hot oil."

"Just potato?"

"Spices. A bit of Lemon juice and chili paste on the side. I suppose you could find some full of meat if you looked but I prefer them simple."

"I would like to try them someday, perhaps if I get my courage up," Fiona said nervously.

"I'm sure I could just make them for you." Lucille said with a smile.

"Is this a dessert or dish?" Lucille held up a small gold cookie with brown and green flecks on the top.

"That's an herb parmesan cookie." Fiona explained.

"Ah, the best of both worlds." Lucille said, biting down on it. "Mhmmm. Yes, ah-"

"You are so vocal." Fiona said, tugging on her cravat.

"Am I?" Lucille said coyly.

Was Lucille playing with her? Fiona glanced at Marty who was standing by the door, he cocked a brow and nodded ever so slightly.

Lucille

"An important aspect of confectionery is eggs," Fiona said. Lucille noticed she was wearing riding boots.

"Do you keep chickens?" Lucille asked, wondering why in all her time she hadn't seen or heard any of them. She had simply taken for granted that when she needed eggs there was always a cold clay jug filled with liquid eggs. Lucille had assumed it was some enchantment of the house like the furniture.

"Goodness no," Fiona said.

"Quail?" Lucille asked. Goose were too dirty, people hardly kept them unless there was no other option.

Fiona sighed. "Let me take you to our coop." She pointed down the hallway.

"We're not going outside?"

"No?" Fiona said evenly. She was walking so quickly Lucille had to jog a bit to keep up with her.

Fiona swung open a door that Lucille thought led to a parlor. A wave of sand rolled over their feet.

Lucille blinked, trying to figure out what her eyes were seeing. It appeared to be sand dunes as far as the eye could see. Before she could give it a second thought, Fiona was dragging her up the closest dune.

"Hurry up." Fiona said playfully.

A giant bird stalked past them. It had a snaking neck, small head and a pair of long skinny legs.

"What is that?" Lucille shrieked and cowered down.

"It's called a dostrichure."

Lucille struggled to pick apart the syllables of the name.

"They're mixes of dodos, ostriches and vultures."

"That is nonsensical."

"You're standing in a room full of sand dunes and this is what you find nonsensical?"

Another dostrichure appeared and charged towards them, it head-butted Fiona and sent her flying into the nearest pile of sand. Lucille picked up Fiona's discarded cane. "Shoo-shoo!"

Fiona laughed and held up her outstretched hand. The dostrichure flew back as if being dragged, its feet grasping at the sand. Lucille tried to gather her wits and control her breathing.

"Alright," Lucille said, handing Fiona her cane back and helping her up. "Lessons over for the day, let us retire."

"No, not at all," Fiona said with a laugh. "We're making too-sweet cakes."

"How many eggs do we need for that?" Lucille said exasperated.

"Just one," Fiona said, still laughing. "Lemons, yogurt, coconut…."

"Oh, shut up; tell me when we're in the kitchen, and I've gotten all the sand out," Lucille said, shaking her skirt.

Lucille sighed at her paper, the rough outline of a city block was taking shape. There was a gentle knock at her door.

"Yes? Come in." She called out.

The door swung open and in one hand Fiona carried a small tray. "I know you're drawing, I wanted to leave these for you." she said, placing the tray on the desk and walking back out.

"Thank you," Lucille called out, returning to her poorly rendered cityscape. The lines of the townhouses were wonky; the bricks and cobblestones were the wrong proportions. It was hopeless. *Take a break,* Fiona's nagging voice played in her head. Lucille got off the bed and stretched. Then she walked over to the desk. The tray had cold meats, cheese, crackers, and an assortment of candied violets, lavender, and lilac. The crystalized blooms glistened like gems in the low amber light of the bedroom. She took a bite and nearly moaned at the sensation of the crunchy softness and the floral taste.

There was another knock at her door. "Come in!"

She turned expecting Fiona, but Perry stood there.

"Hello Miss Waters."

"Hello Perry, did I leave a mess somewhere?" She sighed.

"No, I've come to help you package your sketches." He held up a leather folio.

"I believe I know how to post a sketch."

Perry shook his head. "Please take no offense but I am trained in how to send proper correspondence. We will make a beautiful impression on these artists and institutions."

"Alright," Lucille said finally; really, she should accept any help she could get. "What do you suggest?"

Perry walked over to the desk. "In addition to packaging each one in a folio, we should sign each sketch more delicately and seal it with the Fondant family emblem."

Lucille watched Fiona rinse off her hands in the cleaning bucket and continued to stare as Fiona promptly started scratching at her knuckles.

"Stop scratching." Lucille pulled her hand away.

"They're not contagious, the patches," Fiona said, embarrassed. Lucille followed her into the parlor.

"I know. I have a salve for this." Lucille said.

"Do you have a salve for everything?"

"Truly, I do. Mixing remedies is very similar to mixing paints. It's a passion of mine."

"Stay right here," Lucille said, and then she bounced up the stairs to her room; her moisturizing salve was still on her nightstand since she hadn't bothered putting it away this morning. She slid down the railing and landed on her feet. Fiona was exactly where she'd left her. Lucille rubbed the salve on both of Fiona's hands, although the right hand was raw and more scaly than the other.

"May I roll up your sleeve? I want to rub the excess on your inner elbow." Lucille asked.

"Of course, there's no part of me I would deny you," Fiona said with her signature lopsided grin.

Lucille glanced down. "You forget yourself; you should choose your words more carefully so they're not misconstrued."

"There's nowhere you are prohibited from touching me…" Fiona the smirk not leaving her face.

Lucille searched her mind for a subject to change the conversation too. "Thank you for sending Perry to help with my submissions."

Fiona cocked an eyebrow. "He must have done that on his own accord."

"Oh," Lucille said. "How sweet of him. I've been meaning to tell you." Lucille said, wiping her hands on a cloth.

"Yes?" Fiona asked.

"I received this letter from the school, Kenna had it forwarded. Can you read it for me?" Lucille asked.

"Uh sure, my hands are a bit greasy." Fiona said.

"No matter." Lucille said.

Lucille watched as Fiona broke the wax seal and unfolded the letter. She watched as Fiona's lips moved soundlessly.

"It is a rejection," Fiona said carefully. "But a warm one; they've asked for more samples."

Lucille jumped up on the sofa in excitement.

"Are you always this excitable?"

"Me? No. Hardly ever."

Lucille sat back down and crossed her legs at the ankles, looking very demure and proper. She rolled her shoulders back and giggled. She patted the sofa gently. "Sorry, sofie."

Dearest Sauce Ladle,

I feel unwell, please read up on the Pontefract Cakes and produce a perfect set for me to taste them. Marty and Perry can assist you but please do the assignment yourself.

Regards,
Lady F

Lucille made her way to the library. After comparing several recipes she quickly discovered that word *cake* was a misnomer. This was not a cake at all, it was a licorice lozenge or disc. She scribbled a few notes in her journal. While she was fond of Marty and Perry, she wanted to do this on her own. It took her about three tries to find a suitable kitchen. Perhaps if Fiona continued her absences, she would leave her a map. After carefully thickening the licorice with flour and a bit of oil, she pressed out small discs until they were about the size of her thumb. The only stamper she could find had a small swirl. The first one she pressed too hard and it flattened the disc too wide. The next few came out perfectly. Once they hardened, she placed a bit of parchment paper onto an embossed Fondant Family tin and then she gave it for Marty to deliver.

She sat in her room, not certain of what to do. You could be drawing, she thought to herself. Instead, she ate the snack that Perry had prepared: little tarts with slices of fresh strawberry floating in a pool of yellow custard. The lemon flavor perfectly complemented the tartness of the strawberries, she wondered how much Fiona spent on fruit alone. It seemed as if some sort of fruit was served with every dish.

It had been two long days since she had heard or seen Fiona. Sure, there had been a couple of cute notes and instructions on how to make fudge. But it was certainly not the same. Lucille begrudgingly made the fudge and was nearly done when she felt a pair of strong arms wrap around her waist and tighten. A shudder of panic coursed through her for a moment then she inhaled and smelled burned almond and vanilla.

She felt a slight pressure as Fiona placed her chin on Lucille's shoulder. Lucille sighed deeply; she was so glad Fiona was back. She allowed herself to breathe Fiona in for another moment and then she said. "Here. Taste." Lucille said, twisting in her arms.

She squished a fudge round against Fiona's lips.

"This has more flour," Lucille said.

"Mhmm," Fiona said, chewing.

"This is the more bitter traditional chocolate," Lucille waited until Fiona had swallowed and fed her another piece.

Fiona said something indecipherable.

"Try this one again," Lucille said, slipping a sliver of fudge into Fiona's parted lips. Lucile felt her fingertips graze Fiona's tongue.

"It has a vaguely nutty flavor," Fiona said; she was so close that her breath was warm and soft against Lucille's face.

Lucile pushed away from her. "This is more delicate." She said, feeding Fiona the rose water infused chocolate.

Fiona gently nibbled on Lucille's fingertips.

"Lovely," Fiona said. "You've been busy."

"Truly? It's lovely?'

"Yes, I believe so."

"You believe?"

"I don't care for fudge," Fiona said with a shrug.

"Not mine?"

"None at all," Fiona said, pulling Lucille into another hug.

"Oh, why did you allow me to shovel it into your face?" Lucille murmured against her.

"It was a pleasant experience."

"What will I be making today?" Lucille trying to change the subject.

"Truffles," Fiona explained.

Lucille carefully followed Fiona's instructions, heating up the chocolate, coconut milk, and vanilla to a boil.

"I'm roasting," Fiona said, motioning to the vat of chocolate. "Do you mind if I-" Before Lucille could respond, Fiona was untying her cravat and untucking her shirt.

"Lady Fondant!" Lucille exclaimed. "Really, we should maintain some semblance of decorum."

"There's no one to talk to; Marty and Perry won't gossip."

"Still, it is improper."

"I believe you're closing the barn doors after the horses have escaped." Fiona said but she stilled her hand.

"I'm nervous." Lucille blurted out. "It makes me nervous."

"That was not my intention." Fiona said as she turned away from Lucille to pour the chocolate into a series of bowls. When she looked up, her expression was unreadable. "We'll let this cool a bit then we will roll them into balls." She made a circle with her fingers. "About ye big. Then we'll dust them."

They sat in silence and then rolled the balls in cocoa powder, the only sound between them, the sliding of porcelain plates against the wooden table.

"Close your eyes," Lucille said excitedly.

Fiona took another bite of her macaroon and then did as she was told. She heard something as it was set down in front of her.

"Open them!" Lucille said.

The dish in front of her was a crispy golden-brown patty with flecks of green herbs. It smelled of onion and garlic. On the top was a sprinkle of fresh cilantro. It was a simple meal but she could tell that Lucille had put a great deal of care into preparing it.

"What is this? It smells divine." Fiona said.

"Saucer fritters. I did my best. Hopefully, they're good. The cook was out of turmeric so I made do."

"They'll be delightful."

"Because you have no comparison," Lucille said nervously.

"No, because you made them," Fiona said firmly. She dipped the patty in the light green sauce that accompanied it and took a large bite. The crispy shell gave way to a creamy, spicy potato filling. "This is amazing." She said, her mouth full. She covered her mouth with her hand. "You must make these every day."

Fiona

"We really should study each other more," Fiona said playfully. "Your parents will be upon our doorstep before we know it. And I doubt they are as aloof as you say."

"They don't believe me deserving of love. I'm sure they'll interrogate you." Lucille said. She was tracing the recipe with her fingertip.

"You deserve love. You deserve someone who would offer you their heart, and if you tore it to shreds, they would have it sewn up and stitched back on their sleeve." Fiona said.

"Why are all your love metaphors so gruesome?" Lucille said finally looking up.

Fiona smiled, more of a wince. "I fear it is my only point of reference in matters of love. I had my shot, she loved me in spite of everything, and I lost it."

Lucille opened her mouth and then closed it.

"Speak!" Fiona said.

"Don't talk to me like I'm a hound," Lucille said, her dark eyes flashing with anger.

"I would never. You just don't ever-"

"Fine. You're always saying I deserve this or that… it's my turn to make a declaration." Lucille said loudly.

"Fine," Fiona said. "Go ahead."

"I don't need your permission," Lucille said; Fiona could hear the anger rising in her voice. She should have taken a moment to breathe, but she was too annoyed.

"You're being intentionally obtuse." Fiona countered icily, she tried to keep her town civil.

"Stop insulting me," Lucille said; the intensity of her seething response took her completely off guard. If Lucille had been smoldering moments ago, she was now white hot.

"Luce!" Fiona said, trying to quell her anger. After it was too late, Fiona realized she had called Lucille by her familiar name. *Don't do that, she's not yours,* a nagging voice in Fiona's voice reminded her. But luckily Lucille seemed so upset she didn't notice. "Please continue, I'm sorry."

Lucille shot her a cold look but took a deep breath and blew it out dramatically. "Firstly, you should stop speaking as if you know me well and my self-worth. You deserve someone who loves you not in spite of who you are but because of it." Lucille said finally.

"I-" Fiona wasn't sure what to say. Instead, she stood there stupidly and rubbed a dry patch of skin on her neck. Lucille grabbed her hand.

"I have very sensitive skin," Fiona said, swatting her away.

"I have a material I use to exfoliate, to remove the dry skin," Lucille said tentatively. "You'll love it. It involves sugar," Lucille said. "Take a bath, and I'll come to your room."

"Okay," Fiona said carefully. Was that all? Bree had been quick to anger and held onto grudges for weeks on end. At the most minuscule perceived slight, she would wall herself off. Then the cycle had proceeded to groveling and negotiations. No offering had been quite good enough. Lucille did not seem that way at all. *Why am I comparing them?*

Lucille

"I'm mixing up a warm paste; just molasses, honey, sugar, and a dash of lemon juice. I'll just try it on your arm and see how you react." Lucille explained to Fiona who was laying in her stays and a pair of short drawers. She had carefully covered Fiona's bed in a towel in case there were any drips. Lucille tried to keep her composure. She rubbed the warm glob along Fiona's arm.

"Ahh," Fiona said softly.

"Is it too warm?"

"No, it feels good. You rubbing my arm."

"I don't want to add more since I don't know how your skin will respond," Lucille said. "We'll see how your arms and neck react; then I'll do more."

"Right, of course," Fiona said, sitting up slightly. Lucille carefully pushed her back down.

"Was the shea butter I gave you soothing?" She asked.

"Yes."

"I'll use that then," Lucille said, digging around in her basket.

Fiona closed her eyes and Lucille enjoyed the sensation of rubbing the cream into her skin and then rubbing her tense muscles until they relaxed under her fingertips. The warmth and softness of Fiona's skin beneath her hands was sending jolts of desire through her as she tried to concentrate on the task at hand.

"Your hands are huge," Lucille said, kneading Fiona's knuckles and spreading the thick butter over her hands.

"Are they?" Fiona said, opening her arms. She splayed her fingers out wide in front of her face as if she'd never seen them.

"They're big and strong, great for handshakes, whisking, holding…." Lucille trailed off and glanced down. "I imagine all sorts of things." She was wringing her apron in her hands. Then she dropped it, and smoothed it out across her thighs. Lucille twisted the lid back on the shea butter tin and put it in its pouch before placing the pouch into the pocket of her apron.

"I'll let you rest; you look half asleep," Lucille said before Fiona could sort her thoughts and respond. The massage had seemed to make Fiona sleepy and achy in the best possible way. Instead of protesting, Fiona leaned up and kissed the tip of Lucille's nose. "Thank you,"

Fiona

"What is your favorite confection?" Lucille asked as Fiona gathered the molds they needed for the day. They were standing in a little cluttered kitchen, with Fiona's scribbles laid out on the table. Fiona was chewing on the back of a pencil, trying to figure out the best way to explain the techniques to Lucille.

"Blood bars?" Fiona said after a moment of thinking.

"Do they sell those in your family's shop?"

Fiona laughed. "No, they're not typical fare."

"I want to make them," Lucille said excitedly. "I want to make them for you."

Fiona put down the mold she was inspecting and pulled Lucille into her arms. Fiona tried to not to outwardly show how excited she was that Lucille hadn't pulled away. "It's not a misnomer, there's actual blood."

Lucille shrugged. "I don't care. You need it. I'm not squeamish."

"Fine." Fiona relented, "Change of agenda."

Fiona stirred the boiling vat of jammy blood. Lucille craned her neck over Fiona's shoulder. "Miss Waters, I told you to stay behind me, I don't want you burned." She said for what felt like the thousandth time.

"I am behind you," Lucille whined.

That was technically true, Lucille's chest grazed her back and the ends of her braids ticked her neck, she could feel her warm breath on her ear.

"You have to step back," Fiona said firmly.

"Why? I won't be able to see anything.

Because I won't be able to resist clearing the table and laying you on the table, Fiona thought to herself.

"I have to add milk, sugar, vanilla, and…"

"Syrup!" Lucille supplied eagerly.

"Mhmm." Fiona nodded. "Hand me the ingredients in turn." This seemed to appease Lucille.

After everything was well mixed Fiona stood up. "Now we wait for it to set up and tomorrow we make it into bars."

"Oh, I wanted to try them," Lucille said, pouting.

"I have some," Fiona said, pulling a tin down from a shelf.

Lucille took one out and gave it a hesitant nibble. Her face contorted. "It tastes fine at first, but it's like chewing on a handful of coins."

Fiona laughed and Lucille fed her the rest of the bar. *Had her hands always been this soft?* Fiona wondered.

"C'mon, let's get started on our actual lesson," Fiona said, closing the tin. "You get started, and I'll bring the veg from the greenhouse."

"Oh," Lucille said, reaching for her as she stood up.

For a moment Fiona thought Lucille was reaching for her pants but instead she looked down to see Lucille's finger hooked through Fiona's watch chain.

"You're missing a charm here. Has it fallen?"

"Huh?" She tried to look clueless but knew the space she was referring to.

"There's a biscuit charm, a pencil, a coin, and then a ring with no charm," Lucille said, concerned.

"There was a locket. I removed it."

"I see," Lucille said with a funny look on her face.

"I'll be back with the greens," Fiona said quickly. In truth, they didn't really need the veg until the end of the recipe, but she needed some air before she said something foolish. Fiona took her sweet time getting the garnish from the greenhouse.

"I couldn't find the clippers," Fiona said as she entered the kitchen.

"Oh Fiona, don't come over! I don't want you to slip and I've made a mess."

Fiona froze and watched for a moment as Lucille's body shuddered and her mouth opened as if to release silent sobs. For a moment it looked as if she was dry heaving or choking. Lucille shook her head vigorously from side to side and took an audible death breath. Then she pushed out a loud sigh.

"I broke a bowl, I'm so sorry, this mess."

Fiona looked down, there were in fact shards of what was probably once a large porcelain bowl and then some eggy mixture puddled on the floor and splattered across the walls. Lucille sat in the middle of the mess like a fallen star in the center of its crater.

Naturally, Lucille's eyes were already wide for her face but they were currently huge.

"I broke a bowl, I'm so sorry, this mess," Lucille repeated. "I was done. I was done."

Fiona used the handrails to make her way over to Lucille and then sank to the floor to awkwardly pull Lucille into her lap. She rocked her as best she could. Lucille was stiff and heavy. Fiona realized the custard had already cooled and was solidifying to sludge. It was strange to Fiona that Lucille hadn't simply cleaned up the mess and started over. But that wasn't important currently. Fiona took Lucille's arms and wrapped them around her neck. After a long while, Lucille buried her face into Fiona's jaw. Fiona could feel the hot tears as they fell from Lucille's eyes and hit her own face. After a while the shudders stop.

"I'm so sorry about your bowl and your clothes and the floor," Lucille said finally. She sounded exhausted, and her words slurred slightly, but she wasn't yelling anymore.

"It's alright, we've literally had an oven explode. It's one of the benefits of having several ovens." Fiona said evenly.

"I grabbed the bowl; it was too hot." Lucille all the words blending together.

"It's alright," Fiona said.

Dark splotchy hives began to ripple across Lucille's skin. "Are you allergic to custard?" Fiona asked.

"Oh no, it happens when I am overwhelmed or in distress," Lucille said, still talking incredibly quickly.

"I'll run you a warm bath," Fiona said.

Fiona tried to stand and gain her footing but slipped slightly only just she correcting herself at the last moment.

"Oh, please don't hurt yourself," Lucille said, scrambling up to her feet.

Fiona clutched the butcher block countertop and used it to hold her weight. She felt Lucille's hands on her hips. Normally she would have brushed off the assistance but she didn't want to injure herself and her cane was upstairs. Together they eased their way out into the hallway.

"Let's take off our shoes so we don't track custard upstairs. Alright?"

"Mhmm." Lucille nodded and looked dazed.

Walking in stockinged feet, Fiona guided Lucille to her personal bathroom. Her large clawfoot tub was gilded in gold, the sides were etched with swirling icing motifs and it had more than enough room for Lucille and herself. She pushed that naughty thought to the back of her mind. She needed to focus. Carefully, Fiona navigated the two steps to reach the tap. The last thing they needed was another accident.

Fiona filled the bath, adding plenty of soap to form a thick layer of bubbles and then she turned away. "You get in, I'll change and bring you a nightshirt."

"Relax. I'm not angry with you." Fiona said softly, tracing the dark constellation of moles on the top of Lucille's shoulder. Her eyes were closed and her head was laid back. Fiona rolled up a towel and placed it behind Lucille's neck.

"I'm angry enough with myself for both of us," Lucille said finally as she seemed to shrink further into the bath.

Fiona leaned forward and kissed her forehead. "Then I'll be gracious enough for both of us," Fiona said softly.

When Lucille was dried and dressed in Fiona's nightshirt, she nearly bolted for the door. Fiona raised her palm and pantomimed closing the door and it slammed shut.

"Ahh." Lucille gasped.

"Please?" Fiona asked.

"Please what?" Lucille said quietly.

"Stay with me for a while."

"I'm fine," Lucille said with a quivering smile.

"I'm not. I...I would like the company," Fiona said quickly.

The bench from the front of the bed scuttled towards Lucille.

"Alright. I'll sit for a while." Lucille said, petting the tufted back of the bench before sitting down.

Lucille

*T*he strawberry shaped clock chimed twice. Oh no, she was late. She took a final glance at the sketch she had made of an upside-down peach tart she had been sketching. It was a bit stiff looking and she thought the peaches looked more like mangos than the fruit they were supposed to be. She could fix this later. It was good progress, she told herself. Lucille carefully wiped her hands on a handkerchief. She had spent so long choosing this pink cotton dress and she didn't want any graphite on it. Kenna would be amazed if she knew that she had enough dresses to spend time debating between them. Lucille pinned her apron on and slid on her detachable sleeves. Fiona was already at the table in what had recently become their favorite kitchen. She was straddling the bench, looking languid and handsome as ever.

"This door has been appearing to me so often," Lucille said.

Fiona nodded. "Me as well. It knows where it's needed."

"My apologies for being late, I was wrapped up in my drawing."

"No worries," Fiona said; per usual, she seemed vaguely amused by Lucille simply existing.

"What's all this?" Lucille motioned to the strange assortment of tools.

"Materials for sugar paste. We'll start with the basics, you'll need a baller, palette knife, blade, needle and a rolling pin." Fiona said, pointing to them in turn.

Lucille gathered them into a pile. "What are the molds for?" They were wood, unlike the metal ones she was used to.

"You put the dough in." Fiona motioned to a ball of sugar paste. "And then add the details. When or if you master that, you can make figures from scratch.

"Seems easy enough," Lucille said confidently.

Fiona

"Dinner!" Marty called out to them from across the room. Fiona looked up at him; he was leaning against the doorway, his arms folded, a bemused smile twitching on his lips.

"How long has he been standing there?" Lucille whispered. Fiona shrugged. They both had been so enthralled in their sculptures.

"Coming," Fiona said to Marty, wiping her hands on her trousers. She picked up her cane and then waited for Lucille to finish putting the eyes on a goose. Just as expected, Lucille had thrived at crafting the animals. Fiona sniffed the air. "We're having my favorite dinner."

"What's that?" Lucille asked as they made their way through the house.

"Chops and liver, ginger biscuits, kidneys, and rice," Fiona said.

"All of that?" Lucille asked.

Fiona slid open the pocket door to the dining room "And dessert of course."

Their respective chairs pushed themselves out. Fiona looked at the indents of dishes in the tablecloths, she could tell from the shapes that she was right about their menu. Marty liked to lay out the dishes before dinner to ensure the cooked dishes would be arranged just the way he liked. The gingerbread attendants filed in; Fiona watched as they matched each plate of food to its outline on the tablecloth. Fiona observed Lucille take tentative bites of the food, searching for her reaction. "Mhmm, delicious." She said after a moment.

"Don't sound so surprised," Fiona said teasingly. She surveyed the table, she had floral arrangements placed down the banquet table. Hopefully Lucille was pleased.

Lucille shrugged. "I've never had chops and liver."

"There's many things you will have to try in your time here." Fiona smiled at her over her wine glass. "I've been meaning to ask: would you like to tell me about your art plans?"

"I want to study at a university or perhaps..." Lucille paused as if thinking very hard. "Or perhaps I would prefer to be an apprentice. If I were to study at university I would be prohibited from many pursuits. For example, drawing live figures in the natural." She giggled softly after she said the word 'natural'.

"Is that a limitation on female artist students?" Fiona said, not bothering to hide her disgust.

"Yes." Lucille with a shrug. "Unless you're wealthy. Then they don't care if you're seeing a tool."

Fiona nearly spat out her wine.

"My apologies," Lucille said, lowering her gaze demurely. "I forgot myself for a moment."

"I appreciate your candor. Forget yourself as often as you would like." Fiona said, giving Lucille a warm smile, "What other things will you learn as an apprentice?"

"Hmm," Lucille said, taking a bite. "Preparing paints and canvases, the proper technique for composition and lighting."

"Fascinating." Fiona said. "What would you like to paint?"

"Big things," Lucille said, spreading her hands wide.

"Buildings?" Fiona asked.

"No, just..." Lucille frowned then used her fork to point to the painting of Fiona's great aunt that hung on the dining room wall. "Large scale paintings, not like the little watercolors or sketches I make."

"How wonderful," Fiona said; she motioned for the gingerbread attendant to bring more wine.

"I believe I'll also paint portraits of animals. Just the animals. Not the dogs with their owners. Just the dog. Or the cow or whatever. I believe that would be whimsical. I would gladly paint deer and livestock."

"I've never heard anyone doing such a thing. You're so creative." Fiona said.

"I've noticed creativity is mainly freedom, freedom to do and think as you wish," Lucille said. "Your mind's imagination is one of the few places that your social status or monetary situation matters very little."

"I feel as though you're teaching me so much more than I'm teaching you," Fiona said softly.

"Oh, shut up. Have I been going on?"

"Yes, well, no," Fiona said with a laugh. "I like listening to you."

Lucille giggled and then raised her hand to her mouth as if that would contain it.

"I'm being earnest," Fiona said. "Are you tired?"

"Not particularly; what do you have in mind?" Lucille asked.

"A recipe for shortbread." Fiona said, "I wanted it to prepare them for tomorrow." The lie slipped easily off of Fiona's lips. She simply wanted to spend more time with Lucille, basking in the warmth and humor that was her companionship.

Lucille

"If you looked at what you were doing while you were doing it, you would make less of a mess," Fiona said, her top lip curling up, pulling her mouth into an asymmetrical sneer.

"Hmph." Lucille scoffed, wiping the side of the bowl, and then she began to stir the mixture slowly.

Lucille wasn't sure if she should be offended by Fiona's bluntness or if she was being sensitive. While Lucille never considered herself particularly tactful or eloquent, Fiona seemed wholly unconcerned with anyone's feelings or how her words affected others. After it came together, Lucille moved the dough from the bowl to the flour covered table.

"Wow," Fiona said, taking a step back. She was clearly staring at the lumpy slab of creamy dough in front of Lucille.

"What?" Lucille asked, looking over at Fiona and then back down at the dough she was rolling.

"This may legitimately be the worst roll out of dough I have ever seen. You realize the purpose was to get the slab even, yes?"

Lucille's mouth opened slightly. "Uh? Well…are you going to fix it?" She said putting the rolling pin down.

"No, I'll show you how." Fiona retorted.

Fiona reached into a drawer and produced two long dowels.

"Are those rolling pins?" Lucille asked, they looked too skinny and it seemed quite odd that there were two of them.

"No, they're guides" Fiona said as she placed the dowels on either side of the slab of dough. "Here," she said, coming up behind Lucille and placing the rolling pin back in her hands.

Then Fiona placed her hands over Lucille's and maneuvered the rolling pin across the dowels like a track. "Roll along them until you get used to how much pressure to apply," Fiona instructed.

"Oh, I see." Lucille realized she had been applying more pressure at the beginning and end of each roll instead of applying the pressure evenly.

"And you've got to be confident," Fiona said, her voice husky.

"The dough can tell?"

"Well, no, but the world can," Fiona whispered gently in her ear. "It can smell the fear on you like the sweet smell of cocoa butter."

Lucille shivered as Fiona brushed against her earring, causing it to graze her neck and while her breath gently caressed Lucille's skin. The familiar prickle of erupting goosebumps began to cascade across her body and she trembled.

"Cold?" Fiona said, wrapping her arms around her and dropping her head onto Lucille's shoulder.

"Freezing," Lucille said; despite her racing heart, it seemed as though all the blood had drained from her body. Her fingers were cold as if someone had molded them of sherbet, and her head was light.

Fiona gave her a firm squeeze. "After this, we'll get cozy, have a chat, and have a spot of tea by the fire. We just need to…."

Whatever Fiona was saying was soft and far away. *Focus,* Lucille told herself so as not to ease into the panic.

"….and we'll use the molds and punches." Fiona said, releasing her.

"Does that sound good, my little candied peel?" Fiona asked.

"Yes, lovely," Lucille said, taking a moment when Fiona's back was turned to compose herself, wiping her apron across her face and taking a deep breath.

"Let us use these," Fiona said, returning with a tray of silver cookie cutters. "This recipe spreads a bit. So I don't want to bother with the molds; it won't show the details."

Once they were done, Lucille politely excused herself, explaining she was too tired for tea.

In the safety of her room Lucille tried to work on her art. She sat at the small table that was covered in a silky fabric, careful not to stain the delicate fabric. Perhaps there was somewhere else she could work other than her room? Both the little table and her desk seemed far too fine to use as a workstation. As she sat scribbling, her mind wandered as it often did. The table had two seats and she wondered what the purpose of such a little round table would be. Did the wealthy entertain people in their rooms? There were so many sitting rooms and parlors, that seemed unlikely. She was half tempted to ask but did not want to appear foolish. Sugar Lump Manor had an inordinate number of little tables, some bare, some covered, some with little statues sat on them. Some moved themselves about but most were stationary. If there were spare drawing rooms and parlors perhaps there was a room Fiona could allow her to use as a studio. *Ah, Fiona.* Instead of thinking of Fiona, she tried to focus on the form she was drawing. These pencils were smoother than any others she had used. They blended easily, and Lucille was quite satisfied with the result. She studied the faceless, stout, muscular figure. The realization slowly dawned on her…she had drawn Fiona, or at least what she imagined Fiona looked like under her well-cut suits. Lucille shoved the likeness to the back of her other drawings.

The parlor door was slid open, but Lucille knocked on the wooden door frame. Fiona was sitting at the desk, which was covered in tiny dishes full of spices.

"I'm going to gather recipes and ingredients in the greenhouse. Is there anything you need?" Lucille asked.

"No," Fiona said, then she thought about it. "I'll escort you."

As they walked, Fiona caught Lucille's hand and laced her large fingers in between Lucille's long slender ones. Fiona gave her hand a gentle squeeze and then loosened her grip slightly.

Lucille waited for Fiona to pull away but she didn't. Instead, they fell into an easy stride, their steps falling into sync, their clasped hands swinging between them. Once they had made their way back to the kitchen, Lucille began thumbing through Fiona's Great Aunt Alberta's journal.

Lucille had skimmed through the recipe book twice before looking up. "Am I advanced enough for baked apples?"

"Certainly," Fiona said with a laugh. "I, however, will be making shortbread cookies. Have you never hand-baked apples?"

"I've purchased them, I didn't have a bake house before attending Brittlebone and the school never served them."

Fiona reached over and covered Lucille's large hand on her own. "Now you have everything," Fiona said.

Lucille opened her mouth and then closed it as if she was considering what Fiona had said for a long time.

"Can I show you something special?" Fiona asked, squeezing Lucille's hand gently.

"Of course," Lucille said.

"Oh my, you have a cavern in your wine cellar?" Lucille looked about and realized she was actually mistaken. The cavern was the wine cellar with niches carved into the walls to hold the bottles in place.

She felt Fiona's long fingers interlace with hers.

"Come, let me show you the swamp."

They walked down the tunnel-like hallway which led to a massive clearing at the end. Slightly off center was a large pool of what appeared to be mud and to its left was a small pool of water with a fountain or some sort in the center. It resembled a geyser and the jet alternated height and thickness.

"This is my chocolate oasis," Fiona said proudly.

"Is it chocolate?"

"Yes. Hence the name. What did you think it was?"

"Mud."

"Ew. Goodness no." Fiona said, wrinkling her nose. "Care to go for a swim? It feels divine and works wonders for the skin."

"Will you undress me?" Lucille said before she could fully form the thought. "I meant could you assist me in undressing. I don't want my long dress to weigh me down. Would it be alright to swim in my chemise."

"Yes?" Fiona said with a smirk. "To both."

Lucille turned around "There's a drawstring at the neck and waist."

"Thank you for telling me."

"I'm sorry, I wasn't attempting to question your intelligence."

"I was being sincere." Fiona's hand had settled on Lucille's waist but she made no move to undo the drawstring. Fiona leaned forward and whispered in Lucille's ear. "I've never been tasked with such a wonderful mission."

Lucille covered her face with her hands. She felt her dress go slack as Fiona undid the ties and she pushed it off her shoulders.

"Please, pardon me. Pretend as if I did not open my mouth. My thoughts were wholly inappropriate and I hadn't fully processed them before I spoke…" Fiona said after a moment.

"Shocking."

"That I have inappropriate thoughts?"

"No, that you process any of the things you say. I had assumed you spoke without thinking."

Fiona gasped.

"Ah, so the lady pauses for a breath," Lucille said with a wink. "Will the chocolate stain my chemise?"

Fiona shook her head. "No, it sticks to the skin but the other spring will wash it off."

Lucille turned around and watched as Fiona leaned her walking stick against a stalagmite.

Suddenly Lucille felt very bold. She pushed off the jacket Fiona wore. Then she worked her way towards Fiona's high waisted pantaloons. Lucille carefully undid the buttons and watched the front flap fall forward. She made quick work of the six buttons on either side of the flap and then she kneeled down to undo the buttons at the ankles. "So many buttons." Lucille giggled.

She looked up at Fiona who had a tight smile on her face. "In a hurry, eh?"

"You should have worn breeches."

"Should I?"

"That was an attempt at matching your bawdy humor."

Lucille wondered if Fiona was as nervous as she was. As she tugged the pantaloons down, she realized they were carefully padded. Fiona took a step back and wiggled out of the pantaloons and stood there in her muslin shirt, its hem barely grazing her knees. Lucille stood there simply staring at Fiona. It was rude but she could not help herself.

"Ready?" Fiona asked.

"I, you-" Lucille said.

"Oh, my stockings," Fiona said, removing them. "Let us wade in."

The velvety liquid chocolate was not as viscous as Lucille expected, and her bare feet sunk comfortably into the sandy bottom of the pool. It was slightly thicker than water and came right under her bust. The smell of cocoa was heavy in the humid air, and it was comfortably warm. Never could she imagine such a perfect place or moment, but if she were more creative, she would have imagined this. She watched as Fiona floated on her back, the thick, gooey substance clinging to her clothes and skin. Paddling over to her, Lucille dabbed a bit of chocolate on Fiona's nose.

"Hey," Fiona said, laughing. "You stop that, or I'll dunk you."

"You wouldn't dare," Lucille said in mock indignation.

Fiona splashed her. "I would dare, instead though–" Fiona hooked her arm in Luculle's, "Let us float together for a while. The chocolate does wonders for the bones." Together the two women floated, peering up at the craggy ceiling, cocooned by the gently lapping waves and a soothing silence.

Fiona

*I*t was becoming more and more obvious that Lucille had no interest in model making. Fiona had been trying to explain to her the construction of cookie houses and furnishings but the conversation continued to wind its way back to a discussion of Lucille's parents.

"We must make a convincing couple. Which will be difficult." Lucille sighed.

"How so?" Fiona said.

"They will be skeptical. Someone of your status would not be interested in me."

"Odd," Fiona said, spinning the tray around to get a better angle on the cookie. She was trying hard to master this sugar cookie house, and this was the only batch where the dough had cooked properly without any burned or raw spots. After cooling, the walls, windows, door, and panels remained intact, with only a few patches of icing needed.

"Also, my family has carefully documented all of my short-comings," Lucille said, fiddling with a piping tip.

"They must be creative." Fiona began creating a flower box at the bottom of the window shaped cookie.

"It is not a stretch of the imagination," Lucille said, tapping the metal tip on the wood table.

"If prompted I can think of a long list of…" Fiona started.

"My failings." Lucille interrupted.

"No, as I was saying…. I can think of a long list of the reasons you are a most suitable partner and quite lovable." Fiona said not breaking concentration from piping rosettes onto the pan.

"I..." Lucille stopped. "I believe the others were too brittle because you over whipped the batter."

Ah, so she had been listening, Fiona thought, chuckling to herself. Lucille often managed to redirect conversations where she was being complimented.

"I see," Fiona said, putting the piping bag down. "What brings your parents to mind now?"

"I dunno. I have been avoiding thinking about it. Now it is all-consuming." Lucille said.

"Help me," Fiona said.

"What?"

"I need you to hold the walls while I ice them," Fiona said, motioning to the cookies.

"Oh yes, of course. I'm sorry." Lucille said, her face clouded with nervousness. She held up the pieces while Fiona piped icing where the pieces met.

"Think nothing of it. What normally distracts you?" Fiona asked. "Clearly it is not cookie architecture."

"Well, my art," Lucille said, slowly releasing the cookie pieces.

"Why don't we finish this, and we can sit, you paint, and I'll read," Fiona said.

The cookie manor came together easily. There were a few things she would improve upon; the columns were a bit blocky. Perhaps she would replace them with a rolled wafer cookie, the hard candy that had been used for glass was a bit cloudy. Fiona doubted she could get them any clearer so she would dust them with powdered sugar to give them a frosted look. She added shaved lime peels to look like veg.

"I'm as done as I will be," Fiona said. "Do you need to stop by your room for your materials?"

Lucille nibbled absentmindedly on a slightly burned cookie. "Mhmm, I left a pad and pencils in the parlor."

"Of course you did," Fiona said; she almost teased Lucille about how often she left her items around, but she didn't want her to feel self-conscious and stop.

"C'mon," Fiona said. "I'll get you a real treat. You'll make yourself sick off burnt cookies."

"Nuh-uh" Lucille said. "I ate some raw ones too."

"Delightful," Fiona said, guiding her out of the room. The fire in the parlor was warm and Lucille curled up in her armchair and began to sketch away. Fiona pretended to read her book but she was more interested in what Lucille was doing than any story that had been printed on the pages. Every so often she absent-mindedly flipped the page.

Lucille looked up after a long while and her eyes met Fiona's. "Did you want to see the sketch?"

"Yes," Fiona said, hoping her tone didn't reveal her guilt. Lucille sat down beside her, holding up the sketchpad. "I am sketching Marty and Perry."

"You did not have to tell me," Fiona said, slipping her arm around Lucille's shoulder. "Can you still draw?"

"Mhmmm." Lucille nestled into her shoulder. *We fit perfectly,* Fiona thought with satisfaction. She watched as Lucille added more details into the sketch, Marty and Perry's features coming through more clearly in the sketch. Eventually her pencil began moving slower and slower. Then it stopped and she began to gently snore. Fiona took the pencil out of her hand so as not to ruin the drawing with scribbles and set it aside. She knew Lucille well enough to know she would be waking up soon but Fiona would enjoy her laying heavy in her arms until then.

Lucille

t seemed as if all her mornings moved so much faster and more pleasurably than her time spent at Brittlebone. It was probably the lack of lessons, uninterrupted art time and delicious food. *Ah, food would be wonderful.* She stared down at her sketch of sister buns and wondered if Fiona had ever had one. They were always her and Kenna's favorite. She didn't know the first thing about making them but she was sure it was just dough flavored with coconut. Perhaps she could describe the pastry to Fiona and she could help her get the braided shape down. They could discuss the pastry over a snack. She bounced down the hall to Fiona's room, in her excitement she forgot to knock and instead opened the door.

Fiona was holding a curved piece of wood with a piece of rope attached to either side of one end. It was almost like a sled. She was clothed save for her stockings, both of which were laying across her lap.

"What's that?" Lucille asked.

"I use it to dress. I slip my stocking on it. It holds it open and then I slip my foot in and pull it up. It saves me from bending down." Fiona said, then she put the stocking onto the contraption and slid her foot into it.

"Why don't you just ask for help? I would gladly assist you-" Lucille said, stepping forward.

"I am more than capable." Fiona said angrily, she raised her hand. Lucille felt a pressure on her chest and she had to gasp for breath.

"Sorry," Fiona said. "I did not mean to be so forceful. I can do it." Her voice softened.

"Well of course but it would be faster and more efficient if I were to-" Lucille said, trying again.

"Stop," Fiona said dismissively. "Please leave."

"Alright," Lucille said curtly. "I'll make myself useful elsewhere."

It took her a few moments but finally she found Marty. He had a feather duster in his hand.

"Hello Miss Waters!" Marty said in his typical warm tone.

"I'll draw the curtains," Lucille said helpfully. The instant her fingers touched them, she realized they were not fabric.

"Taffy," Marty said as if reading her mind. "Best for blocking out the sun and keeping in the heat. They're not terribly fashionable, but it's been years since there's been a feminine touch at Sugar Lump Manor."

"Of course," Lucille said as that was the only polite thing she could muster.

"Does something trouble you, Miss Waters?" Marty said. His handsome features were awash with concern.

"Uh." Lucille tried to hide her surprise. "No." She moved to fluff the pillows but then realized perhaps Marty could offer her good advice.

"I fear I have insulted Lady Fondant," Lucille said, replacing the pillows to where she had found them.

Marty nodded "Perhaps, she can be rather sensitive. It is best to leave her alone for a bit. I'm sure she'll be right as rain by dinner time."

"Thank you, Marty. Which room is next?" She asked, reaching for his basket of cleaning tools.

They cleaned one room, then another, then another. But apparently there were not enough dirty rooms in Sugar Lump Manor to avoid being called for nuncheon. When Perry appeared to tell them lunch was ready, Lucille begrudgingly followed.

Nuncheon was nearly silent. Even the gingerbread attendants seemed to move as little as possible to maintain the palpable silence. Lucille looked about the dining room. It seemed as if endless portraits of the Fondant family members frowned down at her. She smiled nervously at one particularly distinguished gentleman who was holding a whisk. He frowned at her and twisted so that his back was facing her. Wow, apparently all the Fondants were sensitive, both living and deceased.

"You can't just tip toe around me. I'm not made of glass." Fiona said finally.

"I see you. I'm not looking past you." Lucille said, snapping her gaze back to Fiona's face.

"That's not what I meant."

"If you spoke clearly and not in metaphors and riddles, I would be able to follow along," Lucille said with a sigh. She pushed her buttered potatoes around her plate. In the center of the table was a peculiarly colored cake. She realized after a few moments of staring that it was actually three layers of watermelon adorned with slices of fruits and clusters of berries tumbling down the side.

"I meant I'm not fragile, I won't break. If you have a question, ask. I don't want your pity." Fiona said.

"It is not pity. It is care." Lucille said, stabbing a potato.

"You feel sorry for me," Fiona said, her voice tinged with disgust.

"You're wealthy, handsome and have no relations to speak of! You're not exactly a portrait of misery. It's not as if I sit around worrying you'll drown in champagne and bank notes." Lucille snorted. She did nothing to disguise her mocking tone.

Fiona cracked the first smile Lucile had seen the entire evening. "Are you going to thank me for your clementines?"

"Oh?" Lucille looked at the crystal bowl full of peeled and separated clementines, each fruit had been placed so that it resembled a blooming flower and there were sprinkles of flower petals and spices for garnish. "I hadn't realized they were for me."

"Ah?" Fiona said, taking the crystal bowl down from its silver stand and placing it in front of Lucille. "You m'lady are the only reason we clear the garden and the hot house for."

"Oh." Lucille said stupidly. She had noticed the extra flowers, garnishes and fruit but she thought perhaps it was typical. The citrus fruit was delectable, just as she expected, the salty dusting creating the perfect contrast to the zesty juice.

"Let's take the air," Fiona said, rising and holding out her hand. They walked across the lawn and down a stone path. "This is my garden. I like to walk here when I'm stuck on a recipe."

Lucille noticed the pathway was soft, springy even and looked like smooth buttercream icing but it did not stick to her slippers. It looked like a permanent layer of snow was paved just for them. She looked at the trees and bushes that lined the path and immediately she could tell something was slightly off. Instead of smelling floral or earthy, the air was filled with an almost sickly sweetness. The leaves of the nearest tree had a bluefish tint and in place of berries were bunches of jellybeans.

Fiona used her cane to motion to various plants as they walked. "That is a patch of gumdrops, they grow like tulips. That's to say that it grows from a bulb and regrows. Or you can harvest it with the bulb attached. That way the gum drops stay fresher longer."

"Oh, I hadn't realized that is how gumdrops grew," Lucille said.

They turned down a narrower path that led to a circular opening. They sat in the center. All around them the pink bushes had been cut into bakery related shapes. One was a spoon, another she thought was meant to be a piping bag. Others she wasn't quite sure of.

"This is Perry's new hobby," Fiona explained. "Hopefully, it improves quickly.

"They are a wee abstract," Lucille said with a giggle.

"Does it bother you?" Fiona said.

"The crooked bushes?" Lucille said, she tilted her head to try to make out what the conical one was, "No. I think he really did his best."

"My limp," Fiona said. "It is worse some days more than others."

"Oh no, that doesn't bother me." Lucille said, taken aback.

"I have special shoes to disguise it." Fiona continued.

"Oh goodness no, don't wear those, not on my account," Lucille said, stopping her. "You're perfect."

"Alright," Fiona said, still eyeing her skeptically. "Let us continue our promenade."

"I've never been on an official promenade," Lucille said as they passed a plant with cubes of some kind growing in place of blooms.

"You can eat those," Fiona said. "It's a jelly; it melts in your mouth and becomes a chewy, sticky paste."

"Perhaps another time." She was having a difficult time processing all of these new items. Interspersed with seemingly normal patches of grass were tufts of what looked like spun candy that trembled in the slight breeze.

As they walked, something small hit her head and then another and another and another. She looked down, they were hard candies.

"The squirrels." Fiona pointed up to a massive tree that loomed overhead. "They bury the candy to plant more candy trees."

"Oh," Lucille said. "

"Are you alright?" Fiona said, her tone serious.

"Fantastic, superb, amazing." She said trying to convince herself even more than Fiona.

They had reached the center of the garden and Fiona guided her to one of the stone benches with legs shaped like waffle cones and the marble had a swirl pattern that reminded her of meringue.

Fiona sat beside her and reached her hand to the side of Lucille's face, leaning in ever so slightly. *Is she going to kiss me? Calm down. Calm down. Calm down. Control yourself. Control yourself. Control yourself,* Lucille's thoughts raced. She felt as if she could not control her limbs, she leaned back and then her arms and legs flailed out in an attempt to grasp something. Instead she just fell back into the short hedge.

"Miss Waters!" Fiona said, peering over her. "Are you alright?"

"Yes, yes," Lucille said, picking herself up; instead of climbing back onto the bench, she stalked through the hedge.

"Wait," Fiona said.

"Thank you for taking air with me. I am a bit tired; I'll go to bed now." Lucille said and practically raced towards the house. When she was finally inside, she took the steep servant stairs up to her floor. The stairs were uneven and she had to grasp at the rough wooden wall to keep her balance. When she reached the top, she pushed the door open and was completely disoriented. If she had been in this wing of the house she couldn't remember and she had no clue how to get back to her room.

She stood there pondering where to go when she heard the tell-tale sound of Fiona's walking stick tapping ever closer. Lucille opened the nearest door and ducked in.

She closed the door gently behind her. This room like most others was lit with glowing amber chunks that were cradled in sconces on the wall. The walls were lined with armoires and in the middle were five large trunks. At first glance she thought it was a dressing room but there was no vanity or even a bench to sit on. She tiptoed over to the nearest armoire and opened it. It was filled with gowns. She opened the armoire in turn, each was filled with gowns, cloaks, and Spencer's. A cursory glance of the trunks revealed them to be filled with accessories. Lucille made sure not to disrupt anything and then went to the door, opening it a crack. The coast seemed clear and she scurried out into the hallway and into the servant's staircase. She'd barely made it to the foyer when the bell rang for dinner.

She took her seat at the table trying to still her racing heart.

"Is everything to your liking? Fiona asked sweetly.

"It's wonderful as always…" Lucille said quickly. "I'm sorry about earlier, my nerves are terribly frayed at times."

Fiona nodded. "All is forgotten. I am anxious at times as well."

Lucille paused for a moment. "Might I ask you a frivolous question?"

Fiona reached over and placed an extra dinner roll on Lucille's plate. She winked. "You can have as many as you'd like."

"Thank you." She said demurely. "However, I was actually curious about your fashion. Have you always dressed in a masculine style?"

"Yes. I find it more comfortable,"

"I see."

"Will that bother your parents? Perhaps I could find something else." Fiona looked disgusted as if she hated this idea more than anything.

"No, no," Lucille said, nibbling on the roll. "They won't think about any of that. Just your money."

Fiona laughed. "I have more of that than good sense. I'm not used to socializing but I believe I will manage."

"So, do you not have friends?" Lucille asked.

"I have Marty and Perry. Others are a liability."

"Perhaps I am not one to talk; I truly only have one friend."

"Mhmm," Fiona said.

"Do you not get lonely?" Lucille asked.

"Do you?"

"I'm too busy surviving, and I had assumed loneliness was a luxury you could easily afford."

"The cost is far too great," Fiona said, laughing bitterly. "Even for myself." Fiona motioned to the whipped syllabub. Lucille squirmed under Fiona's intense gaze.

"Why are you looking at me like that?" Lucille said, popping her spoon out of her mouth.

"Your net dress leaves little to the imagination, and while I'm not an artist, I would gladly share my most creative impressions of what is shielded, but you might slap me, and I rather like my face intact," Fiona said.

"Lady Fiona, you say that as if you haven't seen practically everything save for the tuzzy-muzzy. You don't have to be terribly creative to picture that." Lucille said mockingly.

Fiona's upper lip quirked; Lucille was actively playing with her and based on Fiona's face she was enjoying it.

"Miss Waters, why do I feel as if you're goading me."

"Lady Fondant, I believe you feel that way because I am. It's a taste of your own medicine or perhaps a more apt metaphor… it is a taste of your own confections."

"You find my teasing sweet?" Fiona said, not bothering to guard the surprise in her voice.

"On occasion,"

"Tell me, Miss Waters, what do you think of me?"

"The world." Lucille said softly.

"Hm?" Fiona said, leaning forward.

"I think the world of you." Her somber demeanor returned. "Is that the wrong answer?" She said quietly, unsure.

"No, there is no wrong answer. You did not inquire, but I think very highly of you." Fiona said, patting her hand.

"What are all these scribbles?" Lucille said playfully.

"I am attempting to create a treat that will be more accessible to the masses, perhaps served by an attendant with a cart or perhaps on a tray with a neck strap," Fiona said, gathering the notes up. Lucille could tell she was nervous.

"I've made you more silver bars," Lucille said. "Have all my tales of street food inspired your newest treat?"

Lucille watched as Fiona slowly unwrapped the silver bar from its wrapping made from wax paper. She took the smallest nibble and then took another small bite.

"Are the bars awful or are you simply trying to avoid telling me of your newest creation?" Lucille asked.

"No, well, yes," Fiona said sheepishly, brushing a hand over her short hair. "The bars are delicious."

"Let me see what you have." Lucille said taking the notes back "Roasted and sugared nuts, hmm, what if we use a pecan or walnut? I believe everyone is familiar with chestnuts, almonds and hazelnuts. The pecan or walnut would be novel."

Fiona nodded, scribbling a note. Lucille watched as she dug around the pantry. She pulled out a jar of pecans.

"Can you take notes as I cook?" Fiona said gathering up brown sugar, butter, and milk.

"Of course," Lucille said. She watched Fiona combine the items in a hot pot. Stirring it constantly, Lucille looked at the clock and made a note of the time; she also made note of how hot the fire on the hearth was.

"What are you doing now?" She asked Fiona.

"I'm going to place a dollop on this marble slab and let them cool," Fiona said. Then she carefully ladled out a small bit of the gooey mixture onto the marble cutting board.

"Is that all?" Lucille said.

"Yes, do you not think that will be well received?"

Lucille thought for a moment. "I believe a sprinkle of coarse salt."

"For balance! Brilliant!" Fiona said, nodding and looking around for the canister.

She called me brilliant, Lucille thought to herself, internally shrieking with joy.

On her day off from confection lessons, Lucille put a great deal of effort into making herself busy to avoid following Fiona around the entire time. It was an endeavor more difficult than it first appeared. Everything from the linens to her sketches, to her skin care reminded her of Fiona. She noticed that the fresh brown silk pillowcases were the same tone as Fiona's skin, the sketches too resembled Fiona and the vanilla in her mixtures overpowered all the other scents. Lucille made it until midday when she cracked. She was so proud of the texture and smell of her newest salve that she knew she must show Fiona. She didn't bother putting the lid on the jar as she hurried down the hall. She opened the door and Fiona stood there half dressed, her shirt in her hands and her breeches undone and slung precariously low on her hips. For once she wore a full corset but it was in the style of a man. Instead of emphasizing her bust and waist, it flattened her chest and skimmed over her hips.

"I-" Lucille started then stopped.

"You're staring at me as if you'd like to take my underclothes off," Fiona said after a moment, pulling her shirt over her head.

Lucille almost choked on her own tongue. "I made this for you." She fiddled around in her apron pocket trying to pull out the jar lid and when she finally fished it out of the fabric, she tried to take a deep breath. "Here let me put the lid on." Her hands trembled and she couldn't manage to align the lid with the threads on the neck of the jar. The lid slipped out of her hand and skittered across the floor.

"May I assist?" Fiona said, flashing her wide smile. Fiona squatted down and picked up the jar. Lucille tried not to stare at Fiona's shapely bottom in her fitted white breeches. She straightened up and Lucille averted her eyes.

"Here you are," Fiona said, holding the jar lid out.

Take the lid, Lucille thought to herself but her hands didn't respond. Thankfully Fiona took the jar out of her hand and screwed on the top.

"My apologies if my crass joke offended you," Fiona said, running a hand down the back of her head and looking sheepish.

"Oh no, I am sorry. I was curious about your stays." Lucille explained.

"They're lazy stays," Fiona said, pulling up her shirt and twisting around. "They wrap and don't have boning but offer good shape,"

"What a curious name," Lucille said.

"They're named by those who don't know what it is to be ill." Fiona said, shrugging.

"I can imagine they don't but it's still a horrid name." Lucille said firmly.

"Well-" Fiona started.

"I'll be off. I'll see you tomorrow." Lucille said with a curtsey before backing out of the door. *Why did you do that?* Lucille chastised herself. *Why are you so foolish?*

The mornings where Lucille found a note on her nightstand were either wonderful or horrid and there was rarely any in between. She stretched and scratched her hair under her scarf before unwrapping it. She read, her heart sinking and then she read it again.

To My Dearest Flour Sifter,

I am unwell. Please study the techniques and history of the macaroons. We'll make them when I am well.

> *Much love,*
> *Lady F.*

Lucille tossed the note to the ground. This was absurd. "This would not do," Lucille said angrily to her empty room. What would Fiona do? If she was unwell, Lucille would care for her. It's not as if she would be strong enough to protest. She pulled on a simple muslin dress, not bothering to unwrap her hair. Then she slipped on her house shoes and plodded down the hall to Fiona's room.

Fiona

"My dear, you're burning up." Lucille said. Her hands felt like two blocks of ice on either side of Fiona's face.

The sheets around her were drenched, and the air of the room was thick with the sickly-sweet stench of her sweat.

She pushed Lucille away with as much force as she could muster and then closed her eyes and laid back. After a few moments there was a wet rag resting heavy on her forehead and another one around her neck.

"I'm pulling down your stockings," Lucille said, enunciating slowly.

The next time she woke up, Fiona was cold and clammy, shivering as if her body had never known warmth. The damp clothes were gone and the sheets around her felt crisp. She heard a distant rustling past the curtain canopy of her bed.

"Sweetie?" The hoarseness of her own voice startled her.

"I'm Lucille. I haven't left you. I'm just tending to the fire."

She sounded so far away but before Fiona could manage anything else she fell back to sleep.

Lucille

"Lucille, you and the gingerbreads should rest. It's so late." Lucille said to Marty. He looked haggard and she could tell his mouth was twitching to contain a yawn.

"Let us know if you need the Lady transferred. A fall would injure you and her." Marty said firmly.

"I won't move her. The linens are fresh, I'll just sit right in this chair and keep watch." The chair wiggled beneath her as if in agreement.

"Alright, the scullery maid should be up soon to tend the fire. She comes round four in the morning so you're not startled and-" Marty was interrupted by Fiona crying.

"My love," Fiona called out; they both looked over to her where she was writhing in her massive bed, eyes tightly shut.

"I'll be fine, Marty. Sleep, please. Or you won't be able to manage the household tomorrow and I certainly cannot." Lucille said softly.

Marty nodded and with one more forlorn glance left.

The door had hardly closed when Fiona sat up in bed. "Is there a draft? I've caught a chill." She asked groggily.

Lucille stoked the fire despite being so warm she felt as if she was roasting and her skin itched and prickled with sweat.

"My dear, come to bed," Fiona said groggily.

Lucille walked over and pressed her back into the pillows.

Lucille stroked her face. She couldn't tell if Fiona was cooler or if she was just so hot that the other woman seemed cooler.

Fiona caught her hand and squeezed it.

"Please. Come to bed…"

"I'm not who you think I am." Lucille placed Fiona's hands on the duvet.

"Lucille Waters. Come to bed," Fiona said, her eyes closed as she leaned her head back on the headboard. "If that's even your true name."

Lucille could not help but laugh.

"My flesh is trying to kill me, but I'm not out of my wits," Fiona said. Lucille hesitated.

"I smell awful." Fiona raised her arm and inhaled. "Is that why you won't hold me?"

"Now, Lady Fondant. You asked for me to come to bed. Nothing of holding," Lucille tried to muster a straight face but instead she laughed. A wave of relief washed over her at Fiona coming back to her own flirtatious self.

"Please?"

Lucille nodded and crawled up into the bed. "Marty will be in by first light so I must leave before then."

"The lamps will tell him; they'll tell the whole house" Fiona said with a laugh. They were both asleep in a matter of moments.

Lucille chewed on her bottom lip. This was her second attempt at too-sweet cake. Something about the simple nature of the recipe which only consisted of sugar, coconut, vanilla, honey and yogurt was hard to master.

"You're doing great," Fiona said; Lucille noted that she sounded far away, as if she had a lot on her mind.

Once Lucille had placed it in an oven that she hoped was moderate, like the recipe stated, she sat beside Fiona.

"Miss Waters," Fiona said softly.

"Mhm? Was the ratio that off?" Lucille said with a laugh. She played with the almonds that would top the dessert. "Do you think I should cut it into squares or diamonds?"

"Uh diamonds," Fiona said, then she removed a letter and slid it across the table.

"What's this?"

"I'm not sure but it's from your parents so probably not good."

"Can you open it for me?" Lucille said, sliding it back. Fiona opened it, unfolded and then passed it back to her.

Lucille skimmed her mother's familiar cramped handwriting. Lucille felt hot tears fall down her face. She closed her eyes in an effort to contain them and when she re-opened them, Fiona had pulled her close and she felt Fiona's lips on her forehead.

"Shhhh," Fiona whispered, her warm breath prickling Lucille's scalp.

"They..." Lucille hiccupped. Fiona pulled away, picking up the letter from the ground. "They'll be late, some silly thing for my sister, they called me inconvenient and..."

She suddenly felt cold as Fiona crossed the room. With doubled vision she watched as Fiona tossed the letter into a fire.

"Rubbish," Fiona said; she took her by the hand and led her down the hall to her private parlor.

"Come sit," Fiona said, settling in an armchair.

Lucille gathered herself up and walked towards the second armchair.

"No, come here. I'll hold you until you feel better." Fiona said, patting her knee.

Lucille sat on her lap and Fiona wrapped her arms tightly around her.

"It's alright." She felt Fiona's hand slip into the slit in the side of her dress, it was meant for a pocket but she wasn't wearing one. It was perfectly sized to fit a hand and she felt Fiona's cold hand through her thin chemise. Never had she felt so thankful for old fashioned little details.

"Is this alright?" Fiona said softly.

"Mmmhmm," Lucille murmured softly, sinking against Fiona.

"Did you read it?" Lucille asked.

"What?" Fiona said, her face was buried into Lucille's shoulder.

"The letter."

"Oh no." Fiona rubbed her nose against Lucille's collarbone.

"It said all sorts of things about my personality or lack thereof: They said that I'm a strumpet, that I'm dull and-"

"Hush, hush." Fiona said. "None of that is true."

"They're terrible, and you must put them out of your mind," Fiona said, pressing a kiss to her cheek.

Lucille began to unbutton Fiona's shirt with trembling fingers.

Fiona sighed and closed her eyes. She pressed two fingers to her lips. "No. Not tonight. Not in this way."

Lucille pushed away and stood up. She felt Fiona catch her shirt sleeve.

"No, stay, let me hold you. I'll make you feel good in a different way."

Lucille chuckled ruefully. "I feel rotten. Clearly, I am not the seductress my family believes I am."

Fiona sighed again before rising. "Let us forget about them until they rear their ugly heads on our doorstep. Come to my room, I'll read to you, it's late."

"Lucille?" Fiona said softly.

"No, it is late." Lucille started to walk away.

"It was not a rejection," Fiona called after.

Lucille spun around. "It was."

"Well in the most technical sense. It is my moral duty as your friend to take care of you. Not to take advantage of you because you're upset. I want to-" Fiona said trailing off.

"Hm?" Lucille sighed; she was tired and frustrated.

"I think you're gorgeous," Fiona said finally.

"Your politeness is unnecessary."

"My honesty is wholly necessary."

"Are you being honest?"

"I swear I am. Not taking you feels like torture," Fiona said so softly Lucille almost thought she imagined it.

Lucille nodded several times in rapid succession. "And yet you have objections."

"You're not aroused. That is not an objection. It is a fact. What you want is connection. You want comfort." Fiona said firmly.

"Your moral superiority is not comforting," Lucille said, turning back around. Fiona followed behind her.

"I can comfort you if you trust me," Fiona said. She felt Lucille wrap her arms right around her.

"I trust you," Lucille said after a long pause. The walk to Fiona's room seemed even shorter than normal. Fiona closed the door and then locked it.

"Undress. Lay on your stomach" Fiona motioned Lucille over towards the bed.

She undid the drawstrings that cinched her dress to her body and then Fiona undid all of the laces of her stays.

Lucille lifted up slightly so Fiona could slide the corset out from under her. She lay there in her chemise waiting.

Lucille hadn't realized how drawn up and tense her body was until she felt Fiona's firm hands on her thighs and backside. Fiona worked at her tense muscles; she worked her balled fists in tight circles. Lucille gasped and sucked in a breath as Fiona rubbed her inner thighs.

"Sit up," Fiona said after a few moments.

Lucille let herself be maneuvered in between Fiona's legs, the buttons of Fiona's shirt rubbing against Lucille's spine. She leaned into the gentle pressure as Fiona wrapped her arm around her neck. Then her firm hands pressed around Lucille's jaw. Lucille felt herself go limp as Fiona cradled her. Lucille shifted down slightly as she leaned back on Fiona and Fiona began rubbing her arms and shoulders.

"Mhmm." She felt herself growing tired. Her eyelids would not stay open.

"Rest," Fiona whispered against her ear.

Lucille used the last dredges of her energy to say. "Stay."

"I will," Fiona said, kissing her forehead.

Lucille woke up tightly wrapped in a blanket. She freed her arms and patted the area beside her. Nothing. Thank goodness Fiona had left. Mortification seeped over her.

"Are you looking for me?" Fiona's warm baritone called out from somewhere to her left. She was in Fiona's very large bed.

"Oh my." Lucille buried her face in the mattress.

"It's alright," Fiona said gently.

Lucille felt the mattress shift ever so slightly. After a moment a fabric landed on her head.

She sat up pulled on the shirt. It smelled like burnt almonds and clean soap.

"Is everything alright?" Fiona asked.

"Yes, I'm clothed. Well not precisely but I'm more clothed."

Fiona pulled open the curtains to the bed. "I meant do you hate me?"

"Oh no, I appreciate you thinking. One of us has to. I would hate to damage our friendship." Lucille said, looking down at the sheets.

"You're all lopsided." Fiona climbed into the bed and straightened out the collar of the shirt Lucille wore.

"I'm sorry about last night," Lucille said, still not making eye contact.

"I'm not. I had a wonderful time. You're normally the one with the roaming hands. It was a good change of stride." Fiona said.

"I-" Lucille couldn't bear to look at her.

Fiona cupped her hands in her face. "However, I must warn you, if you ever offer yourself again to me so wantonly,"

"I-" Lucille started again.

But Fiona cut her off. "I will not be able to resist you."

"You're needed." Marty's voice said through the door.

Lucille practically ran down the stairs. To her surprise, a row of people stood in matching livery.

"Ah, Miss Waters, come." Fiona said, waving her down.

"What's all this?" Lucille said, descending the rest of the steps slowly.

"I am examining the new shop uniforms and providing instructions for the spring tasting. In a couple months, this fine lot will deliver confections for inspections."

"These are some of the best employees of the shop. Latisha, Carmichael, Frances, Ebony, Ichabod, and Maria." Fiona said, pointing to each of them in turn. "And this," she said, turning to Lucille, "is my fiancé, Lucille Waters. She is learning the family trade."

"Lovely to meet you all," Lucille said remembering her manners. She waited for a moment to be dismissed as she did at her parents' home.

"Are you prepared to take notes?" Fiona asked. She held up the piece of paper and a stub of pencil she'd been holding. "Or I can make notes and you can share your observations. We're paying special attention to fit various body types."

"I'll take the notes," Lucille said, regaining her composure.

Lucille watched as Fiona examined each attendant in turn. These uniforms were a bit more vibrant than the ones she had seen at The Pebble and Fig. There were more trimmings, and she noticed that faux golden sashes had been added. From a distance, it looked as if the band of fabric wrapped around the jacket, but it was actually a carefully placed double layer of ribbon.

"Does this pinch?" Fiona asked, stopping at Frances and motioning to her arm.

Frances nodded and then motioned to the area around her collar. "This is tight as well."

"Can everyone raise their arms?" Fiona asked. Lucille watched as everyone did and then noted that all the jackets rose up quite a bit.

"New patterns," Lucille muttered to herself.

"Excuse me?" Fiona said, turning to Lucille.

"Oh, I'm sorry. I'll be quiet."

"No, I meant excuse me as in, please repeat yourself."

"Oh, I just believe we may need new patterns," Lucille said softly.

"Patterns?" Fiona said, quirking a brow. "With an s?"

"You'll need more than one pattern," Lucille said; her mouth fell open, and it took her a moment to regain her composure. *Had they really been using the same pattern for all their employees?*

"Okay," Fiona said, nodding slowly. "Is there anything else?"

"Yes? These are very pretty, but they're heavy wool." Lucille said hesitantly. Hopefully, Fiona did not think she was usurping her.

Fiona turned back to the attendants. "Is that true?" she asked.

There was a grumble, and then Latisha stuck and stepped forward. "My lady, forgive me if I'm being forward, but last year I got sun sick as these are so hot."

Lucille stepped forward and motioned to Latisha with her stub of pencil. "If you'll notice, Latisha's shape is very angular, she's tall, and her torso ends here." Latisha nodded and motioned to her waist, which was much higher than Lucille's, although they were the same height. "And Carmichael is short in stature and has a full figure."

"What do you suggest?" Fiona asked.

"I would have the modiste design a pattern and then create variations of it."

"We offer tailoring."

"Look at the gaping at the bust on Maria and Ebony's jackets. That will not be solved by simple tailoring. We want them to be comfortable and functional."

"Do we?" Fiona said with a playful smirk.

"Mhmm," Lucille said, grinning.

"It sounds as if we should discuss this more," Fiona said, turning back to the attendants. "Let us have refreshments, and you all can share your thoughts with Lucille and I."

"If I may," Lucille said, clearing her throat.

"You always may," Fiona said, nodding.

"Perhaps we should allow our guests to change before the refreshments and discussion," Lucille said.

The group of attendants all nodded and murmured in agreement. Fiona laughed, the booming sound filled the room, and Lucille could not help but join in. Once everyone was changed into more comfortable ensembles, Lucille guided them to the dining room. Marty had selected an excellent assortment of beautiful dishes, and the table was dotted was small, bright floral arrangements in the shape of pineapples.

Fiona leaned forward over the table, smelling an arrangement. "What a creative use of daffodils and succulents."

"Thank you," Marty said with a curt nod before he took his usual post in the corner of the room.

"Please, sit. Eat." Lucille said to the attendants, who stood in a clump on one side of the table,

"Oh, forgive me," Lucille said, whispering to Fiona.

"You're doing fabulously." Fiona said, placing a reassuring hand on the small of Lucille's back. Per usual, Lucille's breath hitched.

Lucille sat down and helped herself to a glass of orgeat. It was an especially tasty drink that Marty made. Typically the beverage was made with barley and almond in rose water, but he had used hibiscus in this variation. The tropical addition made the drink light and airy. Discreetly, Lucille nudged Fiona under the table. Taking the hint, Fiona piled her plate high with cold meat, a slice of bread, and several berries. Ichabod was the first to help himself to coffee and then to a croissant. Thankfully the awkward silence only lasted a few minutes, and soon the dining room was full of conversation that was as free-flowing as the champagne. They talked for what seemed like an hour, but when Lucille looked over at the clock, several hours had gone by.

She tapped Fiona on the hand softly. "We should let our guests relax a bit, perhaps go into town. I'm sure they are pleased to be away from the hustle and bustle of the city, I know I am."

Fiona nodded. "Yes, I seem to have forgotten myself." She wiped her hands with a napkin. "Thank you all for your sharing your thoughts. If you have any more concerns, leave a note for myself or Lucille. But for the remainder of your stay, please focus on relaxing."

The group cheered their thanks and then quickly exited the dining room.

Lucille poured herself a cup of coffee, adding a drop of milk to the sludgy liquid. "That was fun; I can't remember the last time I just sat and chatted with nice people and delicious food."

"Oh, so you think me nice?" Fiona said, intertwining her hand with Lucille's. "And my food delicious?"

"I was referring to the guests," Lucille said, trying to suppress a grin that she knew would make her look terribly foolish.

"Shall we–" Lucille started, almost asking if Fiona wanted to take a carriage into the village.

"Yes?" Fiona said, smiling at her expectantly.

"Shall we retire to the parlor and read?"

"That sounds wonderful." Fiona said as she finished the mead in her glass and wiped her mouth with the back of her hand.

"Ready?"

Lucille nodded. "Yes, I cannot think of a more pleasant way to spend the rest of our day."

Fiona

he next morning, Fiona felt as if she were being boiled alive. Her normally cool skin was hot, and she pressed it against the looking glass to feel the cool relief. When that didn't work, she sat in a cold bath for a quarter of an hour, waiting for her blurry vision to refocus. When the room finally came into focus, Fiona dressed for the day and then immediately regretted it. She called for Marty and told him to send word to Lucille that she would not be needed that day. Then Perry arrived with his cool rags and herbs.

"Lady Fondant, if I may offer you a piece of advice," Perry said as he helped her out of her jacket.

"If I decline, you'll still give the advice," Fiona said, letting her annoyance soak into the words. She felt awful, but Perry continued.

"Miss Waters seems rather sheltered." he said.

"I believe she is quite capable of handling herself. She handles me quite well, in fact." Fiona said.

Perry nodded. "Perhaps, but be careful with her heart. Emotions are not a thing to be trifled with…" He sighed. "As you know."

Fiona thought for a moment. "Of course, I have the purest of intentions with Miss Waters. I take my role as her benefactor and friend very seriously."

"Friend?" Perry said skeptically.

"Warm acquaintance?" Fiona said, she sat down, ripping at her cravat. It felt as if it were strangling her. "Perry, did Marty tell Lucille we won't have our lesson today? I need to rest." Before he could answer, she stumbled to her bed and lay down.

When she woke up, there wasn't an inch of Fiona's body that felt like it wasn't being scalded from the inside out.

"Lady Fondant," Lucille said, rushing into the room.

"I'm sorry," Fiona said, wincing as she sat up. "I thought I told-"

Lucille nodded "Yes. He conveyed your message but when I heard you were unwell, I wished to see if there was anything I could do to assist you."

"Oh? It's nothing. I feel a bit under. My joints are swollen. I'll be better in a day or two." Fiona said evenly.

"Shall I run you a hot bath? Or soak them in cabbage leaves?"

"No, it's quite alright."

"I'll read to you then?"

Fiona didn't particularly like being read to but there was a searching soulful look on Lucille's face.

"You could come sit with me," Fiona said, patting the bed beside her.

Instead of sitting back, Lucille pressed her firm cold lips to Fiona's burning forehead.

"You're burning up. It's probably because your fire is so high."

"I'm cold." Her head was swimming and she laid back.

"Lay down." Fiona felt Lucille's delicate hands on her ribs and back easing her to the mattress. "Come, Lucille."

Her lids were heavy and as her eyes fluttered open and closed, she saw Lucille up on her knees struggling to pull the curtains around the bed. The bed posts nearly reached the ceiling. There was a stick with a hook on it somewhere but her mind was so foggy she did not remember where she sat it.

Mustering all of her energy, Fiona propped herself up on her elbow. She flicked her wrist and the curtains curled around the bed frame. With a sigh she collapsed down, sinking heavily into the mattress.

"Save your energy," Lucille said.

Fiona grunted and closed her eyes, sighing deeply. She felt Lucille lay beside her, she smelled earthy and sweet as always.

"I'm right here with you," Lucille said, her body curved around Fiona's but not touching her.

Fiona wondered if Lucille could feel the spasms. She tried to be still but it felt as though her muscles were twisting and writhing so hard, they were going to break through her skin at any moment.

"I'm going to be alright; this is no worse than the other," Fiona said; she wasn't sure if she was comforting herself more than Lucille.

"If you tell me what you need, I'll do it. Is there anything I can get?" Lucille asked.

"Hold me as tightly as you could manage." As soon as she had said it, Fiona remembered that Lucille was not used to closeness. Was she asking for too much?

Before she could tell her that it was alright, Lucille's body enveloped hers. Lucille held her tightly and squeezed. "Breathe, breathe with me. I'm here. I'll be here."

Fiona felt warm tears trickle in her hair and drop into her face. It was vaguely comforting since Fiona was too exhausted to produce the sobs that were shuddering through her. She stayed in bed for what felt like weeks but when she returned to teaching Lucille's confection lessons, she was informed it had only been three days.

Lucille

"*I* am a bird that is free but here I stand by my cage." Fiona stated, sighing as if she had made a profound statement regarding the state of her life. Lucille sighed in response. Fiona may have recovered physically somewhat but she was still mentally sulking.

"Have you considered you are a bird guarding its nest?" Lucille asked.

"Honestly, no," Fiona said, frowning.

"Thirty eggs?" Lucille said, reading the recipe.

"Don't forget your conversions." Fiona

"One dostrichure egg should be fine," Lucille said.

"Mhm," Fiona grunted.

"Four pounds of flour, two pounds of sugar?" Lucille said horrified. "This must be a mistake…"

Fiona shrugged "It's very dense. Plum cake is very dense."

"I believe plums are the only ingredient not on this list!" Lucille said.

"Currants, raisins, almonds. Two types of almonds? No wonder you always smell like almonds," Lucille muttered to herself.

"I smell like almonds?" Fiona cocked a brow. "You smell me?"

"Uh, not intentionally," Lucille said. "I'll get started on this; it does not say how long to mix."

"Mix until I return," Fiona said and with that she was gone.

Lucille stirred the thick mixture. She tried to keep her mind on practical matters like art vocabulary or all of the new techniques she was learning in her confection studies. Instead her mind wandered to think of Fiona. For a moment she let her mind wander to the idea of Fiona feeding her warm sponge with fresh berries then gently wiping the crumbs from the corner of her mouth, calling her something ridiculous like the prettiest cut of cheese cloth she had ever seen.

"I'm tired; it's been over an hour," Lucille said when Fiona returned.

"We'll bake it. Then let's soak it in rum, wine, or brandy."

"Brandy," Lucille said quickly.

"Why?"

"It's already here and I'm too tired to fetch anything else."

Once they were done, Fiona tried to excuse herself but Lucille offered to follow her, worried about her melancholy. Once they were in the parlor, Fiona tried to ignore her but Lucille asked her a question so often until finally, Fiona snapped.

"I'm working." Fiona said annoyed.

"What is this?" Lucille said, walking over and craning her neck over Fiona's shoulder, which given the other woman's short stature, was not hard. It seemed to be a poem or song of some kind.

"Uh, nothing. Recipe notes." Fiona said, trying to cover the paper with more papers and her large hand.

"No." Lucille said, snatching the paper out from under the stack. She scanned the poem quickly.

Oh, sweet confection, how you entice
With your sugared scent and your creamy guise
You are a delight to the senses, a feast for the eyes.
A symphony of flavors that my heart cannot disguise.
In your presence, my heart flutters and sings
Like a bird on the wing, with unfurled wings
I am entranced by your beauty, your form.
And with every bite, my love for you is born.

"This is lovely, although I must admit it is quite the shock. You love confections enough to write poetry about them." Lucille said laughing. "Or perhaps it is not,"

"It's not-" Fiona grumbled and snatched the paper back and then she stalked out of the room. Lucille sighed, perhaps she had gone too far.

Fiona

*F*iona grumbled under her breath to herself, Lucille was so frustratingly annoying and beautiful and funny, it was so irritating. In the comfort of her room, she opened her journal and quickly flipped past all of the half written recipes and the errant diary entry. Carefully, Fiona copied the first stanzas of the poem she had been working on. Then she continued on, thinking only of Lucille. She almost laughed at the fact that Lucille hadn't realized the subject was herself. *Who literally writes about sweets? That is absurd.*

Oh, sweetest of delights, dessert divine,
How thy flavors tempt this heart of mine.
For in thy sugared sweetness, I do find,
A taste that lingers on my tongue and mind.
But 'tis not thy sweetness alone that doth inspire,
For in thy very essence doth burn a passionate fire.
A flame that kindles in the heart and soul,
Oh, how thy layers of flavor do unfold,
Like petals of a rose, so delicate and bold.
Each taste is a mystery, a wonder to behold,
For in thy delectable and heavenly taste,
I find a love that cannot be displaced.
A love that's pure and true, beyond compare,
A love that's sweeter than the richest fare.
So let us share this dessert divine,
And taste the love that's truly thine.
For in each bite, we'll find a love so rare.

It was perhaps not the best poem she'd written but no matter, she did not plan to show it to anyone. Perhaps if she put her feelings on paper she could banish them. The oil lamps on her nightstands began thumping in unison. "I know, I know, it is late." She grumbled to herself then got ready for bed, lamenting the fact that she could not fall asleep with the weight of Lucille's head on her shoulder, the silk of her bonnet wrinkling her nose. Fiona tied up her hair and imagined Lucille's nimble fingers neatly arranging the flaps and knots of the headscarf.

*L*ucille

*D*awn found Lucille anxious and wide awake, and her mood had not improved throughout the day. She stared down at the table full of baking ingredients and sighed. *What had Fiona said?* Lucille had made several variations of shortbread cookies since she arrived at the manor and while they were not difficult, they were tedious.

"I must sift the flour, the sugar and cornstarch?" Lucille asked.

"Yes." Fiona said, wiggling her brows at her.

"All three?" Lucille asked incredulously.

"Just wait until you have to chop the butter and knead the dough, it's almost as if you're making cookies." Fiona said grinning.

Lucille frowned. "I'm simply tired."

"Then we'll take a break. There's always time for tea." Fiona said gently.

"Oh, I almost forgot." Fiona handed her a pendant. Lucille held it up curiously, looking at it in the light, forgetting her manners for a moment. It was a massive pink gemstone that spun in its gold mount, the bail it was attached to was a gold moth.

"Is it a necklace?" Lucille said stupidly.

"A watch fob, actually."

Lucille went to hand it back. "I don't wear a watch, it would be a terrible item to waste."

Fiona pushed her hand back. "You can spin the stone, it's very quiet and will give you something to do with your hands while you're anxious."

Lucille hesitated, surely she did not fidget that much. Suddenly she felt very antsy. There were enough bells ringing in her head to put every church in Monarch's Field to shame.

"Thank you." Lucille finally managed. "I don't believe I have a taste for tea. I actually just remembered I should be picking flowers." She stood up, the fob held tightly in fist.

"From the hothouse?"

'No." Lucille said.

"The garden?" Fiona said, rising and picking up her cane.

"Uh, no, the pasture." Lucille said.

"I can come."

"No." Lucille said quickly.

Fiona shifted uncomfortably.

"What I meant to say was I don't want you to be uncomfortable, it is a way away."

"It's still my estate." Fiona said with a little shrug. "I'll be able to see the house from the field."

"You can see the manor from the town square."

"Not the same." Fiona said, strolling past her and out the door. Lucille sighed and followed her. There was no avoiding it, did she want to avoid her?

To Lucille's surprise, the back pasture was relatively normal. She half expected for the grass to be sugarpaste but it was just plain grass dotted by the wildflowers she had come to pick. A white goat with mottled spots like a dairy cow was eagerly chewing away at grass. The only thing curious about the little goat was that its spots were a light pink color as were its horns. As they stepped closer the goat raised its head and eyed them warily with its bulging eyes.

"Is she friendly?" Lucille asked.

"How would I know?"

"It is your goat, is it not?" Lucille asked incredulously. "Your land, your goat."

"Well, technically. But you're in my house and that doesn't make you mine."

"At the very least you should know its temperament."

"I hardly know your temperament and I see you on a daily basis. I am the lady of the manor, not a goat minder."

"Why do you keep comparing me to the goat?" Lucille practically shouted.

Fiona shrugged. "Perhaps you have goat-ish characteristics."

Lucille half-heartedly tossed her wicker basket. "Ridiculous."

"Says the girl who is throwing baskets," Fiona picked up the basket. "What is it you're looking for?"

"Dandelions." Lucille said, starting to gather the fluffy yellow flowers.

"Let us hurry before the goat eats them all or us." Fiona said, beginning to help her. Once they had gathered half a basket's worth, they made their way back to the kitchen. Lucille did her very best to ignore Fiona while she prepared the dandelions. *Clean the dandelions. Fill the jar with dandelions. Add oil to the jar with the dandelions.*

"Now what do we do?" Fiona asked cheerfully.

"We wait. This must infuse them. We'll make it into soap."

"Lovely." Fiona said, that means we have time for-"

"Tea." Lucille finished for her. Perhaps the day would improve. They would have tea and chat and that felt more comforting and familiar than Lucille would care to admit.

Fiona

"This candy smells awful," Fiona said, limping into the kitchen. She hadn't bothered changing out of her large cotton nightshirt and wide linen pants or removing her sleep cap before coming downstairs. She adjusted the cap as it had come loose in the night, pulling it until it was fitted tightly around her head. Then she tied a knot at the base of her neck, letting the excess fabric flow down her back. Lucille did not look up from stirring her pot, so Fiona repeated herself. "These candies smell awful."

Lucille still didn't respond so Fiona spoke a bit louder. "I hope that is not the dandelion soap. It smells horrid. Rancid really."

"Oh hush." She turned around and made a wave, almost as if she she was just noticing Fiona. "The dandelion soap is all cured. And this, this is a poultice," Lucille said proudly.

"It smells horrid; what's in it?" Fiona said.

"Onion, dandelion, turmeric, garlic, aloe vera."

"Ah, just half the garden and the pantry." Fiona said, wrinkling her nose.

"I'll soak cabbage leaves in the mixture and then apply it to your joints."

"Alright," Fiona said. "I trust you."

"Undress and lay on the table," Lucille said.

"The table?"

"It's your table."

"Uh, yes. But you would like to apply the cabbage leaves now?" Fiona said, slowly realizing what Lucille meant.

"Yes." Lucille motioned to the stack of cabbage leaves that were on the sideboard. "Will I have to ask you twice to undress?"

Instead of replying, Fiona sighed and then she flicked her wrist, slamming the door closed.

She shimmied out of her clothes to her undershirt and laid there. After what felt like an excruciatingly long time, Lucille began to lightly touch her skin. Fiona was certain Lucille was simply being as gentle and delicate as she could be so as not to cause Fiona more pain but Lucille's fingertips barely grazing her calves were sending shivers up her spine. Goosebumps began to prickle across her skin. "I'm rubbing the balm on your skin first then I'll move on to the paste and wrap your joints."

"Cold?" Lucille asked.

Fiona realized she was trembling, "Uh, no, chills."

"I'll hurry," Lucille said sweetly.

"Take as much time as you need." Fiona said lying through clenched teeth, much longer of this and she was liable to say or do something foolish.

Fiona cringed slightly as Lucille smeared the thick, gritty paste on her ankles and knees, then wrapped them in warm wet cabbage leaves.

"We should leave these for a while. Would you like me to keep you company?" Lucille said, patting her arm.

"No, thank you, you've done enough" Fiona yawned dramatically. "I'll take a nap, then we can discuss recipe names this evening."

Lucille smiled and nodded, wiping her hands on her apron. "When you're done, you can just put the leaves in the compost. Nothing will hurt the worms." Fiona could have imagined it but she thought Lucille had glanced back wistfully before she left.

The time to test the poultice had arrived and Fiona met Lucille in her chambers, not knowing whether to be excited or anxious. She watched as Lucille unclasped her small gold hoops and removed her rings. Then she lotioned her hands and elbows.

Her rich brown skin glowed and shimmered, catching every bit of amber light.

"One moment," Lucille said, holding up her hands. "I don't want to get your papers oily. Kenna hated that."

"Was Kenna in your room often?" Fiona spoke too quickly to have time to mentally rephrase the question in a less jealous and possessive form.

"Of course, Silly," Lucille said. "She was my roommate. I've never had a room alone in my life. Well, except now." She gestured nonsensically into the air around the jam suite.

Fiona hadn't considered this.

"I imagine that you have never had to share a room," Lucille said with a smirk.

"Uh, no. My rooms have always been my own." Fiona said sheepishly. "I hardly use my sitting room though, I use my parlor more."

"Is that supposed to be noble?" Lucille said, pushing Fiona playfully.

Fiona giggled. "You practically share my room, for all intents and purposes." Fiona had to control herself and not sniff the air.

"You constantly invite me," Lucille replied.

"It's been a long time since I've had the company of someone my own age," Fiona said, embarrassed at how ashamed that made her feel once spoken aloud. Hopefully, Lucille did not think her too pathetic. Did she really invite her that often?

"You mean Marty and Perry aren't the epitome of youth and frivolity? I for one am shocked." Lucille said with a laugh. "Let me wrap up my hair and then I'll help with those recipe names."

"Here, let me," Fiona said. She sat on the bench at the foot of Lucille's bed. It took Lucille a few moments of adjusting and wiggling to sit in between Fiona's legs. Fiona divided the braids into two sections, then twisted them over each other and wrapped the length around Lucille's head. She tucked the ends in and tied Lucille's scarf on.

Fiona couldn't resist rubbing the back of Lucille's neck and down her shoulders. Instead of relaxing against her, Lucille trembled.

"I'm sorry," Fiona said softly.

"No, please, don't apologize. I just get so nervous."

"Of?" Fiona said as she waited for Lucille to turn around.

"Everything," Lucille said quietly, her head still down. "Or I don't get nervous at all and ruin everything; there seems to be no relief."

Before Fiona could reply Lucille stood up. "Now those recipes, we should get to those before one of us dozes off."

Lucille

$\mathcal{D}$espite having been at Sugar Lump Manor for weeks, Lucille still hadn't grown accustomed to the openness and sheer number of windows that the massive estate possessed. Overhead a late winter storm raged. Bits of hail skittered across the glass ceiling and Lucille kept looking up, half expecting the rain to come pouring in through the stained glass. Fiona didn't seem bothered, she was engrossed in her list of recipe titles, scratching them out and scribbling in the new names.

"We can take a break today," Fiona said after a sip of wine.

The remnants of their macaroon and drink tasting littered the table. There was a line of tiny glasses, with half eaten little cakes sitting in front of each one.

"Is this about the macaroons? I know not to make the batter too runny but they turned out fine …" Lucille responded. She thought she had impressed Fiona by pairing them with the sweet wines and liqueurs. Perry had suggested she do it as a "display of practical application of theoretical knowledge."

Fiona squirmed. "I wanted, I had hoped…well…"

"Hmm?" Lucille said nervously gathering up some errant crumbs and sweeping them to the floor.

"I thought you might want to show me your watercolors," Fiona said finally.

Lucille hesitated. "I don't have any more watercolors. I sent them and my oil paintings for my applications."

"Have you just not been practicing?" Fiona asked horrified.

"I use my pastels and sketches," Lucille explained. "I'll work on more pieces when I replenish my supplies."

"You should have ordered them," Fiona said, clearly annoyed. Lucille watched as she sighed and rubbed her temple as if she suddenly had a headache. "Never mind, what do you like to paint? Interiors? Flowers?"

"Yes, I paint from life. Picturesque scenes from nature. I'm not one for portraiture." Lucille said.

"Then what will you learn at school?" Fiona asked, frowning again.

"If I get the scholarship, I'll learn to prepare canvases, learn proportions, lighting, mixing colors and the like from master painters."

"You'll have to paint something for me," Fiona said.

"Oh, I am not that accomplished. Even the youngest ladies of your station probably have more mastery of techniques."

Fiona frowned. "I don't want their art. I don't care about them. I would love for you to paint something for me, I'll send for more paints and supplies. From the city so there will be more variety."

"Well, I could paint you a triptych or a screen, perhaps," Lucille said slowly. "Really, I don't need more supplies."

"Maybe a portrait?" Fiona said.

"I could certainly try to paint you."

"I meant a self-portrait," Fiona said.

"You flatter me." Lucille said, looking down demurely.

She noticed that Fiona winced as she reached for a scone.

"What is it?" Lucille asked firmly.

"Just a few patches on my back," Fiona said.

"I'll tend to them, let us go to my room." Lucille said, rising.

Fiona stood there in the center of the room, shifting awkwardly from foot to foot.

"If you want me to do your back, you'll have to let me unwrap your stays," Lucille said. She gathered up her basket of herbs and medical supplies.

"Okay," Fiona said, lying down.

With trembling fingers, she undid the two large flaps that held the corset together, then she removed the undershirt beneath. She examined Fiona's back carefully, the sores were healed, crusted over and none of them had broken back open.

"Does this hurt?" Lucille asked, rubbing Fiona's shoulder blade gently. It looked larger than the other one and the skin around it was puffy.

"Yes."

"It's swollen." Lucille applied a cream to the swollen shoulder and then dressed the rest of the sores on Fiona's back.

"Let this dry down," Lucille said, blotting the excess salve with a bit of cotton. "May I rub your neck?"

"Of course," Fiona said. "You can do anything you would like."

"That's the second time you've said that," Lucille said with a sigh.

"It's the second time you've not taken me up on it."

"Stop teasing me," Lucille said. "I'm trying to take care of you."

Lucille hoped the last bit of cream disguised her sweaty hands. She trailed the valleys and knobs of Fiona's spine, tempted to kiss each bump, but she thought better of it. Lucille noticed Fiona had gone rigid beneath her outstretched palms. "Perhaps discussions of affection should be had at a more appropriate venue and time," Lucille said softly.

Fiona laughed nervously. "It's understandable, being a carer doesn't elicit the most romantic feelings." Lucille watched as Fiona twisted herself back into the corset careful not to expose herself.

"You're being terribly unfair," Lucille said. "Do you not consider yourself a carer for me?"

"You showed up on my doorstep in need of help." Fiona said, pulling her shirt on. "What would you have had me do? If I did not care for you, who would?"

Lucille glared at her in response.

"Well." Lucille said after a moment, "I'm thankful for your charity." Her gratitude sounded like a curse. She knew she was being ungrateful but she didn't care. "You may leave now."

Lucille huffed as she pinned on her apron and tied up her detachable sleeves. The last thing she wanted to do was have a lesson on baking. But she was a lady of her word and she had already offended her hostess. *I should try to be more agreeable,* she reminded herself. Lucille had half expected to wake up with a note asking her to leave. Instead there was one instructing her to join Fiona if she "felt up to it." She had smiled at that despite herself.

"What are we making?" Lucille tried to sound cheerful as she entered the small cozy kitchen. Of course the house would choose a kitchen that was a quarter of the size of the rest. It looked as if it belonged in a remote country cottage.

"A tart," Fiona said politely.

"Oh, Marty and I baked these crusts yesterday," Lucille said. All of her false cheer melted out of her when Fiona spoke.

"Yes," Fiona said, filling the piping bag with jam. Her face was flat and unreadable.

"Is that the berry jam we made last week?" Lucille asked although she knew it was.

"Hmph." Was all Fiona said. She tied the bag off and held it out to Lucille.

Lucille pretended to squeeze the bag out. "How should I do this?"

"Squeeze a thick layer into the bottom, covering it completely," Fiona said; Lucille could see she was trying not to smile.

"Should we not make the cream first? Lucille asked, making her eyes large.

"No," Fiona said. The smile finally emerged. "Jam goes on the bottom because it is heavier than cream, and we don't want the cream sitting about."

"Oh, of course. I see now." She held out the piping bag to Fiona. Lucille half expected to make a magical gesture and the jam to go oozing out. Instead, Fiona came up behind Lucille, wrapping her arms around her. Fiona placed her hands over Lucille's and gently guided her into squeezing the jam to fill the tart shell. Then together they made the cream and spread that on top of the jam. Lucille could feel Fiona's breath on the side of the face, her chin jutting into Lucille's shoulder, per usual Fiona was cool but Lucille's temperature rose several degrees whenever the other woman was nearby. Lucille leaned back ever so slightly.

"Can you manage to fan out and place the pears if I slice them?" Fiona asked, finally releasing her. Immediately Lucille missed her, which was absurd. Fiona hadn't left, she was barely two steps away.

"Yes," Lucille said, trying not to reveal her true feelings.

"I'm sorry I was angry," Fiona said, not looking up at the pears she was slicing so thin that they may as well have been pieces of parchment.

"It's fine to be angry." Lucille said softly. As Fiona sliced the pears, Lucille carefully began to arrange them in a spiral.

"I didn't say what I meant and it all got twisted and wrong. I got scared and vulnerable and insecure." Fiona said the words came tumbling out of her quickly.

"I believe, I understand." Lucille paused her decorating. "I believe you insulted yourself."

"Oh?"

"No," Lucille said, waving her hand. "I'm sorry, I meant… you assumed…" Lucille said. "It is not that I don't find you attractive because you are unwell sometimes. It's simply that I don't-"

"Find me attractive." Fiona finished.

"Allow me to finish," Lucille said with a groan. "It is not that. I am just overwhelmed with so many conflicting feelings. It is all very new to me."

"Wrong."

"What?" Lucille said.

"You're mixing up the pear slices, instead put one color at a time so it creates a gradient."

"Oh," Lucille said, peeling off and reapplying the pear slices overtop the cream.

Fiona sighed. "There's no obligation for anything, Lucille. You know that?"

"Yes. I just want you to know how I feel. Well, to the best of my ability. You're the most captivating woman I've ever seen." Lucille said.

"I clearly must put more looking glasses in your room," Fiona said with a smirk.

Lucille averted her gaze and glanced over at the half finished tarts.

"Do you need help?" Fiona said, nibbling on a pear slice.

"Sorting out my feelings?" Lucille asked.

"Filling the hole in the center of the spiral with cream," Fiona asked. "Or is the piping bag working now?"

After they were done cleaning and putting away the desserts, Fiona retired which was just as well. Lucille had too much on her mind to be good company. Sternly, Fiona had reminded her to send for food at a reasonable time.

Fiona

For probably the second time in her time living at her manor, Fiona locked her door. On occasion, Marty, Perry, or other servants checked in on her health during the night. Normally she did not mind, but this time she did not want to be disturbed. This would not be a quick endeavor. She drew the curtains around her bed and then lay very still, nervous that the soft rustle of her sheets would echo through the manor, whispering her activities to the rest of the household.

She hesitated, pausing only for a second. Sure, she knew what she enjoyed and how to satisfy herself, but what she did not know was how Lucille would satisfy or be satisfied. Fiona explored her body, grounding herself with the feeling of her calloused hand sliding against her clammy skin; simultaneously, she mentally explored Lucille's figure. Fiona pictured that Lucille would be the same as she was in the day; responsive, sassy, playful, sweet, eager to please, and a quick study.

Fiona went tumbling over the precipice quickly, and she shouted out Lucille's name gutturally. *Fiona, Fiona.* She could practically hear Lucille's sweet voice echoing her name. Wait, that was Lucille's voice, and the handle of Fiona's door was rattling.

Tap. Tap. Tap.

Lucille had started knocking on the door gently but urgently.

"Fiona? Are you alright? Are you decent?" Lucille said, her voice slightly muffled through the door. "Are you decent? Should I get Marty?" That last question sounded like she was asking herself. Fiona wiped her slick hands on the hem of her nightshirt, then she pantomimed, unlocking the door and the lock unlatched.

The door flew open. And Lucille rushed across the room.

"Oh, are you unwell?" Lucille said, perching at the edge of the bed.

"Yes. What is it?" Fiona asked.

"You called me." Lucille said, her voice high and anxious.

"What?"

"I was going to fetch a glass of water, but my pitcher turned out to be cake, and you called my name."

"Oh? I was dreaming," Fiona said quickly. "I believe."

Lucille nodded. "I have nightmares. I'll sit with you."

"I was – I-" Fiona said hesitantly.

"Was your dream embarrassing?" Lucille asked sympathetically.

"Uh, yeah," Fiona said.

"I have those," Lucille said, chuckling, then she shifted awkwardly. She was leaning over the edge of the bed, and in the dim lights, Fiona could see her face was upturned eagerly.

"Are you comfortable if I close the door?" Fiona asked.

"Yes." Lucille climbed up on the bed. With a flick of her wrist, Fiona closed the door gently and pulled back the blanket.

"Come, lay here," Fiona said, patting the cool pillow beside her.

"I'll just stay until you sleep," Lucille said, wrapping the blanket around herself. She scooted forward. "You're so cold she whispered."

"I'm always cold," Fiona said, laughing nervously. "Even when I take to fever."

"Well, yes, but the room is warm," Lucille responded.

"I hope not overly so." Fiona said.

"No, the weather is fine," Lucille said in a whisper.

"The weather?" Fiona asked, confused.

"The climate," Lucille said, laughing softly. "Can I-"

"Yes," Fiona said, interrupting; whatever she asked, it would be yes. Lucille gently rubbed Fiona's face and then snaked her hand under the blanket, down Fiona's shoulder. Finally, Lucille intertwined her fingers with Fiona's. Lucille gave Fiona's hand a tight squeeze.

Lucille

Lucille yawned. She had left Fiona's room early in the morning but still too late to avoid the disapproving glance of the scullery maid. She shrugged off the awkward encounter and made her way to her room, getting ready for the day and then she went to the kitchen to prepare the gourds she would be using for her soap. Much like Fiona and everything else at Sugar Lump Manor, the gourds that grew in the garden were not what they seemed. Lucille wagered that if she had tasted the pink flesh it would have been sweet but she hadn't, instead she had carefully peeled, cored it, removed all the seeds and rinsed it thoroughly. It had been frustrating to wait for it to dry in the oven but now it was ready. She began to slice the long straw-colored spongey tube into discs.

"I have never seen this kitchen," Fiona said from the doorway.

Lucille looked over at Fiona. "It is not a kitchen…. I believe."

"Are you not cooking?" Fiona said, craning her neck. "Is this a secret of some sort?"

"It is not," Lucille replied.

Fiona walked over and sat on the bench across from her. "What is this?"

"I am making you soap bars." Lucille said.

"I have soap."

"This to help you exfoliate."

"It looks scratchy," Fiona said skeptically.

"Hush, you worry about baking and I'll worry about making you feel good."

"Yes, Miss Waters!" Fiona said beaming.

She wanted to chastise Fiona but she remembered that she needed to check her soap mixture. If the blend was not kept at just the perfect temperature it would not set correctly. She hoped she had the proper ratio of water, ashes from cocoa pods and banana leaves to palm oil and shea butter. Lucille looked at the mud like concoction. The consistency seemed perfect.

"Can you place the slices in the bottom of those molds?" Lucille asked. Lucille wrapped rags around the handles of the pot as she carefully removed it from the stove.

"The teacher becomes the pupil," Fiona said excitedly. Lucille watched as Fiona carefully put the gourd slices in the bottom of the molds.

Lucille ladled the mixture into the molds.

"How long until we can use them?" Fiona asked.

"A few weeks," Lucille said.

"No, not that long." Fiona groaned dramatically. "I would never make you wait that long."

"I have some that are already cured," Lucille said.

"Wonderful, you can bring it to my room. I have a fire you can watch." Fiona said with a flirtatious wink.

Lucille sat the soap bars down on Fiona's nightstand and then settled herself down in front of the fire, slowly Fiona lowered herself to the plush rug beside her. Lucille took a long look at Fiona. Typically, Lucille had relished in all the little details of her through sneaking glances while they were working. She was a masterpiece. Lucille loved Fiona's long broad nose and those full lips that were nearly always curved into a smirk. Now that they were sitting so closely, so quietly Lucille could hardly tear her eyes away. Fiona stared back at her with an expression that Lucile couldn't quite place. Fiona began to fiddle with a spring of her kinky yellow hair. Lucille watched intently as Fiona pulled the strand which expanded and then shrank back and then she ran her hands down the sides which were shaved so short, they were nearly straight. Lucille used her eyes to trace Fiona's soft round jawline and tiny delicate ears. Fiona reclined back slightly, holding herself up on her elbows and rolling her head in a circle. Lucille looked closely at Fiona's chest in the dim light of the fire. There wasn't the slightest hint of a curve, she knew Fiona's chest was flattened by her wrapped stays. She also knew she should drag her eyes away but she couldn't help herself. Fiona sat back up slowly and then reached over and gently took Lucille's hand and pulled it towards her chest. Lucille felt her fingers make contact with a slight bump.

After a moment, Fiona guided her hand over, to another slightly smaller bulge under the ridges of the stays. Lucille moved her hand from under Fiona's and reached for the button just below Fiona's chin, thankful Fiona had forgone a cravat. After Lucille had undone the button she hesitated, gently tracing the edge of the button with her fingertip.

"I'm sorry," Lucille said, suddenly feeling the need to whisper; she pulled her hand back. She was mortified she had been tempted to undress Fiona. *How rude, how forward, how indecent. Fiona can hardly stand me,* Lucille thought to herself. *Why did you do that?* The voice in her head screamed. *To be rejected for a second time, how embarrassing. Obviously, Fiona had noticed me staring and wanted to tease me by making me uncomfortable. But then I went and did that.* Lucille could not stem the flood of negative thoughts that gushed into her brain like a flood.

Fiona looked down for a few long moments, and when she looked up, she had a forced-looking, closed-lipped smile plastered across her face. Her eyes shone, not with their usual playful gleam but with the sheen of unshed tears. "I misunderstood; I took your kindness and friendship as an advance; my apologies," Fiona said quietly.

"It was not my intention to..." Lucille struggled to find the words. "I was not attempting to fondle you."

"I know" Fiona said, Lucille could've imagined but she thought she saw her winced.

"If I had known you were interested, I certainly would have done my best to flirt. It simply had not occurred to me that you might be interested in me, in that way. I'm rather plain, uncultured-" Lucille said, the words were spilling out from her with such force she could not contain them.

Fiona held up her hand. "You do not have to let me down, gently. I had thought perhaps you might be interested in deepening our friendship based on our conversation the other day. But if this is not the case, I will still continue to entertain your family until they leave."

"I know you will," Lucille said with more frustration than she intended. It sounded as if it was a threat.

She watched as Fiona wrung a handkerchief in her hands, twisting it as if trying to squeeze water out of it. *You're making a mess of this,* Lucille thought to herself.

"I didn't mean it like that," Lucille said, sucking in a deep, ragged breath. "Please don't be upset with me."

"I could never," Fiona said, her voice sounding as awkward and stilted as Lucille felt. "Perhaps you should take a deep breath, I get the impression you're not expressing how you feel. Is that correct?"

Lucille nodded, a brief wave of apprehension coursing through her. She forced it down and took another deep breath.

"I was just taken aback, that's all." Lucille closed the distance between them by scooting forward. She pressed her forehead against Fiona's and interlaced their hands. "I did not want you to know of my unseemly thoughts. I was so embarrassed and then my old ways of thinking returned."

Lucille felt Fiona's forehead wrinkle as she smiled.

"You should never feel embarrassed with me," Fiona said. "You read the situation correctly, you need not doubt yourself."

Lucille felt her shawl slip off her shoulders as if pushed.

She pulled away from Fiona and looked at their intertwined hands. "You used your powers! You silly goose."

Fiona laughed. "My sweet, it is a shawl. Those tend to fall on occasion. Especially when one is being kissed."

"But we were not..." the rest of her sentence was swallowed by a soft moan as Fiona pressed her lips against hers. Unsurprisingly, Fiona tasted sweet and nutty like marzipan. Lucille felt Fiona pull away, she wished the moment did not have to end. Lucille leaned forward and flicked her tongue across Fiona's bottom lip, craving the softness.

Lucille yelped and covered her mouth with her hand. "I'm so sorry, I've never done that before."

"It's alright. I was not expecting you to lick me but it was not unpleasant." Fiona said then pulled Lucille back towards her, she nibbled on her earlobe, then she kissed a whispering path down her shoulders and back up her neck. After so many near-kisses, this was almost too delightful. A shudder of anxiety pulsed through and she had to pull away. Fiona was speaking gently to her, their hands still intertwined. She stole a glance at Fiona's dark eyes. They glowed with a tenderness and passion that almost unsettled Lucille.

".... Lucille? Are you alright, do you need water...." Fiona was whispering slowly. Lucille could only half-listen as her mind was too hazy to truly grasp what Fiona was saying. But she could tell from the soft sounds, it was meant to be gentle and reassuring.

"I should go to sleep," Lucille said, standing up, her voice husky. Before Fiona could respond, Lucille left, practically running to her room. *Remember,* Lucille reminded herself, *none of this is real, and she is only kind to you because she is rich and bored and lonely. When she gets tired of you, she'll discard you like a toy with all your new trinkets. But she kissed you, and you kissed her and together you all kissed in unison, as one, together!* The little voice said happily. It was true, Lucille realized, she had been kissed. There was kissing.

Fiona's words buzzed in Lucille's mind like an orbiting gnat. She tried to push the echoing thought from her mind but it continued to return to the forefront. *Perhaps you might be interested in deepening our friendship...deepening our friendship...deepening our friendship...deepening.*

Fiona

*F*iona had gone to Lucille as early as she dared but far sooner than what was proper. The sun had hardly shown its face and not even the gingerbread men were about. Begrudgingly, red-eyed and puffy-faced, Lucille had opened the door and ushered her. If spring was coming, no one had told the weather gods. It was cold and despite the warm amber lights and fires, there was a chill in the jam suite. Fiona laid very still in the silence, shivering slightly as Lucille's hand worked her way over the topography of her twisted body. She felt naked despite being in short stays and trousers. It was not a feeling that made her feel the least bit aroused. Between the pain and the astringent smell of mint, sage and lemongrass, any enjoyment from Lucille massaging her sore muscles was completely eclipsed by the utility of the interaction. She was actually surprised that Lucille answered when she knocked on her door and asked for a massage. Part of her had expected Lucille to think it was some sort of ploy but instead, Lucille readily agreed, apologizing for her cold hands as if Fiona's skin was not already as cool as the watermelon sherbet they had enjoyed the night before. Secretly though, Fiona hoped that once Lucille was done, they would be able to talk. Lucille for her part was being agonizingly slow as if she sensed Fiona's eagerness and was attempting to counteract it. Lucille worked her hands across a knot below Fiona's shoulder blade for the third time. Fiona was uncertain if she was being thorough or if she was stalling.

Finally, Lucille sighed and patted her shoulder to signify she had finished. "I'm glad we can still be close after my indiscretions yesterday." Lucille said as she stood up and wiped her hands with a wet rag. Fiona was surprised by the sudden noise interrupting the silence they had been wallowing in for the last hour. It took her two long beats to process what Lucille had said.

"Indiscretion? Oh you, meant the kiss. You're so darling." Fiona said, rolling over to her back. Lucille draped a towel across Fiona's exposed skin. Fiona shifted indignantly. *Why was Lucille being strange? She's seen nearly everything, it's a bit odd to act shy now.* As much as Fiona liked Lucille, her behavior baffled her sometimes.

"My little spoon, you are going to have to start using your brilliant mind a bit more, why would we not be close? Did I give you that impression?" Fiona held the towel up as she propped herself up on the headboard not wanting to make Lucille anymore uncomfortable.

"I was worried you wouldn't want me to care for you anymore," Lucille said, sitting on the edge of the bed as far away from Fiona as possible.

"Do you think of yourself as my career?" Fiona asked.

"No, but I enjoy caring for you," Lucille said, twisting her hands.

"You don't think your friendship and physical affection helps? Your kiss was very healing." Fiona said, she shot Lucille with an impish grin.

"Don't patronize. Have you kissed very many times?" Lucille asked.

That was not what Fiona had been expecting her to say. Instead of answering, Fiona looked down at the tapestry on the wall. She remembered the warnings both Marty and Perry had given about Lucille. Quickly, Fiona tried to figure out what the best way was to handle the situation without lying or hurting Lucille's feelings.

"Oh, you have" Lucille said flatly. *Clearly, my mind is not working fast enough,* Fiona thought bitterly.

"It's alright," Fiona said, scooting over so she could cup Lucille's chin. "How about I make you a deal."

"What's that?" Lucille said. Her warm dark brown eyes looked more afraid than hopeful.

"You'll be the last person I kiss." Fiona hesitated not wanting to carelessly give away the promise of forever so she continued. "For a very long time."

"I'll take that deal," Lucille said. The velveteen dress she wore clung to her generous hips and rolls of her stomach delectably.

"Come, lay beside me, please." Fiona said letting go of the last scraps of her self-control.

"I've never—" Lucille started.

"We'll just kiss," Fiona said, reaching for her. "Or I'll just hold you. You like that. I do that all the time." She was whining now, and she didn't care.

"Alright." Lucille said, "a few kisses and a snuggle. Then you need to rest."

They lazed about for most of the day, taking their meals in Lucille's room until she announced she would like to dance. Fiona was not one for dancing but they made their way to the parlor nonetheless and the pianoforte played itself, producing an upbeat, lively melody. Fiona was excited that her joints were cooperating enough to dance with Lucille. Neither of them knew the most popular dances or were particularly coordinated, but they were having a good time. It was a most refreshing change from drawing or baking.

"This should be our song," Fiona said, twirling Lucille around.

"Hardly, it's a heartbreaking song. Have you listened to the lyrics?" Lucille responded.

Fiona shrugged. "I've never heard it performed, only the instrumental. It's quite upbeat."

Lucille pulled away. "Let me show you the lyrics,"

"You have the sheet music?" Fiona said, surprised Lucille bothered purchasing such things. She was terribly frugal, albeit very lively out of necessity.

"Oh no I do love music, but I could not justify such an expenditure" Lucille said, laughing. "My pianoforte instructor allowed us to copy the songs in our books."

Fiona frowned. "Would you like me to send for sheet music?"

"No, don't be foolish. I'll find the lyrics for you, I'll be just a moment." Lucille said hurrying out the room.

Fiona stared after her.

"Here," Lucille said, opening the book on her return. "It's about two lovers who aren't meant to be, but when the reckoning is near…. they choose each other because there are no consequences."

"That's not heartbreak," Fiona said firmly.

Lucille tapped the page and then began to slide her fingertip along the sentence as she read.

"A winter and a summer have passed, just now I've let your name past my lips without tears shed."

Fiona moved her hand and guided her to trace another line "if my heart could choose, I would choose you, again, again, again and then, again."

Gently, Lucille moved their hands back to the chorus, "Champagne stays locked in the cellar."

She read it out loud twice and then announced, "Obviously they are star crossed lovers."

"Who choose each other when their world ends" Fiona said, enunciating each word as if it was the most obvious thing in the entire world.

"Precisely, but the world does not end," Lucille said.

"Perhaps they simply created a new world together. Away from societal expectations." Fiona said.

"Not everything is a metaphor," Lucille said; there was a vague annoyance in her voice.

"It's a song," Fiona said, flicking Lucille's nose. "That is typically the perfect medium for a metaphor."

Lucille snapped the book closed tightly. "Alright. It is late, I am tired. We should retire."

"We should retire because you are tired?" Fiona said playfully. "The two of us, to our separate rooms."

"Mhmm." Lucille said standing up.

"When did you become the queen of when to turn on."

"Just this moment." Lucille said, raising a brow and nodding to the door.

"Yes, your highness."

Lucille

here was no bell to mark dawn at Sugar Lump manor like there was Brittlebone but Lucille still managed to get up, dressed and to the third floor reasonably early to work on her art. Only an hour seemed to have passed when the sun stopped trickling into her makeshift studio. She rose, stretched, and then turned the amber stones in their sconces. Then she sat back at her easel and returned to her drawing. Perry had been kind enough to let her borrow a bust from one of the lesser-used hallways. She wondered if this person was a relative of Fiona's. There was nothing candy related to the woman's dress, and there was no inscription. Whoever the lady had been, she was beautiful. The sculptor had done an especially fantastic job at reproducing a tight, curly hair texture in stone, and the woman also had a prominent nose with a gentle slope and warm eyes with wrinkles at both corners. Lucille recreated her plump, pillowy lips as best she could but took a bit of liberty with a facial expression. She could tell from the crinkles around the statue's face that she would have smiled often. There was a gentle tap on the door.

"Mmhm?" Lucille said, not tearing her eyes away from her picture.

"Luce," Fiona called out.

"Yes, Lady Fondant?"

"Open the door, Luce," Fiona said firmly.

"Oh?" Lucille said, wiping her hands on her apron.

Lucille opened the door. Fiona stood there with a handled tray in one hand and she held her cane in the other, leaning slightly to one side. The tray held a teapot, cups, a rice dish, fruit, cold meats, and cookies. It took Lucille a few moments to register what was happening. "Oh, come in." She said finally, stepping aside. Lucille motioned to the drafting table in the center of the room. "Just sit it on top of those sketches; they're no good." Fiona looked skeptical but placed the tray down.

"You've been in here for hours," Fiona said, her voice thick with concern.

"I have not." Lucille said.

"It's almost eight," Fiona said; she looked around. "Where's your timepiece?"

"I dunno," Lucille said, nibbling on a piece of salami.

Fiona went to the desk and closed a case full of paint tubes, revealing a small clock.

"Oh," Lucille said. "I'm sorry, did you need me? I thought we had a break from our lessons."

"We did," Fiona said. She sighed loudly. "And yet, you did not take a break of any sort. Did you eat? Did you take tea?"

"Lady Fondant, not everyone takes tea thirty times a day."

"You must eat, you must drink, even if it's port or nectar. I don't care." Fiona said, a serious dark edge creeping into her voice. "I'll make you a pot of drinking chocolate every fifteen minutes if I must."

"I don't need you to take care of me," Lucille said, waving her off. "What is this?" She asked, motioning to an unfamiliar dish with rice.

"If you do not take care of yourself, I must do it myself. I am not above treating you like a babe. Say the word, and I'll have leading strings stitched onto every garment you own." Fiona said.

"Stop it, Lady Fondant." Lucille bit into a plum dramatically, "I'm eating," she said, not bothering to chew or swallow before answering, so her words came out garbled. Once she finished the plum, she poured herself a cup of tea. Lucille took a big swig. "I am nourishing!" She said loudly.

Fiona rolled her eyes in response.

"Are you satisfied?" Lucille said, curtsying deeply. "Or is there something more I can do to please you?"

"Do not tempt me," Fiona said, her voice still stern and low. Before Lucille could formulate a response, Fiona pointed to the rice dish. "It's sticky rice; it's made with coconut milk. That's mango, papaya, and apple."

"I know my fruit," Lucille said, taking a big spoonful. "Even if I haven't tasted half of them. I know what they look like." She moaned. "This is amazing, and it's salty, sweet, creamy…Was this dinner?"

Fiona laughed at her normal playful demeanor, seeming to return, "No, it's a dessert."

"I could eat a pile of this," Lucille said.

"You would have to ensure it makes it to your face," Fiona said, brushing a grain of rice off of Lucille's face.

"Did you bring that with you?" Fiona asked, pointing to the bust with a cracker.

"No?" Lucille said, "It was on a pedestal in a hallway."

"Ah, it's nice." Fiona shrugged.

"Well, yes, what do you think of the likeness?"

"Nearly identical," Fiona said, studying the grayscale sketch. "I want a miniature of you,"

"I…" Lucille stopped and then started. "I don't believe I could produce such a likeness."

"Try?" Fiona said. "For me."

"Perhaps an eye?" Lucille offered. *An eye could not be that difficult,* she thought.

"Wonderful; I look forward to seeing your oil rendering of your deep brown orbs, vast like the starless night sky."

"You flatter me," Lucille said, looking down and then quickly back up.

"Ah, and my heavens. How they shine." Fiona said. "I hope you can capture your humor."

Fiona leaned forward and although Lucille was expecting it, when Fiona's lips hit her own, it was as if every coherent thought was knocked loose and went hurtling from her mind.

She tried quickly to reorganize her thoughts, flipping through them as she did the pages on her sketch pad. Fiona's fingers snaked to the nape of Lucille's neck, stroking the thick coarse patch of hair there. Fiona's touch was decadent, familiar and vaguely possessive. Lucille wondered if Fiona could feel her clattering thoughts as she tickled her scalp and traced the curve of her skull. *Focus,* Lucille said to herself, *respond to her.* Fiona tasted of mangos and her typical toasty reassuring smell of vanilla filled Lucille's nostrils, it was a rich experience Lucille could normally get lost in.

Fiona broke the kiss leaving Lucille panting and confused.

"Where are you?" Fiona asked. "Are you here with me?" Her face was clouded with concern.

Look her in the eyes, tell her the truth, Lucille thought to herself.

"No," Lucille asked. "I want to be. However, my mind is in chaos."

"Come here," Fiona said, pulling her into a tight embrace and rocking her back and forth. Lucille could feel the chaotic pounding of Fiona's heart. *Is my heart hammering louder?* Lucille wondered. When she tried to relax with Fiona, she let go too completely. Lucille slumped forward. In perfect rhythm, Fiona stepped backward, pulling them both onto the small sofa that was pushed off to the side.

Somehow, Fiona managed to contort Lucille's body in a small package and tightly wrap her arms around her. But it was too tight, Lucille wrenched out of Fiona's vice like grip and tumbled out of the room, she bolted down the nearest staircase and took a sharp left and smacked straight into her bedroom door. She threw herself onto her bed, tense and exhausted. She quickly cleared her mind and gave herself over to a deep, death-like sleep, safe from any emotions or her own scattered thoughts. When she awoke there was a note on her nightstand.

Miss Waters,

We will take a break from our lessons today. My apologies for hurting you yesterday, I personally find compression to be very reassuring. In the future we can discuss what you find soothing. I care for you deeply. It was not my intention to hurt you and it pains me greatly that you were uncomfortable.

Lady F

Fantastic, Lucille thought. *You've done it now.* When she was too high strung or hysterical at Brittlebone she was relegated to her room with no interaction for days to "soothe her nerves." Her fingers traced over the formal moniker "Miss Waters" where something silly and ridiculous should have been written. It should have said "to my little cheese grater" or "my sweet cutting board."

Lucille lay back on the pillow and was perfectly still, staring at the canopy and listening to the gentle woosh of her own breathing. Lucille hadn't been hurt; she'd been overwhelmed. There was a gentle tap on the door and she swung her legs over the side of the bed.

"Oh." She said, not bothering to hide her disappointment that it was Perry.

He held out a tray with a small teapot, a singular teacup, and the standard tray Lucille had come to expect: an artistically arranged array of cold meats, cheeses, and fresh fruits. It was all beautifully arranged and the sight of it caused the tears she had been holding back to burst forth. Perry walked past her, placed the tray on vanity and then gave her a weak nod and a pat on the head. Then he closed the door and she was alone again. She didn't have long to wait for soon there was another knock, this one more fervent. Lucille ignored it, Perry had probably sent Marty up.

"Lu- Miss Waters. If I may, come in?" Fiona's voice was garbled and soft through the wood door.

"Yes, of course," Lucille said, but she couldn't bring herself to open the door.

"I'm sorry," Lucille said when the door eased open. Fiona did not come in but instead she had opened the door a bit and pushed her head and neck in.

"Don't apologize, I'm sorry to bother you. Perry was concerned." Fiona said.

"Oh no, I'm fine. Just embarrassed and sad that I was put up." Lucille said hiccupping. She swallowed hard, trying to manage to say something coherent to explain her concerns.

"Put up?" Fiona said as she pushed the door open a little wider.

"Yes, when I have my upsets at Brittlebone, I'm sent to my room or a spare room for a long while," Lucille said.

"No, no." Fiona said coming in. "We wanted to give you space and not overwhelm you. You're not relegated to your room by any means but if you would like more space to be alone we can clear the floor."

"Oh." Lucille said stupidly. "That would not be necessary, I'm alright now."

"May I hold you?" Fiona asked hesitantly.

"Mhmm."

Fiona pulled her in a warm embrace and whispered into her arms.

"I don't want to stay in my room." Lucille hiccupped, crying all over again.

"You never have to worry about that again." Fiona said, rubbing her back. After a long while Fiona asked, "Would you like to have tea with me?" pulling away just a bit.

"Of course," Lucille said, her voice breaking slightly.

After the tea had been drank and Fiona's multiple reassurances, Lucille retreated to the quiet of her makeshift studio. For a long time, Lucille sat before her easel brush in hand, studying her own reflection, which wasn't something she did often. She was determined to capture herself in paint, to give Fiona a portrait of herself that she would enjoy.

With a steady hand, she began to sketch her features, capturing the curve of her jawline, the wide bridge and gentle slope of her nose, and the softness of her full lips. She painted herself with rich, dark colors, adding depth and dimension to her features, hoping that Fiona would be pleased.

As she worked, she thought of Fiona, imagining the way her eyes would light up when she saw the tiny portrait, the way her fingers would trace over the canvas as if trying to memorize every line and curve of her face. Or at least that is what she hoped. It could be tossed aside, forgotten in a lonely drawer beside cufflinks and pen nibs.

The portrait was taking shape, and Lucille was pleased with it. She wished Kenna were here to give her feedback, but it would have to do.

Finally, she put down her brush, studying the finished portrait with a critical eye. It was not perfect, but neither was she, and it was her, captured in the beautiful paints Fiona had given her.

Part Three

Presentation is Everything

Fiona

he last thing in the world Fiona wanted to do was drag her aching bones out of bed and downstairs to oversee the preparations for Lucille's parents' arrival. The house had been on edge ever since word had been received of their impending visit but she knew if she did not do it, Lucille would be worried and that would not stand. On her way to her parlor, Fiona was nearly slammed into by a gingerbread attendant. He was carrying a stack of towels so high, she couldn't see his face.

"How are preparations going?" Fiona asked as she passed Marty and Perry.

"Very busy…" Marty said.

Perry motioned to the bustling servants bumping around like bumble bees. "As you can see my Lady."

"Ah, and you must send for the hairdresser, the one who does my hair just so. My roots are a mile long" Fiona said, pushing back her hair to show her hairline.

Perry and Marty exchanged glances. "She is busy, she is traveling."

"Recall her, offer her more money," Fiona said, ducking out of the way of another servant, this one carrying a large potted plant.

"She's at court," Perry said.

"The king's court." Marty said explaining as if Fiona hadn't understood.

"No!" Fiona wailed. "Who will help me with my hair?" Fiona practically wailed.

"I will," Lucille said cheerfully. Fiona looked around until she saw Lucille leaning back against a wall, looking as delectable as ever.

"How long have you been over there?" Fiona said with a laugh. She walked over to Lucille and pulled her in her arms for an unfortunately brief embrace.

"Just a few moments; I didn't want to get trampled," Lucille said; she pulled back. "I will help you with your hair, and I am familiar with beauty products."

Fiona shrugged. "I don't have much choice."

"You mustn't ever call me vain again," Lucille said.

"I only did that once." Fiona objected.

"Twice," Perry said.

Fiona rolled her eyes at him and took Lucille's hand. "Let us work on this mess," Fiona said, patting her head with her free hand.

"What will you do?" Fiona asked once they were in the kitchen, she cocked an eyebrow up, not bothering to hide her skepticism.

"I'm making a saffron tincture, then I'll add a bit of carbonate of soda," Lucille responded brightly. *Clearly, she was confident,* Fiona thought.

"What will that do?" Fiona asked.

"Once I apply the lemon juice and vinegar there will be a reaction and it will lighten your hair to match your currently garish yellow, red color. I'm sure your dresser has a premixed tonic. But I'll have to work a bit."

"It is not garish," Fiona said defensively.

"It certainly is not subtle," Lucille said, shooting her a look over her shoulder.

"Does it please you?" Lucille said holding up the looking glass to Fiona.

"It does," Fiona said, craning her neck to get a better angle at her freshly cut and dyed hair. Fiona had been a bit nervous when Lucille had used her straight edge around her hairline and sides, but the lines were neat and crisp. To Fiona's delight, her curls were still tight and soft.

"Now I must do my hair," Lucille said, packing up her supplies.

"I could help." Fiona offered.

"Are you sure? I don't want you to hurt your hands." Lucille said hesitantly.

"I feel fine today." Fiona said, "Sit," she said standing and motioning to the chair she had been occupying.

"It might be better for me to sit on the floor," Lucille said.

"Ah, yes," Fiona said. "Because you are a statuesque goddess."

"Or you are a short king. Or …?" Lucille's voice raised into a question.

"Whichever," Fiona said, sitting back in her chair.

"You are a short monarch," Lucille said, settling in between Fiona's knees.

Fiona rubbed her shoulders and then unpicked each braid and separated the crinkled clumps of hair until Lucille's coils sprung free. She massaged Lucille's scalp and then gently finished detangling her hair. Fiona stealthily gathered a few of the loose tufts of fluffy hair that had fallen to the floor and on her knees and placed them in her pocket.

"This feels nice," Lucille said.

"Do you like scratches or no?" Fiona asked.

"I dunno," Lucille said absentmindedly.

Fiona raked her hands gently across Lucille's scalp. "How's that?"

"Nice. I like it." Lucille said softly.

"I can flat twist. Or I can send for the village braider." Fiona offered.

"I don't let people touch my hair. Flat twists are fine."

Fiona used a wide-tooth comb to section Lucille's hair. Fiona took a glob of hair grease and placed it on the back of her hand. She carefully applied a smidge to each part, making sure to smooth down Lucille's roots. Fiona worked deftly, weaving the hair into twists. They weren't perfect but they were shiny and thick.

When she was done, Fiona traced the nearly straight part lines with her nose, dragging her face against the slick bare scalp and inhaling deeply. When she opened her eyes and looked down, she noticed a sea of goosebumps had prickled across Lucille's neck, shoulders and chest.

"Everything alright?" Fiona said, pulling Lucille up to sit on her knee.

"Oh yes, I just…" Lucille "I just get a bit nervous; it's embarrassing how much you care for me."

Fiona thought for a moment. "My affections overwhelm you because your family does not care for you. Or do I misunderstand?"

"No, well now that you mention it, perhaps I should be embarrassed. I meant caring for me in a literal sense. Clothing me, feeding me all that." Lucille said.

"You take care of me." Fiona said, wincing as the admission passed over her lips.

"Only when you're in need," Lucille said.

"Are you not in need of loving care?" Fiona said, tilting her head to one side.

Lucille didn't answer so instead Fiona rose, not wanting to push her any farther.

"Let's have a negus," Fiona said, clapping.

"Are you escorting me out?" Lucille said with a laugh.

"How do you mean?" Fiona said.

"Normally you have a negus before you escort a guest out." Lucille said with a frown.

"Oh, I haven't had guests recently," Fiona said. "The impromptu gathering of the attendants was the closest I've been to a party in a long while."

They sat down and drank their beverage. The mug felt incredibly hot in Fiona's hands, and Fiona realized that she didn't particularly care for the drink. It was a tad too thick because of the jelly but she did like the wine, citrus and spices. She had simply offered it to avoid Lucille complaining again about the amount of tea they drank.

"I finished your miniature portrait." Lucille said, clearly embarrassed. She fiddled with her mug and swirled the last bit of her drink.

"You did not bring it?" Fiona said, pouting.

Instead of replying, Lucille took a sip of her negus.

"We should serve your family little Rout cakes?" Fiona said thoughtfully. "Those are very popular in the city I hear."

Lucille still wasn't meeting her eyes, so Fiona kept talking.

"Have you been to a Rout?" Fiona asked. She had always been intrigued by these massive parties but had never gone to one or even been invited. Perhaps she would if she ever left the house.

"Yes, the Duchess of Ater invited some four hundred people." Lucille said and then she added "It was exceedingly boring and hot and crowded. No seats. People were crammed in every nook and cranny."

"It sounds as if you are describing your worst nightmare," Fiona said with a laugh.

"I am not exaggerating. The cutlery closet, the library, the linen closet…it was all full." Lucille said.

"I bet you have a great deal of interesting stories," Fiona said.

"No, well…." Lucille said, snuggling up to her. "I could tell her a few."

Fiona wasn't sure if it was the warm woolen blanket, dwindling fire, the negus or the heat radiating off of Lucille or a combination of all three, but a sense of warmth and ease settled over her. When she awoke, Lucille was gone and in her place was a tiny likeness wrapped in a bit of velvet fabric. Fiona traced it with her finger. It was stunning, just like Lucille. Fiona was in awe at all the details at such a small scale. She couldn't wait to put it in her locket. Only a small portion of the portrait would be visible through the window when the locket was closed. In private, she would be able to enjoy the full image.

Despite the entire staff and both Lucille and Fiona working around the clock to get ready for their guests, there was a nervous energy reverberating through the air of Sugar Lump Manor and it was setting everyone even more on edge. It seemed as if every wave of anxiety bounced into one another and then rippled out endlessly. It reminded Fiona of a molded jelly jiggling aggressively after its dessert table was knocked into. She tried to focus on the recipe but Lucille was making it difficult.

"Are you feeling fine?" Lucille asked. *Dammit,* Fiona thought to herself. *Obviously, she was not doing a good job of guarding her emotions.*

"Yes, my grater," Fiona said quickly.

"I fear I have overworked the dough," Lucille said, pointing to the brown glob that was on the floured counter.

Honestly, Fiona had not been paying attention when Lucille tempered the chocolate or added in the powdered sugar or the golden syrup so she couldn't be sure if it had been formulated properly in the first place. Instead, Fiona had been agonizing over hypothetical conversations with Lucille's parents while the dough was being flattened and left to rest. Lucille's worry seemed infectious.

"Did you use the spatula?" Fiona asked. "And not the whisk?"

Lucille slapped the dough. "You handed me a spoon."

"Of course." Fiona said, judging from the 'thack' sound, the dough had been left to sit too long and was rock hard. "Keep kneading it. It will soften." *Eventually,* Fiona added silently.

"Alright," Lucille said after a few minutes. "And now?"

"You roll into logs and then cut into sections and wrap in paper," Fiona said. "I'll cut the strips of paper while you work on that."

Fiona wrapped the chocolate taffy as quickly as she possibly could. Once they were all wrapped, Fiona stood up.

"Shall we wait in the foyer for my parent's arrival?" Lucille said. She wiped her hands on her apron, brushing off imaginary crumbs.

Fiona took Lucille's hands gently in her own. "Perhaps a better use of your time would be spent correcting this Rout cake recipe. If we plan to serve it to them, it must be impeccable. The humor will not land if they are nasty."

"Of course, of course," Lucille said, then she repeated herself. "Of course," as if trying to convince herself as well.

Fiona gathered the flour, sugar, butter, and egg and passed the ingredients over for Lucille to mix. The instant the ingredients had left her hands, she knew that this had been a mistake. Lucille began mixing so hard that Fiona worried she might crack the bowl. It was a wonder that she had not snapped her wrist with the intensity of her whisking.

"Is there something you would like to discuss?" Fiona asked softly.

Lucille nodded, her shoulders dropping in relief. "I'm so stiff with you, well, with everyone. We barely know each other. Well, we're close. But not overly or improperly so. And what if Mother notices…." Lucille said loudly as the words tumbled out from her. "What if she asks something that we do not know. For example, your favorite poem, do you care for poetry? Perhaps I could just lie…" she said, pausing slightly to catch her breath as the idea occurred to her.

"Calm down!" Fiona said when Lucille finally paused.

"Don't tell me to calm down!" Lucille shrieked.

"You're screaming at me! But more importantly, you've beaten all the air out of that batter," Fiona said.

"No," Lucille said. But she finally released the wooden spoon. Fiona wrenched the bowl out of her hand and gave the mixture a tentative stir to check its consistency. It was a sickly, pale yellow and dripped off the spoon.

"Yes," Fiona said, holding up the spoon coated in the slimy yet watery liquid. "Souls have a better chance at rising from the underworld than this cake."

"Perhaps I was a bit vigorous?" Lucille said sheepishly as she winced and began fiddling with her hands.

"Can I hold you?" Fiona said, reaching for her.

"Please," Lucille said softly, sinking into her.

"Let us see if we can salvage this cake and then we'll go wait for your people." Fiona murmured into her hair.

Lucille

While the cake wasn't salvageable, Fiona laughed it off and offered to make her a hot drink. Lucille quietly watched as she heated up the milk to use as a base, adding honey and dried lavender, and stirring the honey until it dissolved. She topped it with a bit of black tea and then she sprinkled it with cinnamon, nutmeg, and a touch of clove. Just when Lucille thought it was done and Fiona poured it into a large ceramic mug, Fiona added a touch of vanilla and a sprinkle of dried rose petals.

"I created this recipe for you." Fiona said, sitting down at the small table next to her. They shared a warm fruit tart, the creamy custard perfectly contrasting the flaky crust.

Lucille had never been one to believe in love at first sight or even second or third. She had always been a practical person, focused on her studies and her artistic pursuits, and never really one to entertain the whimsical notions of a love match or a grand, epic romance. But as she sat across from Fiona, watching her talk and laugh and move her hands in that expressive way she had with that booming voice and cocky swagger, she felt a strange sensation wash over her.

At first, she tried to ignore the feeling, to dismiss it as a passing fancy or a momentary distraction, gratitude or respect perhaps. But as the hours went on, she found herself thinking more and more about how she felt about Fiona. It got to the point that she couldn't focus on what Fiona was saying and it was then that Lucille realized that she was in love. Or, at the very least, deeply infatuated.

The realization hit her like a carriage clambering across cobblestones. It was loud, it was rough, and all she could do was ride it out. As Fiona made the crepes and recounted stories, Lucille felt the sudden urge to tell her, to share her feelings and see what she thought. To see if their minds met somewhere. But as Lucille opened her mouth to speak, she felt a wave of panic wash over her, even more intense than her feelings of affection. What if she didn't feel the same way? *What if she made a fool of herself? What if she lost her friendship?*

No, she decided. She couldn't risk it. She would keep her feelings to herself, buried deep within her heart, and continue on as if nothing had changed. They would continue this courtship ruse, and once it ended, perhaps they could be friends.

And so, she kept quiet. Though it pained her to keep her feelings hidden, she knew it was the right thing to do. For even though she was in love, she was also sensible. And sometimes, the sensible choice was the hardest one of all. All she had to do was make it through the visit. That is what she should be worried about.

"Can you believe they burned the sugar that bad?" Fiona said, leaning back in her chair, her hands cradling the back of her head.

"No, I cannot." Lucille said quickly. "If you're done, we should go downstairs to wait for my parents."

"Yes." Fiona said, holding up a crepe.

"You have it." Lucille said.

Fiona

ucille's pacing back and forth in the foyer was making Fiona dizzy. The messenger had said her parents weren't due for another two hours but Lucille was acting as though they had seen them down the lane.

"Hey, hey." Fiona said, catching Lucille by the wrist to stop her. Fiona had to stand on her tiptoes, stretching her neck as far as it would go to kiss Lucille as she did not bend down or tilt her head. Still, Fiona's eyes closed in anticipation as their lips met, and for a moment, it seemed as if Lucille's lips were hard and unyielding, but after a breath and a skipped heartbeat, her lips softened. Fiona held her close, one arm around Lucille's waist, the other cupping the back of her head. Lucille leaned down to meet Fiona halfway, their lips meeting in another perfect, gentle kiss. Despite the height difference, the two fit together perfectly.

Lucille pulled away first. She appeared completely unaffected by the kiss. Fiona watched helplessly as Lucille resumed her pacing.

"We must not retreat. We must not be weak." Lucille slammed her fist into her palm.

"Why are you acting as if dinner is a battlefield?" Fiona said, reaching for her fist and uncurling it.

"Isn't it?" Lucille stopped her pacing momentarily. Fiona wished she could hold Lucille still, shelter her from the noise that was her own mind but she knew wherever Lucille was she was partially unreachable.

"It's a meal…" Fiona said. Lucille twisted her hand away and continued her pacing.

"Oh, Lady Fondant, you really haven't been in society. These events are horrid. They are truly horrid." Lucille was actually noticeably trembling.

"I will protect you." Fiona said, taking her by the shoulders.

"I don't understand," Lucille said, twisting away.

"Whatever they say, I'll defend you and distract them; they'll hardly notice you to attack you," Fiona said gently.

"Do you mean this?" Lucille's eyes glimmered with hope, and Fiona could tell she was searching for sincerity.

"Of course. I would keep you from anything that means you harm. Your relations or not." Fiona said firmly.

"You're committed to your role." Lucille sighed and Fiona watched as she dragged a smile across her face.

"I'm committed to keeping you safe. That is not a role." Fiona said, "that is infinite."

Lucille nodded weakly.

"Listen, Luce. You shouldn't be so sensitive. It'll let everyone have the power to destroy you."

"I am not weak," Lucille said angrily. "I'm going to go freshen up." She said pushing past Fiona. Fiona watched her jog up the stairs. She waited for Lucille to look back but she didn't.

Lucille

ucille sat down at her vanity. She had to blink away a few tears that were welling in her eyes, she looked down, there was a thick bundle of paper tied with ribbon. At first, she had assumed Marty or Perry had gathered up her errant sketches but she realized the pages were too small. She picked them up. "Everything is a metaphor" the top page read in Fiona's familiar scratchy handwriting. She undid the ribbon and thumbed through the pages. Sheet music. Sheets and sheets of music. This must have cost a fortune. Before she could put them away, she heard Fiona's familiar knock on the door.

"Come in," Lucille said, not bothering to turn her around.

"I apologize for what I said. It was untrue and I'm not sure why I said that. It was cruel. I spoke in haste. Would you like a hug?" Fiona said to her back.

Lucille considered this for a moment. Never once had she imagined she would turn down the offer of a hug. They were so rare and so precious that the idea of not wanting one seemed absurd. She turned around and shook her head from side to side. *Don't be sensitive, don't be weak,* she thought to herself. "No." She mouthed.

"That's fine. You can say no." Fiona said, tilting her head slightly to the side.

I've done it again, something peculiar, Lucille admonished herself silently.

"Is there some other way you would like me to apologize?" Fiona said. "I am sorry and would like you to feel better."

"I-" Lucille sputtered. "I accept your apology."

"Alright. Are you certain?" Fiona said.

"Uh yes, is there something more I'm supposed to do?" Lucille swallowed hard trying to choke back more tears.

"I dunno. You're the society girl. What's the proper etiquette?" Fiona said evenly but her face was awash with concern, her perfectly arched brows knitted together in concern.

"I believe to move on with grace and decorum." Lucille said. "I've only read about it."

"Do you not accept apologies?" Fiona said playfully.

Lucille shook her head from side to side. "They've never been offered. And you?"

"I'm rarely wronged so there is rarely need." Fiona said.

"How delightful that must be for you," Lucille said bitterly.

Fiona swiped a hand across her face. "I was not teasing, I meant only…"

"I know; I was being sincere," Lucille said.

Perry stuck his head in the doorway. "The Waters are here. I took them directly to the dining room as they were complaining of hunger."

Fiona and Lucille exchanged sideways glances; any tension they had felt now replaced with anxiety.

Fiona

$\mathcal{A}$s their guests settled into their seats around the long, ornate table, a gingerbread servant appeared at the door, carrying a silver platter laden with dishes of steaming hot food. Fiona watched with amusement as Lucille's parents watched the gingerbread servants make their way toward the table, each one moving in a smooth, fluid motion.

Gerald, the head gingerbread man, approached the table first, he carefully placed the platter down in the center, his movements precise and measured. He then stepped back, his hands clasped together in front of him as the guests eagerly surveyed the meal before them. The table was piled high with all of the foods that Marty and Perry had researched and discussed with the house-keepers of the neighboring estates. While she was not familiar with most of the dishes, Fiona knew they had spent such a high amount at the butchers that they had to provide the note upon delivery and there was enough butter sauce drowning the veg to float an armada. Lucille's mother Alma had commented on the massive amount of fruit wistfully. That was probably the only pleasant thing she said. For his part, Lucille's father Simon seemed to only communicate in a series of coughs and looks of vague displeasure.

As the meal progressed, the gingerbread servants moved silently around the room, refilling glasses and offering second helpings. They were an unobtrusive presence, never speaking or drawing attention to themselves, but always there when needed. Gene, the head gingerbread man, flashed Fiona a subtle but reassuring smile.

And as the group finished their meal and began to retire to the drawing room for drinks and conversation, the gingerbread servants disappeared to their wing of the mansion, their duty fulfilled for the evening. Fiona wished she could join them.

"Lucilla!" Alma practically shouted. "You did not tell us you were dining in such luxury, no wonder you're looking so shapely."

"Th-thank you?" Lucille said, shooting Fiona a shocked glance.

Marty and Perry appeared behind Lucille's parent's chairs to fill their glasses.

Fiona took this opportunity to whisper to Lucille, "Your name is Lucilla?"

"No, it's Lucille, they forgot," Lucille whispered back.

"How?" Fiona said. The Waters only had three daughters, hardly enough to forget one's name.

"My sisters' names are Viviana and Tabitha," Lucille said with a shrug; she swallowed the rest of her sherry and held her glass up to Marty, who promptly filled it to the brim.

Fiona was surprised, Lucille's mother actually looked quite like her but with a dour expression permanently contorting her features.

Once they had eaten dessert, Fiona signaled for the cake that Lucille had made to be brought out. The icing was pure white, perfectly smooth and it was elegantly decorated; bare, save for a sugar paste branch that held a sugar paste dove.

"Oh, this is lovely," Alma nearly shrieked. "This icing must have cost a fortune, don't you think Simon?' She nudged her husband.

"Mhmph," Simon said with a shrug.

"Our dearest Lucille made it all herself. She's quite accomplished." Fiona said proudly, she patted Lucille's hand reassuringly. To her surprise, Lucille gave a weak smile.

"Lucille did this?" Alma said, shock etched into each of her exquisite features. "Well, I believe this is probably the best thing she's ever done."

Fiona couldn't help but roll her eyes. "Let us partake."

"Mmmm," Fiona said, taking a large bite. "Possibly the best cake I've ever eaten."

Alma nodded. "It is quite good. I believe you may be the only instructor who has gotten through to Lucilla."

"I thought you were an accomplished student," Fiona said, turning to Lucille.

"I am," Lucille said firmly. "I have nearly perfect marks."

"Lucilla! Do not brag." Alma said.

"Lucille," Fiona said, sighing.

"That is what I said," Alma said. "Isn't that what I said, Simon?"

"Ompf," Simon said, cutting himself another slice of cake.

Fiona felt her mind wandering, she wondered if the sugar she had ordered had arrived yet. It had been delayed and the last time the supplier had sent her wet sacks that were full of unusable sugar that was lumpy and nearly rock hard. She tried to snap her attention back to Alma.

"I must say, it concerns me the need for secrecy...." Alma said for what seemed like the twentieth time.

"I promise you, nothing untoward happened. Lucille wrote to me concerning employment. I was simply taken with her charm and impeccable penmanship. Our relationship grew from there." Fiona said exasperatedly.

"Hmm," Alma said; she did not seem wholly convinced but moved on. "Lucilla," Alma said, turning to Lucille.

"Hmm?" Lucille said, looking up from her venison and baked apples.

"Your sister wrote and is quite...taken aback by your turn of fortune," Alma said.

"Ah-umphf." Simon said. Fiona rolled her eyes; Alma and Simon were increasingly irritating her already frayed nerves.

"There is no linear path to finding love," Fiona said with a shrug.

"Did you know that your sister is close acquaintances with Lady Fondant's former fiancé Bree?" Alma said, waving her speared potato in Lucille's direction.

"Isn't a close acquaintance an oxymoron?" Lucille said quietly.

Fiona could not help but laugh. "My darling Lucille has no reason to think of Bree. As I'm sure you're well aware, Lucille is incomparable. Bree was a childish folly." Fiona hoped her sincerity came through in her voice.

Lucille's full lips formed a perfect "o" in shock.

Simon leaned over and whispered something to Alma.

Alma's face tried to form something that Fiona imagined was supposed to be a smile but more closely resembled a grimace. "We must apologize, the bespoke bracelet that Lucilla gave us to hold, it was lost...in our....travels?" Alma said, shaking her head from side to side dramatically.

"Was it?" Fiona said, shooting Lucille a confused glance over her glass of champagne.

"Later." Lucille mouthed.

"Please, don't worry about it. I have a great deal of jewelry and I will always prove Lucille with more, that was a mere token. A trinket really." Fiona said. Alma looked as if she was about to speak.

"I am exhausted; Lucille walk me to my room, will you?" Fiona said, rising.

"Gladly," Lucille said, rising quickly.

"Stay up as long as you would like," Fiona said with a curt nod to Lucille's parents.

As they exited the dining room, Fiona tripped and lurched forward.

Fiona felt Lucille's hand slip into hers ever so gently in an effort to subtly catch her. As Fiona recovered her balance, Lucille linked their arms together, placed her hand on top of Fiona's, and pressed their bodies together ever so slightly in an effort to support her.

"I don't need your help," Fiona whispered.

"I'm not offering it; I'm terrified." Lucille hissed back.

Fiona pressed a kiss into the part in Lucille's hair.

"Of course, I'm sorry, my little rolling pin," Fiona murmured.

"You did a fantastic job," Fiona said. "What is all this bracelet talk?"

"Kenna and I came across a little bauble at the market. It happened to have an F on it, I used it as proof of our engagement. I'm sure they pawned it the moment they could." Lucille said, rolling her eyes.

"You, Lucille-Lucilla, never cease to amaze me." Fiona said.

"Oh, shut up," Lucille responded. Instead of going to Fiona's room they made their way to the parlor. Fiona wanted to embroider and she was sure Lucille would draw or read.

Fiona settled down into the settee and set up her embroidery hoop and Lucille pulled a book down from the shelf, sitting in her customary armchair.

"Fiona!" Lucille said, shutting the book as quickly as she opened it.

"Yes?" Fiona resisted the urge to smile; she loved when Lucille called out her name, even when it was exclaimed in anger or annoyance.

"There are scribbles everywhere." Lucille held up the open book.

"Annotations," Fiona responded, then she turned her attention back to her embroidery. She adjusted the stand that held the hoop and picked up her needle. She was stitching a sampler, but now she was concerned the gray broad-weave cloth would be too dark for the threads she had chosen, but there was a limited selection of fabric at the modiste that met her requirements.

"Why don't you take notes like a sensible human? What if you sell the books?" Lucille said.

"Firstly, I am not human. Secondly, I have no need to sell anything."

"This is so expensive, and you've ruined it," Lucille said, pouting.

Fiona looked up from her embroidery and pouted back playfully. "If it bothers you, I'll order you your own copies. Anything with a pink ribbon has been annotated. If you're interested, "I'll send for new copies."

Fiona glanced at the bookshelf closest to her. At least twenty books had little pink ribbons sticking up from the pages. None of them were particularly rare or expensive.

"Not, it's fine," Lucille said, huffing.

"Is it?" Fiona said, cocking her brow.

"It is. I chastise you for ruining a costly item, and your solution is to spend more." Lucille said incredulously.

"If it will put your mind at ease, I would gladly spend a fortune," Fiona said. She walked over and took Lucille's hand, kissing her fingertips. "I did not realize it was a problem."

"Perhaps I was being dramatic," Lucille said softly, she looked down and then looked back up at Fiona, looking through her thick eyelashes.

"No need to apologize," Fiona said, giving her a squeeze before releasing her. She returned to her seat and continued her chain stitches.

"Does that not hurt your hands?" Lucille asked after just a moment.

"No, it's a large needle and loose cloth." Fiona didn't bother looking up.

"And the stand?" Lucille asked.

"Yes," Fiona said.

"Oh, I wish I could use a stand," Lucille said. "It hurts my neck terribly when I embroider."

"Why don't you?" Fiona asked.

"Well, I-I'm not..." Lucille trailed off.

"Yes?" Fiona said, staring deeply into Lucille's eyes, who immediately dropped her gaze to the book she clearly wasn't reading.

"I don't know." Lucille said.

Fiona added a few more stitches to the chain. "If there is some device or technology that would make your life easier, then you should use it." Fiona looked up from her stitch and waited for Lucille to make eye contact which didn't take long. "You can use such materials even if you are not disabled."

"Ah." Lucille opened her mouth and then closed it tightly. "Yes, but of course. I'll return to my reading now. I have to stop to take in your notes, so it'll take me twice as long."

Lucille

The next morning, Lucille made her way back to Fiona's parlor; she hadn't been invited, but she knew she would be welcome. Fiona did her work in the mornings before breakfast and had very little interest in talking or generally interacting before her tea had been consumed, but they enjoyed the easy silence. Lucille nodded to Fiona and then took her normal spot in the armchair by the fire. She finished addressing her sketches to the institute that requested more work and one to an artist who put an ad in the paper for an apprentice. She also wrote a letter to Kenna which she could not mail yet, but there was so much going on she did not want to forget any details. Lucille took a bite of her morning snack; she had topped a grilled, flattened, stale croissant with cream, slivers of cold meats, olives, and greens. It was one of the few recipes she had enjoyed at Brittlebone and eating was comforting.

Marty entered the room and glanced Lucille's way without saying anything.

Fiona looked up and stopped writing. "What is it that can't wait until breakfast?" Fiona snapped at him.

Shooting Lucille another furtive glance, Marty leaned forward and whispered something in Fiona's ear.

Fiona cackled. "Let them have it. I don't care for it anyway."

Marty frowned but nodded and then scurried out of the room.

"What was that about?" Lucille asked.

"Your parents are helping themselves to our traditional silver, but I don't care for it anyway. It hurts my hands," Fiona said with a shrug. "So, it's best not to make a scene."

Our. Increasingly, Fiona had been using the word 'our.' She used it to refer to everything from household items to the future.

Fiona closed the book she was writing in. "It is probably time for breakfast." She stood up and walked over to Lucille.

"You're already eating! What is this abomination?" Fiona said, a bemused smirk crossing her face.

"Oh, the croissants were stale," Lucille said. "So I made a little bite."

"Why didn't you give them to the birds?" Fiona asked, but she picked up the treat and put it to her lips.

"That would be a waste," Lucille said with a shrug.

"What did you do to the croissant?" Fiona asked, taking another bite. "It tastes like a cracker."

"I flattened it with the slab roller and toasted it," Lucille said guiltily.

Fiona nearly choked on the bite she was chewing. "You used my slab roller for stale pastry?"

"Mhmmm"

"Well, at least it's tasty," Fiona said. Lucille's eyes were wide, and she had licked her lips several times in rapid succession.

"I'm not upset," Fiona said, rubbing Lucille's arm. "Let us get this over with. Hopefully, your people don't cause me too much indigestion."

Just as she expected, breakfast was exceedingly dull. Her mother was prattling on about something, but Lucille alternated between eating her delicious parfait and staring dreamily at Fiona. For her part, Fiona responded with similarly sweet expressions in between bites of custard. Lucille wasn't certain how many of

Fiona's loving glances were sincere and how many were sincere, but she was relishing in the attention. Perry scurried in and sat a book in front of Lucille. The book was thick with scraps of fabric spilling out between the edges of its pages.

"Hello, Perry!" Lucille said happily, glad for the interruption. "What is it you have there?"

"Oh, my dear, this is part of your surprise," Fiona said.

"A book for a surprise?" Mother muttered.

Perry scooted Lucille's plate out of her way and sat the heavy book down.

"It is sponge!" Lucille said loudly.

"It is not, I swear it. The modiste sent a book of samples for your made-to-order dresses." Perry insisted.

Lucille eyed him skeptically, then tapped the book with her fork.

"Ah, it is a book." Lucille declared.

"Perry, please fetch me a bit of pencil and paper so Lucille may take notes," Fiona asked.

"At breakfast?" Mother scoffed.

Lucille ignored her, already opening up the book.

"We are amongst family, are we not? Why fret about formalities." Fiona said coolly.

"Well-" Mother started but was cut off by Perry loudly clearing his throat.

Perry sat a silver tray down with a few sheets of parchment, a pencil stub, and a sharpening knife.

Lucille picked up the pencil, but when she pressed her fingers to the sides, it snapped in half.

"Oh, Fiona, you've tricked me. Is it the whole tray? No…" Lucille trailed off as she tapped it. It was solid wood. But the parchment and knife crumbled under her fork.

Fiona shrugged. "It t'was not me."

Lucille used a knife to saw into the tray and sheets. The outer layers of marzipan cracked to reveal the cake underneath.

"Is this your work Perry?" Fiona asked.

"Yes, ma'am," Perry said proudly.

"It is impeccable," Lucille said, giving him a warm smile.

"Very well, let us try it!" Fiona said, her tone equally as encouragingly.

Forgetting herself for a moment, Lucille loaded up a forkful of the cake and fed it to Fiona. "Mhmm, it's delightful," Fiona said.

Alma frowned disapprovingly. But Lucille ignored her, loading up another heaping forkful and trying it. "Oh yes, fabulous. Divine. Truly."

Perry nodded. "Thank you, I'll let you get to it," he said, producing a real pencil and scrap of paper from his pocket.

Alma frowned. "If we are discussing matters of business at breakfast, I have a subject I would like to broach."

Simon leaned over and whispered something unintelligible to Alma.

"I don't believe dresses are really a matter of business," Fiona said, breaking her scone in half.

"Don't be silly," Alma said.

"Whatever it is, just say it," Lucille said, making a note of a cornflower blue fabric.

"There is the matter of jointure," Alma said.

"Mother!" Lucille said she grasped the pencil tightly. A wave of embarrassment surged over her.

"Hush," Alma said. Immediately, Lucille's mind was transported to when she was a small child when she was either ignored or constantly corrected.

"What did you have in mind, Mrs. Waters?" Fiona said, seemingly unfazed, but Lucille felt her rough hand cover her own under the table.

"A comfortable amount; god forbid you to die and leave our dear Lucilla a widow," Alma said.

"God forbid," Simon said in a very cheerful tone.

"He speaks," Fiona said softly.

Lucille would have laughed, but she was fighting back tears. This was utterly humiliating.

"Perhaps ten thousand notes a year?" Fiona said tentatively.

"For her?" Alma said, her mouth falling open ever so slightly.

"If you all will excuse me." Lucille dropped Fiona's hand. She stood up and tried her best not to run out of the room. Lucille had barely made it down the hallway before she felt caged in by a pair of strong arms. The smell of toasted almonds filled her nostrils.

"Luce, Luce," Fiona said, her normally warm baritone husky and tense. "I'm sorry. I can give you more. Whatever it is you want, just tell me, and I'll make it so your family will never touch it. It will be all for you."

Lucille couldn't hold back her tears anymore. They flowed from her eyes freely, and she pushed Fiona away so that she could wipe her tears with the back of her sleeve.

"It's not that." Lucille dropped her voice to hardly a whisper. "I know it's not real; it's just so embarrassing. They're just so awful."

Fiona looked as if she was going to speak, but then she didn't.

"I'm going to bed," Lucille said.

"It is not even noon," Fiona said.

"I don't care," Lucille said, pushing away from her.

"Don't close me out," Fiona said; there was a vague whine in her voice. "I'll make you feel better."

Lucille kissed her cheek. "A proper cuddle sounds delightful."

Fiona held Lucille's hand as they made their way upstairs to Fiona's room. Instead of sitting on the bed or the bench at the foot of the bed, Fiona sat on the floor with both legs bent in front of her, one leg crossed over the other.

"Come here," Fiona said.

Lucille scooted towards her but hesitated slightly.

"Sit in my lap," Fiona said, her face warm and inviting.

"How would you have me do that?" Lucille said, moving forward tentatively.

"Climb up, silly. Mount Me." Fiona said playfully.

"Mo-" Lucille's eyes grew wide like she could not bring herself to utter the words.

"Like a horse," Fiona said.

"I don't ride," Lucille said with a little shrug.

"We'll have to remedy that. I'll get you a pony." Fiona said, her face suddenly sobering.

"Horses are too much to maintain," Lucille said, waving her hand as if that would dismiss the silly notion.

"Luce, you can afford to keep a horse." Fiona insisted.

Lucille shook her head from side to side. "I certainly cannot."

"Let us argue about horses later," Fiona said, patting her thigh.

"Will I hurt you?" They shared a smile.

"No, trust me," Fiona said.

Lucille settled herself in Fiona's lap; she bunched her skirts up so she could wrap her legs around Fiona's strong abdomen.

"How does this feel?" Fiona said.

"It feels nice," Lucille said, staring deeply into Fiona's eyes.

They pressed their foreheads together and breathed in each other's air for a long while, their heartbeats synchronizing and their bodies unfurled in the same slow way, the tension seeping from deep in their muscles.

Finally, Lucille lifted her head. "You smell divine."

Fiona wiggled her nose against Lucille's nose. "As do you."

"I could breathe you in for hours." Lucille said softly.

"I won't stop you," Fiona said, chuckling. She rumbled beneath Lucille, sending vibrations through her. To her surprise Lucille dragged her nose across Fiona's neck and across her hair.

Emboldened, Lucille placed a hand on either side of Fiona's face. She kissed Fiona's forehead.

"Mhmmm," Lucille moaned.

Fiona placed her hand on Lucille's throat and the other on the top of her chest. Lucille's body melted against Fiona's; the room seemed to dissipate, everything falling away except the two of them. Peaceful energy flowed between them.

Fiona

"*U*hmmm," Lucille said again, the throaty moan reverberating against Fiona's palms.

"This feels so real," Lucille said, her voice thick.

"It is real," Fiona said, dropping her hands to Lucille's waist. "Our connection is real."

Lucille wrapped her arms around Fiona tightly. Fiona felt constricted in the most wonderful way. She felt Lucille wiggle ever so slightly, and her hips hitched forward.

"I don't know if this position will have the desired effect; laying might provide more friction for you," Fiona said, fantasizing about how more of Lucille would feel.

"I-" Lucille pulled back, splaying her palms out flat on the floor. She balanced her weight precariously on her hands.

"It was an offer; you don't have to accept," Fiona said quickly. She could feel Lucille shrinking away, the parts of her body that were against Fiona's were tense, and Lucille looked at the wall and not at her.

"I am declining now but in the most respectful fashion," Lucille said. "In the future, perhaps you could show me-" Fiona could tell Lucille was struggling with the words. "More?"

"Of course," Fiona said with a curt nod. She rubbed her hand reassuringly.

"I'll be off, then." Lucille giggled nervously. "And off," she motioned to where her legs were still wrapped around Fiona. But taking one hand off the ground caused her to nearly fall. Fiona grabbed her and maneuvered her gently out of her lap.

"You don't have to leave. You can if you want, but I'm not asking you to." Fiona said softly. "I have a book to read, and you could draw."

"Are you certain? I don't want you to think me a chit." Lucille said, glancing away.

Fiona laughed. "No, Lucille. You asked for a cuddle, and that's what I gave." She took both of Lucille's hands in her own before continuing. "If the only lesson you learn in my house is that you are free to do as you please without shame and say no without apology, then I will consider our time a rousing success." This seemed to reassure Lucille.

They were only able to relax for a quarter of an hour before Lucille was called down by Alma. Fiona was sad to see her go but she remembered she should be studying bread recipes for a new roll so she made her way to the library.

Fiona was reading a scientific textbook on bread when Lucille came barreling through the library. Even from across the large room she could tell she was upset. Fiona put down the book and made a beckoning motion with her hand and Lucille flew forward. Fiona held up her hand and Lucille stopped a few paces in front of her. It took a moment for Lucille to steady herself but when she did, Lucille collapsed into Fiona's arms dramatically. Fiona glanced over to Perry who responded with a small shrug.

"Hold me, crush me, smother me." Lucille said her face already burrowed into Fiona's shoulder. She wasn't sure if she should mention Perry's presence.

"You don't like that, remember?" Fiona said awkwardly patting her on the back.

"Not if I'm upset but if I'm sad it helps." Lucille said, her face still pressed against Fiona.

"Oh." Fiona said, squeezing her tightly.

"Thank you, you understand." Lucille said.

"You're wel-" Fiona started but was cut off by Lucille wrapping her hands tightly around the lapels of her jacket and releasing a muffled scream into her cravat. She did it so suddenly, Fiona wasn't sure how to respond. After a few moments, Lucille pulled back and patted Fiona's jacket smooth for her. "Ah, much better." Lucille said with a sigh. "I feel much better, thank you." She stood up and smoothed her skirt. "Mother claims it is warm enough for croquet so I must go. Truthfully, I feel unwell but I must go."

Instinctively Fiona looked up at the ceiling of the library which, like most of the manor, consisted of glass panels. The sky was full of gray swollen clouds and Fiona couldn't imagine it being warm outside. Before Fiona could say anything, Lucille flounced away.

"Wear a shawl." Fiona called after her.

Perry snorted.

"I don't want her to catch a chill." Fiona said indignantly. "It is weather for a chill."

"It is." Perry said, stifling his laughter. "Though, your friendship seems incredibly…warm."

"I don't want to catch a chill." Fiona said with a smirk, opening her book. "So I need a warm friendship,"

"You could wear a shawl." Perry retorted.

Fiona had several recipes to test for the new roll, but instead, she made a posset. It was a thick creamy dessert that she didn't particularly like the taste of. She also didn't care for mixing the hot milk with wine or the smell of the required spice blend. The honey was sticky and scooping the flesh from the lemons to prepare them to use as a bowl was also a hassle. She'd spent the better part of an hour finding the perfect oblong lemons. As she stood there outside Lucille's door, she hesitated. Why had she even made these? They were similar to ices, and she hated making ices. Perry made the best ices this side of Monarch's Field, so she let him handle it. He could have made these, but instead, Fiona had wanted to make them, needed to almost since

Lucille mentioned feeling down. Fiona took a deep breath then she knocked gently.

"Come in." Lucille's voice rang out. Fiona took another deep breath and opened the door. Lucille was hunched over her angled desk drawing with charcoal.

"I made you-" Fiona started, trying to figure out what she should say. Was this a present? A gift? A treat? A remedy?

When Lucille stood up and turned around, Fiona lost any sense of her thoughts. At first glance, Lucille was simply dressed in a silky lavender gown with a darker purple cropped knit cardigan over it. But as she moved, Fiona saw an expanse of supple bare skin flash against the lavender fabric.

"Oh, hi there. Did I miss a lesson?" Lucille asked.

"No." Fiona said stupidly. "Did you wear that to play croquet?"

"No, I changed into this after." Lucille said tilting her head to the side. "I got mud on my dress and I wanted to be comfortable but it's too soon to change for dinner. Is there something wrong?"

Fiona hesitated, there was clearly something wrong with the dress but she wasn't quite sure what it was. "No, no you look amazing." Truly she did. Then it registered to Fiona that the pale purple dress had a plunging neckline with an under-bust tie. Fiona imagined that the dress was meant to be worn with a chemisette or over another dress. Instead, there was just the short cardigan that stopped right under her bosom, almost emphasizing the bareness. The ensemble showed more chest skin than cleavage because of the small size of Lucille's breasts, but it distracted Fiona nonetheless.

"I'll be right with you," Lucille said, hurrying around, organizing her supplies, and closing various containers.

Fiona sat the tray down and then stood there, not knowing what to do with her hands. She stared at her feet and then shifted in her wraparound. Once she was settled, Lucille sat down and then slid Fiona a small stool.

"Did you make me ices?" Lucille said, clearly confused.

"Uh, no possets," Fiona said stupidly. *I should have made ices,* Fiona thought, annoyed with herself.

"Lovely." Lucille said, clapping her hands together softly.

"Thank you," Lucille said, taking one off of the tray. She scooped up a spoonful and moaned.

"Oh, this is heaven. Thank you, Thank you."

"Uh? You're most welcome." Fiona said quickly. She watched as Lucille's small tongue darted out and swirled around the dessert spoon, sucking the last bits of cream off of it. "Well, I must be off." Fiona said quickly, backing out of the room.

The sunrise bathed the greenhouse in a wash of pink and orange lights, settling on the bench where Lucille and Fiona sat, their hands intertwined, their baskets carelessly tossed to their feet. Fiona had been trying to convince Lucille to let her throw a ball for the better part of two hours.

"You really don't have to throw a large gathering…" Lucille said for what felt like to Fiona, for the hundredth time. "Won't the people overwhelm you?"

"No." Fiona tried not to get exasperated, but Lucille just kept repeating herself and making excuses. "I don't care to leave my home. I won't be leaving."

Fiona gathered her up in her arms. "Let me celebrate you. Celebrate how far you've come, how far you're going."

"What if everyone compares me to Bree?" Lucille said, her voice barely audible. *Ah, so that is what this is really about,* Fiona realized.

"There is no comparison," Fiona said evenly. Fiona could tell Lucille was scared, as if she thought she was about to get chastised. So instead, Fiona reassured her. "Bree is a wonderful person in her own right, but you're an amazing person. You're beautiful, smart, kind, and funny. Everyone will see that, and you'll charm them as you have done me."

"C'mon." Fiona said, pulling Lucille to her feet. "It will be a triumph. We'll have it in a fortnight."

"So soon?" Lucille asked.

"Yes, yes." Fiona said firmly. "We should make a test cake, let us begin now."

"Now, as in now?" Lucille whined.

"Yes." Fiona said excitedly.

"I don't want cake." Lucille said as they began walking to the manor. "I have had too many sweets as of late."

"We'll send it to the village." Fiona said with a shrug. "Enough excuses."

Lucille

*T*hey stood side by side at the counter, their eyes locked in concentration as they worked on their task. The scent of vanilla and sugar wafted through the air, intermingled with the sound of their steady breathing. "Harp, play us something, please," Fiona said softly. The huge harp in the corner twisted to life; its strings began to vibrate and strum of their own accord.

With a practiced hand, Fiona dipped a spoon into a bowl of melted chocolate, letting the warm liquid glide over her fingertips as she drizzled it over the cake. Lucille watched with a mixture of awe and desire, mesmerized by the fluid movements of Fiona's hands.

As they worked, the two of them moved in unison, their bodies swaying gently to the rhythm of the harp music playing softly in the background. Fiona's movements were hypnotizing to Lucille, each touch and stroke of the spoon captivating her as it swirled around the bowl. Lucille was tasked with applying fruit; it was a simple enough task, a berry here or a slice there. But she took great care with it.

With each new layer of frosting and a sprinkle of decoration, the cake grew more enticing and tantalizing, the scent of the vanilla and sugar growing even thicker as it mingled with the rich, heady aroma of the chocolate.

When it was done, they stood close together, their bodies almost touching as they leaned over the counter, their eyes locked on the cake in front of them. Around the base of the cake, there were alternating layers of freshly sliced strawberries and ripe, juicy peaches nestled against the icing in a delicate pattern that was almost too perfect to disrupt by eating. At the top of the cake, a cascade of ripe blueberries and raspberries tumbled down in a glorious burst of color. Their deep, rich jewel-tone hues were a sight to behold, and the way they contrasted against the bright white of the icing was simply stunning.

Fiona dipped her finger into the extra bowl of frosting, bringing it to her lips with a smile. Lucille watched; a small shudder coursing through her as they imagined the feel of that finger on her own lips.

"Delicious," Fiona said. "We should get this mess cleaned up."

As they worked, their hands brushed against each other, sending more shudders through Lucille, but she tried to maintain her composure as she sorted the piping tips; they were small and had to be carefully washed in batches to avoid losing them.

"If you're not trying the cake later, at least you should try the frosting," Fiona said, bumping her playfully. "For science."

"Alright, for science, but I am tired of sweets." Lucille sighed, reaching forward. The frosting was soft and creamy under her fingers, but before she could bring the finger to her mouth, Fiona leaned forward and met her lips in a soft, sweet kiss. The taste of the frosting mingled on their tongues, and Lucille moaned softly, lost in the pleasure of the moment. After a moment, Fiona pulled away and returned to cleaning.

"Well I should go, I am tired." Lucille said quickly once everything was back in order.

"Get dressed for dinner." Fiona said, "It'll be just us. Your dress is laid out."

The dress, if one could even call it that without insulting the garment, was laid out on her bed. The gown Fiona had chosen was a masterpiece, shimmering and sparkling in the orange light of her room like a field of diamonds. The base of the gown was a rich, dark fabric so bejeweled that Lucille could not tell if it was cut from velvet or another similar material. The dark color accentuated the intricate embroidery of constellations and celestial forms while planets shaped from rhinestones were expertly sewn right above the hem to ensure the skirt laid just right. The threads themselves seemed to dance and sparkle, catching the light from every angle and casting a brilliant glow. Next to the dress was a pair of net gloves also studded with crystals. She slipped them on carefully so as not to snag them. Lucille felt radiant like a lightning bug or a lantern of some kind. She made her way to the dining room, relieved that it was indeed empty except for Fiona.

"Luce." Fiona said, rising to greet her. "You look amazing."

"It is the dress."

"It is you."

"In the dress." Lucille said.

Fiona guided her to a chair. "It is you, in the dress, who looks amazing."

Lucille averted her glance instead surveying the tablescape. Before her sat a large fruit platter of ripe apples, pears, and grapes. To complement the fruit, smaller plates with sharp cheeses and savory crackers were placed around the display for all to partake. Fiona's meat was off to one side so the pink juices that it swam in didn't touch the rest of the meal. The entire table was so full of fruit and floral arrangements she could barely see the main courses. Lucille began to serve herself slices of roasted fowl and potatoes, hoping that Fiona would do the same and would stop with the compliments.

"What is this?" Lucille asked, motioning to flecks in the creamed potatoes.

"Herbs and mushrooms, have you done your hair differently? It frames your hair beautifully." Fiona said, gazing at her intensely.

"No." Lucille said with a chuckle, she poured herself a glass of champagne and chugged it. Fiona tilted her head to the side and stared at her. It was so easy to get lost in the inky depths of Fiona's eyes. Stop it, Lucille said. As they discussed the plans for the balls and Fiona teased her about her parents, Lucille had several more glasses of the delicious champagne.

"Is it time for dessert?" Lucille said, giggling uncontrollably.

"You said you were done with sweets for a bit." Fiona said playfully.

"I lied; I simply did not want to make cake." Lucille hiccupped. "I am a lying liar. But no matter. I'll have fruit." She pointed at the closest platter dramatically.

Lucille picked up the closest ripe mango, it had already been scored and splayed easily in chunks when she spread it open. Fiona's lips curled into a subtle smile for an instant before it was replaced with a neutral line. With a slow and deliberate movement, Lucille brought the fruit to her lips and took a small bite, letting out a soft moan as the juicy flesh melted in her mouth. She closed her eyes, enjoying the sweetness and the tartness of the fruit as it danced on her tongue.

With as much seductive grace as she could manage, she took another bite, this time more daringly, letting the juice trickle down the corner of her mouth, and her tongue darted out to catch the droplets. Her teeth grazed the flesh, and she sucked gently, drawing out more juice and savoring the flavor.

Lucille leaned in towards her Fiona, the scent of mango lingering on her breath, and whispered, "Want to taste?" with a mischievous smile.

"You've had one too many glasses of champagne to make that an enticing offer," Fiona said firmly.

"More for me then," Lucille said with a shrug.

With a sensuous tilt of her head, Lucille reached for another fruit: a ripe pomegranate. She held it in her hands, feeling its weight and texture, the heft of it, before reaching for a knife.

"Bah!" Fiona said, stopping her. "I won't have you losing any fingertips." Lucille watched as Fiona cracked it open with her bare hands. The skin gave way easily, revealing the deep red arils inside. Lucille plucked one out, placing it delicately on her tongue, and marvelled the burst of flavor that followed.

As she ate, Lucille let out another soft, contented sigh, relishing the sweetness and tang of each juicy seed. She ate the pomegranate slowly, savoring each bite, and her fingers became stained with the deep red juice. She licked the juice from her fingertips, her tongue moving sensuously over each digit.

Fiona groaned. "Bed, now." She motioned to Marty, who took a hesitant step forward.

"I'm not done," Lucille said, pouting. "Besides, you haven't had one piece. Have one piece and send me to bed if you must."

"I must." Fiona said, shaking her head.

"Obviously. You are the Lady of class and virtue. I love it. It's deliriously good. Now, let me feed you." Lucille said, motioning to her plate, which had the last lonely wedge of a clementine.

Lucille held the remaining clementine segment delicately between her fingers, a playful smile on her lips as she brought it to Fiona's lips. Fiona opened her mouth, and Lucille placed the fruit gently on her tongue, watching as her plump lips closed around it.

Lucille felt a rush of desire wash over her. She couldn't help but imagine what it would be like to taste the citrus on her lips.

As Fiona chewed, Lucille reached up to brush a stray coil of hair away from Fiona's forehead; then she slowly moved down her nose until. Finally, her fingers lingered on her cheek. Fiona met her gaze, Fiona's eyes were two dark swirling galaxies, intense and all-consuming, and she knew that they were both thinking the same thoughts.

"Marty, you may take Miss Waters to her room now, be sure to leave her a pitcher of water. I imagine she'll be quite unwell in the morning." Fiona said, waving him over.

Lucille groaned as she struggled to open her eyes, Fiona was right. Her head was throbbing, thankfully the weather was so gray, not much sunlight coming through the crack in the heavy curtains. She pulled on a new gown which was made of sumptuous muslin with delicate embroidery designs of cakes dancing across it. The empire waist and square neckline accentuated her modest decolletage just so. Lucille nervously smoothed the voluminous billowing folds of the skirt that skimmed and draped beautifully over her wide hips and thick legs. The nearly sheer puffed sleeves that were also adorned with lace reminded her of spun sugar. The dress was lovely but also soft and comfortable.

Soon, the scent of beignets wafted up the stairs to Lucille, and she could almost taste the flaky layers of buttery pastry, smell the savory chocolate, and feel the dusty powdered sugar on her fingertips. It was a warm, beckoning aroma, and Lucille followed it to Fiona's parlor.

Fiona was sitting there at her desk, preening like a dragon guarding its hoard, and in front of her sat a small tower of desserts and beside them a smaller tower of rolls, their golden-brown exterior glistening with a glossy sheen of icing.

"Ah, have you come to see me or come for a taste?" Fiona said laughing.

"Are those mutually exclusive?" Lucille said playfully.

"That depends on if your wits are about you or if you're still fuzzy with bubbles." Fiona said, cocking a brow.

"I have as many wits and faculties as I typically do." Lucille said quickly.

"Then I am no match for you then." Fiona said. "I've sent your parents into town for ball supplies."

"They won't return with your coin or decor."

"I know but I imagine you need the rest. Besides, the weather is so awful. Perhaps they'll catch cold." Fiona said, giving a wide smile that exposed all of her teeth.

"One can only hope." Lucille said.

Before Lucille could help herself, she had leaned forward and met Fiona's lips with a soft kiss.

"I thought I was to be treating you, and here you are treating me." Fiona said, then she didn't say anymore, but Lucille could tell she was surprised.

"Let's tuck into these before they cool," Lucille said quickly.

Fiona

he days preparing for the ball went quickly, exhaustingly so and yet the night before what was quite possibly the biggest social event of her life, Fiona sat in her parlor, staring pensively into the crackling fire. She left a wonderfully written book closed on the side table. The events of the evening had left her feeling drained, and she longed for a respite from the endless chatter of Alma and the demands of The Pebble and The Fig that weighed upon her. She was about to retire for the night, but just then, Lucille entered the room, a tray of tea and biscuits in hand.

"Knock, Knock," Lucille said, she wore a dress the color of whiskey and Fiona drank it in greedily with her eyes.

Fiona smiled warmly at her, grateful for the company. She reached for her book. "I was just about to start reading. I'm a bit tired."

"May I join you?" Lucille asked although she was already setting the tray down on a nearby table.

Fiona nodded, and Lucille settled in next to her on the sofa, their bodies close but not quite touching. They sipped their tea in comfortable silence, the warmth of the fire and the company of Lucille a balm to Fiona's weary bones. Soon Fiona's book rested forgotten in her lap. She gazed out the window, even though it was too dark to see, lost in thought.

As if sensing her mood, Lucille moved closer, the softness of her skirts brushing against Fiona's leg. "What a dreadful night," Lucille remarked, her voice low and soothing. "It's no wonder you're feeling sore."

Fiona simply smiled and leaned her head against Lucille's shoulder, feeling the heat of her body as they settled into a comfortable embrace. The sound of the rain outside and the bookshelf-lined walls faded away as they sat together, respectively, lost in the wild landscape of their own minds.

She closed her eyes, content to simply be in the moment with Lucille, feeling the gentle rise and fall of her chest as she breathed.

Fiona wasn't sure when the last time Sugar Lump Manor was the site of a ball but she was convinced this one, in Lucille's honor, was the very best. The perimeter of the ballroom had been lined with long banquet tables; one table was full of nothing but punch, another with ices molded into the most detailed shapes they could manage, a large one resembling almost to each stone, the royal castle. Another had been shaped into a delicate square of lace. Yet another table held the game meats, which were of the nicest cuts the butcher could manage. The chefs had them swimming in butter sauce. For the cost, Fiona thought they should be doing water acrobatics, but she was more than willing to spend the funds to ensure the event was talked about and brought Lucille joy. The dessert tables were also well arranged, with each dish set atop a mirror. She'd worked tirelessly to sculpt a menagerie of animals and realistic plants and bushes. The piece de resistance was the sugar paste temple she and Lucille had sculpted together. Lucille had done the structure, and Fiona had followed behind her with the delicate scrollwork and details. On the back, she had etched their initials. She made a mental note to show Lucille later. In the corner of the room was a raised platform, where a string quartet strummed dance tunes accompanied by the pianoforte. Couples swirled around the dance floor, their movements graceful and precise as they executed the latest dance steps.

The air was filled with the sweet aroma of flowers, which were arranged in large bouquets throughout the room. The scents of lavender and rosemary also perfumed the space. Neither plant matched the pink and yellow color scheme, but Lucille had insisted upon them for their healing properties and to promote proper circulation.

Lucille touched her arm gently, causing Fiona to stop her inspection. "Mm, my little bowl?" Fiona asked.

"Mother asked if the fruit was real or cake," Lucille said sweetly.

"Oh, it's real. We imported it." Fiona said.

"Excuse me?" Alma said, clutching her red coral necklace. Fiona morbidly noted that it looked as if her throat was seeping blood.

"We had it imported," Fiona said again. "Only the best for my future wife," Fiona said, smiling at Lucille. Fiona tugged at the heavy necklace around her neck; it was crafted from a stunning array of jewels, including diamonds, rubies, emeralds, and sapphires, burrowed into links of the thick gold chain that glimmered and sparkled in the light. The center of the chain was dominated by a massive, pear-shaped diamond, easily the size of a small bird egg. Each gem was perfectly cut and polished to catch and reflect the light. It was so heavy it pulled at her neck, causing her to stand a little straighter and hold her head a little higher in order to bare the weight.

"While we are on the subject, how will you all be styled?" Alma asked. She was dressed in the most heavily embroidered gown Fiona had ever seen. Fiona admired that Alma had made an effort to match her dress to the bright pink and yellow of the House of Fondant.

"Impeccably well," Fiona said with another smile. To her surprise, Alma actually smiled.

"I believe the convention is that we'd be the Ladies Fondant," Fiona said. "Or perhaps, for clarity's sake, we would legally be known as Lady F. Fondant and Lady L. Fondant?"

"I see," Alma said with a nod.

"Thoughts?" Fiona said, turning to Lucille.

"I have such a rare few of those. I hate to waste them on frivolities," Lucille said. She was leaning over, examining a pyramid of shrimp that was piled high in a trough made of a carved-out pineapple.

"Noted," Fiona said, trying to contain her laughter.

"Shall we dance?" Lucille asked, opening her fan dramatically.

As Fiona twirled Lucille around the dance floor, she took a few moments to breathe in the gorgeous chaos that was in the ballroom. She couldn't remember the last time they had used this room, but Perry and Marty had shined the floors, chandeliers, and windows until every surface gleamed.

"Is this too much?" Lucille asked in a hushed whisper.

"No," Fiona whispered back firmly. She had dressed Lucille in a net dress, embroidered with hand-beaded moth appliques. The gold and pastel pink glowed on her brown skin, and she created a cascade of reflecting bouncing lights whenever she moved the slightest. There had not been enough amber stones to light the entire ballroom, so they had been supplemented with beeswax candles which both cast the room in a soft yellow glow but also smelled sweet and fresh. Fiona surveyed the ballroom once more; some guests nibbled on chocolate truffles while others sipped on candy cane cocktails. She noted with amusement a couple sneaking a kiss under the rainbow arch of fruit candies.

Perry tapped Fiona on the shoulder.

"Yes?" Fiona asked, annoyed at the interruption.

"Mrs. Waters is trapped in the hall of mirrors. Should I send a gingerbread man to retrieve her? I wasn't sure if you would want the illusion ruined for the other guests."

"No," Lucille said quickly. Then she clasped a gloved hand to her mouth. "I'm sorry, forgive me for interrupting."

"Please," Fiona nodded to Perry. "He'll do as you ask."

"Could you let her stay a bit longer?" Lucille said guiltily. "I believe being trapped with her own reflection might do her a bit of good."

"Of course!" Perry said with a smile then he was gone.

"Let us dance," Fiona said, pulling Lucille back towards her.

"Am I wicked?" Lucille whispered against her ear.

"Yes, terribly wicked. I love y-" Fiona sucked in a breath. "I love it."

If Lucille had heard her, she did not say anything and allowed Fiona to move her around the dancefloor.

"You replaced the locket on your chain," Lucille said when there was a lull in the music.

"I did," Fiona said. She pressed a gentle kiss to Lucille's ear. "I have to make my rounds but then I have a surprise." Fiona gave her a final squeeze before stepping back.

Lucille reached out and caught her arm grabbing it firmly. "No please don't go, it is terribly loud and, and, I-" Lucille's voice began to falter.

Fiona realized immediately that Lucille was in distress. "Come Miss Waters, let us take a turn around the garden." Fiona said, guiding her through the open doors.

The moonlight settled calmly over them, casting a cool glow over the sprawling garden with its winding paths and ornate fountains. Among the blooms and sweet greenery, the two women strolled hand-in-hand, their eyes locked in an intimate gaze. Lucille's eyes were wide and her breath ragged but she was doing a good job of keeping her shoulders back and her steps even. For a while they walked in silence but after a few minutes, Lucille began to chatter excitedly as if nothing was wrong. The words just seemed to spill out of her.

As they walked, Lucille spoke of her travels around her city and hijinks with Kenna, regaling Fiona with tales of her teachers and her friends. Then moved on to discussing how she had been slowly winning Perry over, and when this topic was broached, her speech returned to its normal even cadence. She told the story of her accomplishment with such humor and theatrics that Fiona was enthralled but it was the ease with which she was speaking that really pleased Fiona. Lucille had clearly been overwhelmed by the ball, and it seemed that this was just the respite she needed.

"Fiona," Lucille whispered, as they paused by a bubbling fountain that was carved in the shape of a cake roll. "Thank you for taking air with me."

Fiona's breath caught in her throat, and she turned to face Lucille fully. "Always, I'll always be here to…take air with you if you need it," she replied, placing a hand on Lucille's cheek. And they wrapped their arms around each other; they were totally lost in the embrace, far away from the distant string music and muffled murmurs of the party guests. For a few blissful moments, the world went silent, and they forgot about the constraints of the evening and the expectations placed upon them. But the world had a way of intruding, and Fiona heard a snapping twig nearby, and they reluctantly pulled away from each other. "We must be careful," Lucille said, her eyes scanning the gardens for any sign of prying eyes.

Fiona nodded, hoping the short break would be enough for Lucille to manage for the rest of the long evening ahead of them. It had to be. There wasn't much choice. Fiona's concerns drifted towards musings of the future, past this evening, to when Lucille's parents left. The uncertainty made her uneasy. But for now, they had each other, and that was enough. As they walked back towards the manor, their hands remained intertwined; Fiona forced a smile on her face. She didn't want Lucille to worry or the guests to gossip.

Lucille

"Miss Waters, your necklace. Stunning." A voice called out to Lucille; she had barely had time to register the lightest brush of gloved fingertips on her arm before the woman was flitting away, skirts swooshing.

Lucille resisted the urge to stroke the elaborate piece for reassurance. The necklace Fiona had chosen for Lucille from the Fondant family vault was so heavy it was burrowing into her skin; there would definitely be a floral imprint or bruise tomorrow. Marty had demonstrated that the heirloom could be configured into a tiara with hidden metal screws locking into place, but when it was on her head, it had seemed incredibly heavy. Instead she had chosen to wear the moth tiara because it was lighter. Now as her chest stung, she wondered if she had made the wrong decision.

Calm down, she told herself sternly; she wasn't sure what she should be doing as a hostess. It seemed peculiar to simply follow Fiona around the whole night, but she didn't know anyone else, sure an introduction had been made, but she could hardly remember what had been said. Lucille took a timid step forward and then stopped. At one end of the ballroom, her parents were animatedly discussing something with a tall woman in a dress covered in peacock feathers. She had already taken a break from the festivities and another break would get the gossips started. Perhaps they were already starting. Lucille tried not to take too much notice of the young people her age, their tongues wagging as freely as the champagne flowed. Instead, she tried to focus on the fact that the ballroom was alive with the sound of music and laughter and that most guests were too caught up in their own world of intrigue to notice her or her shortcomings. Lucille tried once more to calm herself down but she was acutely aware of the noise and the thick floral smell, the figures flickering just out of view in the periphery of her vision. She had chosen a corset that gave her chest a lift and then she had shamelessly added a bosom pad. Between the undergarment and the little pillow, her cleavage was heaving but she was also tight and pinched, moving unnaturally stiffly. Lucille turned to search for Fiona and the combs of the tiara dug into her scalp. She thought back to earlier in the evening when Fiona had presented it to her, it had looked incredibly delicate. At its center was a radiant moth made of pink sapphires and yellow diamonds. The jeweler had placed the stones in such a way that the pink and yellow hues almost blended, creating a gradient effect. Lucille had watched with bated breath as Fiona removed it from the red velvet box and held it up to the light. Even the band, which was made of polished gold and dotted with colorful crystals, sparkled in the light. Despite the fact that she was uncomfortable, she was still honored to be wearing it.

Finally, her eyes locked onto Fiona who was standing a few feet away from her parents. Fiona, for her part, was having an equally animated conversation with a small cluster of partygoers. Fiona glanced her way, then back at the guests, then a curious thing happened; Fiona did a double take, locked eyes with Lucille, Fiona winked, and bit her bottom lip seductively. It was so fast; it didn't seem as though any of the guests had noticed. Lucille half expected her heart to burst forth from her chest, soaring up to the glass ceiling like a shooting star. Instinctively she looked up at the night sky; the only thing separating them from the outside was a few crystal-clear panes and some wrought iron, certainly not enough to contain a runaway heart. She vividly imagined the ceiling cracking and it raining hail-like bits of glass down on the guests. She waited for a moment, neck craned up as if her rogue organ had, in fact, escaped, sent shards of her necklace throughout the ballroom, and was now barreling towards the starry sky. Would the pieces ricochet off the walls or get tangled in the floral arrangements, dusting the food like sprinkles? Blood rushed to her ears, and over the whooshing, she could make out screams tangled with the upbeat melody of the dance the string quartet was playing.

"Luce?" Fiona said, appearing suddenly in front of her.

Lucille looked down; Fiona's face was contorted into a looked of concern.

"Yes?" Lucille said, trying to act nonchalant.

"Are you alright? You seem so far away."

"Just daydreaming, I suppose." Lucille said.

"Is that so?" Fiona asked skeptically.

"Mhmm."

"What are you thinking of?" Fiona asked.

"The ballroom," Lucille said quickly.

"Why does it sound as though you're lying to me?" Fiona said, whispering conspiratorially. "You're not going to force me to tickle the truth out of you, are you?"

"Lady Fondant! That would be absurd. There are guests." Lucille said. *Was she serious? Surely not.*

"Scandal by tickling, it would be a society first, and I am a trailblazer." Fiona's dark eyes twinkled with a familiar mischievous glint.

"Fine," Lucille said with a sigh, dropping her voice to an even lower whisper. "I was picturing my heart shot out of my chest and shattered the ceiling, littering the ball in shards of glass and gemstones."

She expected Fiona to be horrified as her friends often were by her anxious fantasies, but instead, Fiona said very evenly. "Was there a crater?"

"In my chest?" Lucille asked in return.

"The floor," Fiona responded.

"The floor?"

Fiona shrugged. "Shooting hearts have to land somewhere."

"You seem quite unbothered," Lucille said as Fiona guided her through the crowd and towards the refreshments.

"We can always repair the floor," Fiona said with a smirk. "On a serious measure, if you need to step outside or take air, no one is judging."

"Everyone is judging." Lucille snorted.

"Well, yes," Fiona said. "But we don't care." Fiona made a subtle nod to their left, where a young man was dramatically brushing his fan across his face. "Everyone is concerned with their own interests."

"You are right, darling," Lucille said with a sigh. She eyed the cold meats, debating if she could manage a plate with trembling hands.

"I'll hold your plate, and you eat whatever you like," Fiona said.

Before Lucille could respond, Fiona piled the small plate with cold meat, crackers, and trifles as if reading her mind.

Fiona

After Lucille was done eating, Fiona pulled Lucille to the far side of the dining room. "It's time."

"For what?" Lucille said, looking around bewildered. Fiona watched as the amber lights and flickering flames twinkled against the shining beads of Lucille's dress.

"The ball is in your honor; we're about to honor you," Fiona said, pulling Lucille towards her. A gingerbread man handed Fiona a flute full of champagne.

"Here, you take this," Fiona said, pressing the glass into Lucille's hand. She noticed Lucille's hands were trembling.

"It's alright." Fiona said, "I need both hands."

Lucille nodded weakly and took the glass from her.

The upbeat tone of the song was roaring towards a crescendo. Fiona glanced over to Lucille, who looked so tense the gentlest of breezes would have knocked her over like a precariously balanced domino. The music reached a fever pitch. Fiona raised her hand and focused on the curtain that covered the opposite wall of the dining room. The tapestry was embroidered with a huge design of the Fondant family crest. The pianoforte struck the final high note. With a flourish of her hand, Fiona had willed the curtain to tug itself. The curtain fell and revealed a mosaic portrait of Lucille, in the style of the old masters, sitting delicately in the garden, a pencil poised in hand.

Fiona glanced over to see Lucille's reaction. Her mouth was open slightly, and when the crowd began to applaud thunderously, the glass slipped from Lucille's hands. Fiona held up her hand, splaying her hands wide, and the glass froze in place.

"I'm sorry." Lucille mouthed, grasping the glass. Fiona released it.

"Do you like it?" Fiona asked nervously.

"Yes, is it a confection?" Lucille asked.

"Yes, hard candy tiles," Fiona said, pointing to the portrait. "Up close, it looks as if it is a random variety of flecks, but far away, you see the painting. It is an enigma of sorts like yourself."

"I-" Lucille began, but she was interrupted by a neighbor introducing herself, and then a man turned to Fiona and said, "Ah, I see you are well, Lady Fondant."

"Lovely to see you again," Fiona said sweetly.

"Lady Fondant?" A voice called out to her; she turned to see the local clergyman holding a sugar paste swan.

"Is this your work? Perhaps you could make them in religious motifs for our next fundraising soiree." he said.

"Of course; what did you have in mind," Fiona asked; she shot a glance towards Lucille, but she had been swallowed by the crush of eager partygoers complimenting the art.

It seemed as if an eternity had passed when the Ton began to trickle outside to their carriages or up the stairs to their rooms. Fiona had asked Alma and Simon to bid goodnight to the departing guests and Perry stood at the landing of the stairs directing the overnight guests to where they would be sleeping. This freed her up to focus on her final duty of the night: speaking with Lucille privately.

"That was rough. Are you alright?" Fiona whispered into the dimly lit room. She waited so long that she felt as though she was only talking to the drawn bed curtains and shadows. She hadn't wanted to risk knocking but now she regretted it.

Then there was a rustle.

"Yes. I don't want you losing sleep over me." Lucille said, her voice mischievous.

"Are you decent? Did you fall asleep in your dress again?" Fiona asked.

"Perhaps, but it is no concern of yours other than lecturing; what is it you need?" Lucille said, giggling. "I would have cut myself on all the pearls and glass beads if I'd fallen asleep in it."

"You're lying," Fiona said.

"I am not…I took off the overdress." Lucille said, laughing.

"I knew it. Why did you leave?" Fiona asked, taking a timid step forward, careful to avoid the spot where the floor creaked. A few of the party guests were staying the night on this floor although she had done her best to avoid it, and she did not want to cause more scandal.

"I was so tired; that was so much," Lucille said. "I appreciate you, though. It was lovely." She added quickly. "What do you need?"

"I needed you," Fiona answered honestly.

"What?" Lucille asked as Fiona heard the mattress creak slightly.

"To kiss you, to touch your hair, to hold you, to breathe your air, to look at your face, I'll take whatever it is you'll give me," Fiona said.

The curtains parted slightly.

"Come to bed just for a bit," Lucille said in a hoarse whisper.

Fiona let her cane fall to the ground and scrambled up into the bed.

Fiona lay at the far edge of the bed.

"Your fingers, how do they feel?" Lucille asked.

"Uh, good, hardly swollen. It was a good night; thankfully, I'm hardly sore from the dancing."

"Could you unlace my stays?"

"Certainly, I could undo stays and whisk eggs; I have almost full mobility," Fiona said playfully.

"No, I'm asking you to. Now."

"Oh, of course."

Fiona yielded to the urge she had felt since Lucille had forced her way into her door and then eventually into her heart. As they kissed Lucille was uncharacteristically quiet, the only sounds coming from her were soft sensual moans, and for once, she didn't guard her body's reaction to Fiona.

"Will you come to me wholly?" Fiona whispered, stilling herself while she still had a few scraps of her self-control in her grasp.

"Yes," Lucille responded eagerly, and then yes again, and once more again. For a moment the only sounds in the room were the sporadic crack and pop of the sputtering fire and the rustling of their bodies pressing against the constraints of the fabric of their night clothes. The hem of Lucille's nightdress grazed Fiona's shoulder ever so slightly as it had been tossed carelessly in the air and Fiona let out a guttural moan, the sensation was too much, breaking the quiet of the room. Fiona felt as if she had walked into a spider web, imagining phantom touches as her skin was oversensitive, prickling at every breath of air. She sucked in a deep breath as Lucille's hands roamed over her body, tracing the curves and contours of her flesh.

Fiona pulled away from Lucille, who mewled in response, grasping at her biceps.

"Space," Fiona said breathlessly. "I need space to work." She kissed her forehead then Fiona snaked her hand in between them, caressing Lucille gently at first, gauging her response before increasing the pressure.

Lucille tightly grasped her face. "Is this alright?" Lucille said, her voice shaky.

"Yes, focus Luce," Fiona said, kissing her softly.

"On you?" Lucille whispered into her ear, her softness, her lusciousness, her gentle sloping curves pressing against Fiona, clinging to her. She trembled under Fiona's exploring fingertips.

"No, on what you're feeling," Fiona said. "You must relax and lose yourself." Fiona watched as Lucille closed her eyes and her head fell back against the pillow. Fiona continued to touch her, to explore every inch of her body until she was writhing with pleasure and then she returned to Lucille's center, working gently until Lucille tensed and cried out. "Breathe through it." Fiona told her before she was lost in her own moment. Afterwards, Fiona laid back, very still not sure what to do or say until Lucille laid her head on Fiona's chest. "And you?" Lucille said groggily. "I am most content. Sleep." Fiona fiddled with the coils that had sprung free of Lucille's silk scarf and were framing her face. Fiona relished in the feel of the soft kinky curls against her skin. Then she straightened the fabric and tied it back into place. "Thank you." Lucille said softly before sleep consumed them both almost instantly.

Fiona woke sometime later, knowing it was nowhere near daylight. The room was chilly which didn't bother her but Lucille was shivering in a fitful sleep. The now mangled sheets were cold and damp with cooling sweat. Fiona peeled herself up, relit the fire and then pulled Lucille off of the bed, depositing her into the armchair before stripping off the sheet, replacing it with a fresh blanket. Once they were back in bed, despite her grumbling protests Lucille promptly went back to sleep.

Lucille

*W*hen Lucille opened her eyes, she was wrapped in a warm quilt enveloped by the smell of toasted almond and soft vanilla tinged with a musk that Lucille pretended was sweat. She took a few moments to gather herself, a memory of last night flashed into her mind, a fresh flash of heat blooming as she remembered the excitement of the previous night. She would have been able to convince herself it was a psychedelic hazy fever dream but she knew her imaginations were not that brilliant. Last night she had become a kaleidoscope, it was as if she had entered her bed chamber an ordinary piece of glass and Fiona had fragmented her into a million fractals until she was transformed into a new person, a new pattern: something spiraling, dazzling and whirling. Fiona kissed her as if she were a paradigm shift.

"You're awake," Fiona said, kissing her forehead.

"Have you been waiting for long?" Lucille asked groggily.

"Well worth it; I need to meet with the tailor's assistant," Fiona said. "I'm already late."

"Oh, I'm so sorry," Lucille said, sitting up, thankful that she was wearing her night dress. She had a vague, dimly lit memory of Fiona covering her with it at some point in the night.

Fiona pushed her back gently onto the pillows. "It's alright, take your time, I wanted to be here when you woke up." Fiona climbed out of the bed and then turned back and leaned over. "May I kiss you?

"Yes," Lucille said, and as soon as the word had left her lips, Fiona's mouth was against hers.

"The meeting will be very dull but come to my rooms with your sketching materials and keep me company, yes?" Fiona said.

"Yes. Yes." Lucille said quickly.

"Let us get you in the bath." Fiona said, stroking her face.

"You're late for your meeting." Lucille said, getting out of bed.

"Never too late to run you a warm bath and ensure that you're not sore." Fiona said, kissing her shoulder.

"How do I look?" Fiona asked Marty. Fiona stood on a small pedestal being fitted for a new shirtwaist.

"You are the very image of a nonpareil," Marty said, clapping his hands enthusiastically.

Lucille stopped her drawing for a moment and wondered once more about how Fiona was referred to; ladies were referred to as incomparables, perhaps nonpareil was not improper, but it was a bit odd.

"Lady Fondant?" Lucille asked once Marty had left.

"Yes?" Fiona was still examining the suiting material. "Aren't we a bit beyond titles?"

"Well, yes, I believe we are," Lucille said sheepishly.

"No worries, my little fork. What was your question?"

"Would you prefer to be pretty or handsome?" Lucille asked.

"Handsome," Fiona said, tilting her head to the side.

Lucille searched Fiona's dark eyes. "I must say I am a bit confused," Lucille said.

"About?"

"You are a woman who acts like a man but is not. It's curious." Lucille asked.

"What brought this to mind?" Fiona said, examining a bit of cloth that had buttons sewn onto it.

"Oh, I don't know. After last night I feel as though I know you completely and not at all."

Fiona put down the button sample. "Do you feel remorseful?

"Not at all," Lucille said. That was not the impression she had meant to give her. *Perhaps she should have written her a thank you note. Or is that odd?* "You did not answer my question," Lucille said frustratedly.

"You didn't ask me a question. You called me curious, and I am no more curious than anything else in this world, Luce. You really must expand your mind. Not everything can be simple." Fiona said.

"I know that…" Lucille said with a sigh.

"May I kiss you?" Fiona asked, gently cupping her chin and tilting her face up.

"Of course," Lucille said.

Fiona pressed a quick peck to her lip. "Mhm. Sweet."

"Why did you ask again?" Lucille questioned.

Fiona had already returned to sorting swatches and buttons. "Hmm? What was that?"

"Why do you always ask to kiss me?" Lucille clarified.

"Do I? I don't want to spook you; you startle like a deer mid-hunting season," Fiona said. She clapped loudly as if you underscored her point, and Lucille automatically flinched. Fiona laughed. "However, I don't always ask." Fiona picked up the sample she had been examining and held it up to the window. "Perhaps this is the one? I'll ask Perry. He'll be honest. Oh, and don't forget we're meeting Marty in a quarter of an hour for mushroom hunting. You should change." Fiona said as she left.

Lucille sat there staring after Fiona. She should be grateful that Fiona gave her any consideration, but she worried she was too delicate or irksome. *Did Fiona think she was immature? Well, I am in a number of ways. Should we discuss it last night in detail? Fiona did not seem as though she thought poorly of me.* Quite the opposite.

The redingote Fiona had ordered for her was a heavy fuchsia wool with light pink silk trim. After some consideration, Lucille paired it with a pastel yellow dress with a large, embroidered moth on the front of the skirt. She examined herself in the looking glass. It was nearly a perfect image, but she noticed the dress and coat both dragged on the carpet. This would not do; there were muddy patches all over. Then she realized they were meant to be worn with riding boots. Once she was all laced up in the brand-new boots, she stood in front of the looking glass again. The open coat beautifully framed the moth appliqué, and the sides of the coat almost mimicked the insect's wings. She straightened her bonnet and made her way to the foyer. Fiona stood there waiting in a pelisse, looking very dashing; Lucille noticed Fiona's coat was the same fuchsia color and the buttons were gold moths.

"Are we a set?" Lucille asked playfully.

"Typically, all members of the household wear the Fondant family colors for outerwear. It was a force of habit to order it for you in Fondant Fuchsia but the dress pairing…. Did Marty dress you?"

"Oh, no. I thought they went well together. I can change." Lucille said, suddenly feeling uncomfortable.

"Don't be silly, we're just going for a ramble. Besides, I always like the way you look in my family colors." Fiona said. Her tone was unreadable.

"Say it," Lucille said, pulling on her gloves and walking towards the door.

"What?" Fiona said, trailing behind her, but Lucille kept walking until she was outside and down the path to the right of the porch.

Lucille spun around and pointed her finger at Fiona dramatically. "Normally, you follow a compliment with something vulgar. I expected you to say I like the way you look in my family colors or your night clothes."

Fiona made a choking noise. "You're overestimating my chivalry. To be completely truthful, I was thinking I would like you in my family's moth tiara again."

"What is unchivalrous about that?" Lucille said, turning back around.

"What if I was imagining you wearing just the tiara?" Fiona said playfully. Lucille slowed down to allow Fiona to catch up. And once they had set down the path, Lucille responded.

"Would I get to keep it?" Lucille said, keeping her tone even.

"Keep what?" Fiona asked.

"The tiara," Lucille said, glancing at Fiona, whose jaw was slack. "I returned it but perhaps if I had worn only that, I would have been allowed to keep it." Lucille said coyly as she looked at Fiona.

"Lucille!" Fiona said, clearly surprised.

"That is exactly how you said it last night. As well, perhaps a tad bit more breathless." Lucille said.

Before Fiona could reply, they came up on Marty, who stood there with baskets. "Hello, Ladies Fondant, I have already scouted out the best mushroom gathering spots. Let us proceed."

Lucille smirked; she knew Marty well enough to know he was teasing them both. So instead of replying, she took her basket, and they set off down the path.

.

Fiona

$\mathcal{F}$iona wondered if Marty had been able to wake Lucille. She felt bad waking her up at this late hour, but after mushroom hunting she had spent the better part of the day entertaining her parents, and Fiona felt as if she'd hardly seen her. If she was too tired, she thought Lucille would feel more comfortable rejecting Marty. Even if she had, she thought he would have been down with the message by now. Just when Fiona was ready to give up and go upstairs, Lucille appeared in the doorway of the study. Her hair was tied up in a pale green silk scarf, and she wore a quilted wrapper that was closed with several bows down the front. Her feet were bare, save for a gold chain that encircled her ankle.

"Luce!" Fiona said, sitting up and gripping her cane.

Lucille slumped down beside her on the chaise.

"Can you make them disappear?" Lucille said hopefully.

"No, I wish." Fiona said, frowning, Lucille's parents were more irritating than the scaly patches that hid just out of sight beneath the confines of her shirt.

Fiona tried to figure out what she should say and so she closed her eyes and leaned her head back, trying to sort out her racing thoughts.

"Can I move this?" Lucille asked.

"Hmm?" Fiona opened her eyes; Lucille had sat up and was peering down at her.

"Your cane." Lucille said softly.

Fiona had already forgotten it was laid across her lap. She flicked her wrist, and it levitated for a moment, then floated forward until it was leaning against the wall.

Lucille straddled her and sank into her lap, not bothering to smooth the bunched and twisted skirt of her wrapper. Fiona noticed the part of her leg that was exposed was unobstructed by a stocking.

"You seem very far away," Lucille murmured against her neck.

"That is what I say to you," Fiona said. "Use your own words."

Lucille laughed. "I have no words, no thoughts, you've completely shattered me."

Fiona sat up, anxiously. "Do you mean-"

"No, no." Lucille said, kissing her softly. "It's silly, I was thinking earlier you've made me feel like a kaleidoscope. I know it sounds silly, it's not important. Forget it."

"I would very much like to-" Fiona said trying to focus but Lucille was squirming against her.

"Tell me, what are you thinking of?" Lucille asked, capturing her chin so Fiona had to look her squarely in the eye.

"I just want everything to go smoothly with this performance, we want to put on a good show." Fiona explained. She hesitated, then laid her hand gently on Lucille's inner thigh.

"Ah yes, the big make-believe," Lucille said, kissing her forehead. Then she moved down and kissed Fiona's open lips. "You taste like a coin," Lucille said, giggling. Fiona cursed herself for eating a blood bar earlier.

Before she could speak, she felt Lucille's soft lips on her neck and slender fingers working at the buttons of her shirt. The cool air hitting her shoulder made her skin prickle as Lucille pushed her shirt down. Lucille's tongue exploring the dip of her collarbone was a sensation of ecstasy so overpowering it drowned out any common sense for a moment.

"Lucille, please." *This is excruciating.* Fiona couldn't tell if she was imagining it, but she felt Lucille shifting forward. Fiona grabbed her thigh to still her.

"Ohhhh." Lucille moaned.

That had not had the intended effect. "Perhaps we should discuss," Fiona started again.

Lucille put a finger to Fiona's lips.

"Just pretend for a little longer." Lucille's voice was soft, breathless, and needy.

Fiona's head swam with her confusing thoughts. She wanted to be with Lucille more than anything, but she didn't know how to say it or if it was selfish. It was too late now, closing the barn door once the horses had escaped, as they said.

"I'm not pretending." was all Fiona could manage to get out. "You're so beautiful—" *Damn it. That was the wrong thing to say.* She should tell her how she made her feel. But this seemed to be enough for Lucille. Lucille nodded then opened her mouth as if she were about to protest.

Fiona kissed her hungrily, claiming her mouth and exploring her with her tongue.

"Don't you trust me?" Fiona asked when she broke for air.

"Yes?" Lucille said, her features awash with confusion.

"I care for you dearly," Fiona said, trying again. "So you know this isn't a game? I want to provide for you and to take care of you."

"Mhmmm." Lucille was peppering her chest with kisses, and her hands were splayed across her ribs. "I want you to take care of me now," Lucille said finally.

Fiona groaned. There was no mistaking it this time. Lucille bucked her hips forward.

"And now, I am certain you know exactly how—" Lucille said playfully.

"The door is open," Fiona said weakly. "And your parents hardly seem to sleep."

"Close it," Lucille said, taking Fiona's hand and wiggling it.

"Stop," Fiona said softly.

Lucille immediately pulled away and dropped her hands to her side.

Fiona made a pushing motion with her hand. "I needed to focus." The door slammed closed louder than she intended so much for focusing.

"That was all," Fiona said, pulling Lucille's hands back to her body.

Fiona toyed with the first tie of Lucille's robe. "So many ties."

"Just three." Lucille said.

Fiona undid the first tie, revealing Lucille's bare chest. "Oh? Where's your night dress?"

"I must have forgotten it," Lucille said mischievously. "Would you like me to go put it on?"

"Goodness no," Fiona said, tugging at the second tie.

"Today, we're making mince pies." Fiona motioned to the assortment of ingredients. She was excited to get back to their lessons; they provided a sense of normalcy and an escape from Lucille's parents. Fiona felt her arms snake around Lucille's waist as she often did. Her body craved Lucille's warmth, where she was firm, Lucille was soft and eased into her. It was like warm butter melting into pastry dough.

"Mince Pies? Is that a confection?" Lucille said, eyeing her warily.

"It involves dough, and at the end, we sprinkle it with sugar."

"Well, you are the expert," Lucille said with a shrug.

"Firstly, we'll have to shred most everything," Fiona said, pulling out a sharp knife and a grater.

"What is included in most everything?" Lucille asked.

"Lamb, apples, raisins, suet, candied peel…" Fiona took a moment to think before rattling off more. "And dates."

"What are we not shredding?" Lucille said, sighing slightly.

"The rose water or the-" Suddenly, a wave of nausea hit Fiona, and she felt as if she hadn't slept in days. She braced herself on the butcher block counter.

"Fiona?" She loved the way Lucille said her name. Like she was unwrapping hard candy from its paper wrapper and twirling the confection in her mouth, it sounded as if Fiona's name was Lucille's favorite flavor. But this was not the time to be thinking of that.

"I'm tired. We'll do this lesson tomorrow." Fiona said. "I'll rest in my parlor.

Lucille unpinned her apron and slipped off her detachable sleeves.

"I'll keep you company," Lucille said.

Once they reached her parlor, Fiona settled into what she considered Lucille's armchair. Normally Fiona preferred the small settee, but for once she felt incredibly cold, and this one was close to the fire, and Lucille, as she expected, sat down in her lap. While Fiona was the smaller of the two women, Lucille liked to sit on Fiona and curl up, being held like a lap dog.

Fiona's mind was fuzzy, and her heart raced even more than it normally did when Lucille was close.

Lucille leaned down and pressed her forehead to Fiona's.

Fiona waited for a kiss, but instead, Lucille pulled away. "You're so warm."

"There's a fire." Fiona nodded towards the roaring fire. She felt Lucille's cold hand on either side of her face. Fiona squirmed away from Lucille's touch.

"There are other uses I can think of for your hands that don't involve taking my temperature," Fiona said, trying to lighten the mood.

"Oh, hush," Lucille said, pressing the back of her hand to Fiona's forehead. Fiona pushed her hand away.

"Lucille, stop," Fiona said, exasperated.

"What?" Lucille said. She was making that pouty expression Fiona had come to love, her plump bottom lip quivering.

"I came to spend time with you, not to have you care for me," Fiona said; she tried to soften her voice. "I want you; I don't want a nursemaid."

"I am not a nursemaid," Lucille said. "Don't be dense. I care for you. What do you expect?"

"I want you to find me attractive and enjoy my companionship," Fiona said, the words tumbling out before she could stop. She took a deep breath and tried to clarify. "I just want you to see me as an equal."

"I do," Lucille responded. "Where is all of this coming from? What does that have to do with caring for you?"

"You cannot do all of those things at once." Fiona said.

"I can," Lucille said firmly, her mouth forming a tight, resigned line.

"I don't need your sympathy or me worrying over me," Fiona said, rubbing her temple.

"Ridiculous," Lucille said. "You're so foolish. Do you treat your family like this?"

"My parents passed when I was younger, and I'm not close to my aunt," Fiona said. "As I told you."

"Oh, I see. Well, you shouldn't act like this. It's unbecoming." Lucille said in a scolding tone. *Had they taught her that in governess school? Fiona wondered.*

"What do you mean?" Fiona asked.

"Telling someone how to feel about you and care for you is strange," Lucille said. "I'm not trying to coddle you."

"I just wanted to be close to you," Fiona said, trying again to explain. "I was surprised when you checked my temperature."

"Are you saying that physical pleasures are the only way to be close?" Lucille said, cocking a brow.

"No, of course not…" Fiona frowned. "That's not what I meant at all."

"Allowing me to care for you is a form of intimacy," Lucille said softly.

Fiona pondered this for a moment. "I hadn't considered that." Lucille kissed her cheek.

"I have something for you," Fiona said. She produced the simple Blue Bonnet necklace she'd sent Marty into the village for. The pendant consisted of two bell-shaped flowers dangling from a short chain.

She spread her thick fingers to better show the necklace. Lucille didn't say anything.

"I believe this is the lariat style; if it's not to your taste, we can have it refashioned," Fiona said, trying to fill the silence with her explanation.

"Oh, it's beautiful," Lucille said quietly. "May I try it on?"

Fiona laughed. "It's yours to keep. Not to try on."

After she had the necklace clasped around Lucille's neck, she traced Lucille's collarbone gently. She noticed there was a trail of goosebumps left in the wake of her fingertips.

"What is the occasion?" Lucille asked gingerly, touching the enamel charms.

"You exist." Fiona said, "No occasion needed."

Lucille laughed. "I've existed for some twenty-odd years, and it's never been an event."

Fiona kissed her palm. "It has always been an event; you simply did not have the correct spectators."

"Thank you," Lucille said softly.

"Now, I must look over this latest batch of accounts from the shop," Fiona said, sliding out from under her and sitting on her settee beside her. Lucille didn't stay there for long. Instead, she moved to her armchair by the fire.

Lucille eyed her warily.

"I assure you, this was a passing spell. I won't keel over doing my books. It's stressful but not that much."

"Fine." Lucille said, gathering her art supplies from a nearby shelf.

Lucille

$\mathcal{L}$ucille watched Fiona sit and read over her letter. Fiona was reading so intently that Lucille felt safe to examine her without fear. Lucille was almost jealous of how easily Fiona could relax, legs splayed wide, shoulders dropped low, in repose as an artist's model sat in front of a small class of feverishly sketching artists.

"What are you thinking of?" Fiona said, flicking her eyes over the top of the page.

"Nothing?" Lucille said quickly.

"Your thoughts are practically buzzing, swarming like a hornet's nest. Your facial expression is very loud." Fiona said, smirking at her. "You're not still worrying are you?"

"I was thinking of art, artists' models," Lucille said quickly as she fiddled with her new necklace.

This seemed to satisfy Fiona as she went back to reading. From her position in her chair by the fire, Lucille couldn't see what the letter said. The writer had cross written, so the page looked more like a geometric pattern on tile than writing.

"What is your letter speaking of?" Lucille asked.

"The Pebble and Fig finances," Fiona responded.

"That's an in-depth letter for sums," Lucille said, cocking a brow. "Hardly any numbers."

"You're clear across the room. Come closer." Fiona said, coolly.

Lucille came and sat on Fiona's lap; the letter, from what she could make out, was about the accounts; the writer had simply spelled out the numbers.

"Look at me," Fiona said. "I'll never lie to you, even if the truth hurts."

Before she could reply, Fiona's lips came crashing onto Lucille's. She let herself savor Fiona. As always, Fiona tasted just like she smelled, warm, toasty, and soft with notes of vanilla and almond. Somehow the familiar flavor was better, more decadent on her lips. When she pulled back, she was gasping for breath and incredibly warm.

"I-" Lucille started, but her protests were swallowed by another kiss.

"Do you believe me?" Fiona said, finally breaking away; her hand was gently on Lucille's neck, her thick thumb stroking Lucille's jaw.

"Yes," Lucille said. "I was trying to tell you as much." She swatted her playfully.

Lucille's heart was a battering ram against her rib cage, screaming for release. Fiona had returned to reading her account book, comparing it to the cramped letter, and it didn't seem like Fiona's world was spinning like Lucille's was. Lucille made a motion to move, but Fiona pressed her hand against Fiona's ribs.

"Keep me company," Fiona said, a slight whine in her voice. That was impossible to resist.

Fiona

"Can I bite you?" Lucille asked.

For a moment, Fiona wasn't certain if Lucille was serious. Lucille tilted her head, clearly waiting for an answer. The hot fire was casting a gold glow over her dark skin and she looked radiant sitting in her armchair, regal even.

"Is that why you're always asking if I'm a vampire? Because you are one?" Fiona said, laughing.

"It relieves the tension in my jaw." Lucille said. Fiona could tell Lucille was struggling to keep a straight face.

"This is for medical purposes or psychological?" Fiona said slowly, trying not to sound overly eager.

"Yes."

Fiona rolled up her shirt sleeve. "Fine."

Lucille hopped out of her chair excitedly. Fiona held her arm out to Lucille, and Lucille bit her gently, barely leaving indents.

"Thank you," Lucille said, clapping her hands happily. Then she stopped "Would you like to bite me back?"

"Mmmhmm." Fiona hesitated. "I might hurt you; I don't want to risk it."

"Oh," Lucille said. She squirmed a bit in her seat.

Fiona reached over to the bowl of fruit on the table and she selected a large orange, holding it up to Lucille and then Fiona bit it into it with barely any pressure, and her teeth easily sank in deeply to the thick skin. She pulled the fruit out of her mouth and showed Lucille. "I wouldn't lie to you."

"I wasn't questioning you," Lucille said.

"I know, I was simply explaining," Fiona said.

"Thank you."

"If you ever need my help with jaw tension or anything else you need, I'm here."

"I don't have needs," Lucille said quickly.

"Oh?" Fiona said, a bit confused.

"Aside from room and board, of course."

Fiona struggled to respond. "It's fine to have needs, you know this, yes?"

"Of course, it's only contrary to everything I've ever been taught." Lucille laughed softly.

"Come here," Fiona said firmly before Lucille could protest; Fiona pulled her towards her and wrapped her arms around her tightly.

"But the books."

"The books are here, we are here. The books will be there." Fiona said as she buried her face in Lucille's neck, careful not to pucker her lips, and instead, she rubbed her lips against Lucille's neck gently and tickled her ribs.

Lucille squealed. "No, no return to your sums and I shall return to my reading."

"You weren't reading, you were staring at me." Fiona said, letting her up.

"Same difference." Lucille said as she pushed herself away from Fiona and returned to her chair.

Fiona shook her head ever so slightly. *She just needs some time to express herself,* Fiona thought. *Patience, that will be the ticket.*

Lucille

*T*he sleepless nights that punctuated the long days of lessons, tolerating her parents and enjoying Fiona were beginning to wear on Lucille. She sighed and leaned against the table as she stirred the sludge in the bowl in front of her.

"Lucille, this pudding is thick. It's going to set up like mortar." Fiona said. Lucille could tell Fiona was trying hard to be patient, but annoyance shadowed her face.

"Oh, bollocks," Lucille said exasperatedly. The first batch had too much orange juice and was orange instead of pale yellow; in the second batch, she'd added too many eggs, and in the third, she hadn't added nearly enough of the isinglass to thicken the milk.

"Is there more isinglass? I'll do it again. Right this time." Lucille said, frowning and looking around the kitchen. She didn't see any more of the clear scaly skin-like flakes. *What had Fiona said they were? Fish swim bladders. That was it.*

"No." Fiona sighed.

"Do we have it in another kitchen?" Lucille said hopefully.

"No."

Lucille chewed on her bottom lip. "Do we have fish?"

"It's not that simple to make fish glue." Fiona sighed again and gave up on trying to stir the pudding. To Lucille's horror, the whisk stood up on its own when Fiona let it go.

"I'm sorry."

"It's alright; we'll make something else. I really think we should speak on where we stand." Fiona said.

"In the kitchen," Lucille said with a nervous laugh. She felt embarrassed about how stupid she sounded.

"I hope I am not intruding." Her mother said cheerfully and in such a way that Lucille was certain that Alma could not care less if she was intruding or not.

"Would you like to help?" Fiona said in an even tone. "We're about to pour the pudding into molds."

"Oh no, I am not made for kitchen work. I have a delicate disposition." Alma said with a chuckle.

"Then why are you in a kitchen?" Lucille said, half muttering to herself.

"I am glad you asked!" Alma said, fanning herself dramatically with an ornate floral fan. "Lady Fondant, you must tell me all about your relations. I could not find a family tree in this entire estate. Can you imagine?"

Fiona finished filling the wreath-shaped mold in front of her, and then she tapped it loudly on the counter and gave it a shake. "Perhaps we could discuss this later? Lucille and I were in the middle of a serious discussion."

"Oh, it is nothing," Lucille said, forcing a giggle. "We can finish our discussion when we take air later. Better to just answer mother's questions so she may continue agitating."

"Excuse me?" Her mother frowned and stopped fanning.

"Continue relaxing, Mother; you are on holiday after all," Lucille said, wiping the rim of the mold in front of her. This may have been the only time Lucille was pleased with her mother interrupting. Alma's incessant prattling was oddly comforting for once. Lucille pretended to fill the molds as if it was very detailed work, even though she knew none of them would be usable. As she made herself appear busy, she kept an ear out to listen as her mother quizzed Fiona. Alma asked about Fiona's education, religion, family history, and finances.

"I don't believe I've seen you at any soirees…" Alma said finally as if she had finally run out of questions.

"I am not much for society, but my family is in good standing," Fiona said evenly. If Alma's interrogation bothered her, Fiona wasn't letting it show.

"I believe I'll retire to my study." Fiona said before Alma could shoot off another question.

"Ah, yes. I should be drawing." Lucille said, unpinning her apron. "Fiona, walk mother to the sitting room for tea?"

Fiona glared ar Lucille but nodded.

Lucille held her breath until she was safely in her room. After resting for a moment, she got out the half-drawn sketch of a Pomeranian that she had started earlier in the week. She was still hunched over her desk, blending, when she felt Fiona's strong, calloused hands wrapped around her neck.

"Is this my end?" Lucille asked playfully.

"Yes." Fiona rumbled, then her hands slipped to Lucille's shoulder, she rubbed the top of her arms and then worked her way back up to her neck. Lucille sighed; the coolness of Fiona's hands was refreshing,

"I have a present for you," Fiona said.

"No," Lucille said playfully. "I refuse it."

A soft ribbon snaked around Lucille's neck, and a pendant settled into the hollow of her throat. Lucille touched it gingerly.

"Thank you," Lucille said softly.

"Tsk. Tsk. You haven't seen it yet." Fiona said, leading her over to a looking glass.

"Ah, ah." Lucille stuttered. The necklace was an explosion of crystals and gems. When she tilted her neck ever so slightly, the pendant cast a rainbow across the room.

"This is far too nice." Lucille managed finally.

"Not nice enough for you." Fiona said sweetly, she kissed Lucille's cheek. "Now, your parents await us."

Lucille groaned but followed her out of the room with one last forlorn glance at her own reflection which she hardly recognized with the finery.

Fiona

If Fiona had taken a swig of wine every time Lucille rolled her eyes at Alma, she would have been comatose. Instead she worked on her handknitting. It wasn't a hobby she particularly enjoyed but it gave her something to do with her hands and didn't require as much focus as embroidery.

Alma was rambling about something, more ardently than normal when Marty appeared in the sitting room. "Apologies for interrupting, but Lady Fondant, your packages for Miss Waters have arrived. Where would you like them?"

"Bring them in!" Fiona said, dropping her knitting and moving to the sofa across from Lucille. "You'll need room," Fiona said to Lucille.

"I do love presents," Alma said, clapping her hands softly.

Fiona wondered if Simon was asleep, it seemed as though he was always nearly silent until he was grunting or whispering conspiratorially to his wife when he thought Fiona wasn't paying attention.

"I don't think these will be of any interest to you, Mother," Lucille said. The gingerbread men began to file in and deposit packages beside and in front of Lucille.

"Lady Fiona!" Lucille nearly shrieked as the piles of packages began to tower over her. "This is far too many."

Simon and Alma exchanged fervent glances.

"No need for the formalities," Fiona said playfully. "Open up your materials."

Fiona watched as Lucille began to gingerly untie the first package and unfold its brown paper carefully.

"These oil paints are so fine." Lucille said, motioning to the swatch papers that came with them.

Fiona had to tear her eyes away from Lucille's excited face and look at Alma.

"What use is oil paints?" Alma said, frowning.

"They're used for painting," Fiona said; she couldn't help but stick her tongue out.

"Fiona is very supportive of my artistic endeavors," Lucille said, excitedly opening the next package.

Fiona watched as Bon Bon crawled across the floor, a small flower overturned on its head like a hat. Lucille must have done that. She is always doing little sweet things like that. Fiona loved Lucille's artist's eye and attention to detail.

Fiona took a chunk of pineapple off the tray of diced fruits and vegetables and held it out to the little turtle.

"Such fine, expensive fruit for a pet?" Alma said, not bothering to hide her disgust.

"We share with you, Mother," Lucille said, shaking the top off a small box. Fiona watched as Lucille's face lit up. The trinket inside was a small pendant notebook; the rectangular silver cover was engraved with Lucille's initials. Fiona was hoping she would flip it over to see the message engraved on the other side, but she didn't.

"What a beautiful notebook, far too fine," Lucille said, examining the front. She traced the flowers on the front and the delicate chain.

"We can replace the paper with vellum or ivory if you would like," Fiona said sweetly, trying to hide her disappointment.

Fiona caught Lucille's arm on the way to the dining room. "I've paid to have a post in the gossip rags."

"Whatever for?" Lucille whispered back.

"I wanted to add validity to our relationship for your sister."

"And Bree?" Lucille said, cocking an eyebrow.

Fiona stopped abruptly, and Lucille took a step but then stopped as well. "Is this jealousy?"

Lucille glanced towards her parents, who were still walking, questioning Marty on some of the furnishings.

"Should I be jealous?"

"No," Fiona said with a wide grin. "You have nothing to be jealous of." Fiona took Lucille's hand and kissed her palm. "If you ever need reassurance, come to me, and I'll assure you that you are peerless."

Instead of looking reassured, Lucille looked as if she might burst into tears at any moment. Fiona pulled her into the nearest room which happened to be the butler's pantry.

"What is this?" Lucille said, looking up and spinning around, momentarily distracted from her upset. Fiona looked at the built-in shelves and large table.

"The butler's pantry."

"It's massive."

"Luce, we haven't got much time." Fiona said, patting her arm gently.,

Lucille's face fell as if she suddenly remembered. "My parents wish for me to return with them to escort my sisters to balls this season. They think I'll be able to make better introductions now that our connection is public," Lucille said, her back sliding down the wall until she was crouched on the floor, her arms hugging her shins and her face burrowing into her knees.

Fiona let her cane fall, and she sank down to Lucille, grasping her by the shoulders. "Gods below Lucille, you can't do this. You cannot just bend and be squished like marzipan, shaped from a lump into whatever is desired of you."

"I am not; I am trying…that's why I am here," Lucille said; her face was turned away from Fiona, but she knew she was crying.

"Try harder. Fight harder." Fiona said, exasperated. "They cannot just talk to you any such way."

Lucille only hiccuped in response.

"Fine," Fiona said, pulling Lucille into an embrace. "We will go; we will make introductions." She rocked her back and forth gently.

"What?" Lucille said, pulling back. "You do not leave your estate. Have you changed your mind?"

"Unfortunately, the mind does not work like that," Fiona said, sighing. "But perhaps we will consult different physicians."

"Oh, no. no. no." Lucille said, pushing Fiona away and standing up. "If we are to consult physicians and change our entire life, then it will be for something that you want to do, which makes us happy. Not for those people." She jerked her thumb towards the doorway. Fiona stared up at Lucille, watching in shock as she wiped her tears and smoothed her dress. "I'll not have it. I may be a marzipan lump, but they will not lump you!" Lucille said firmly.

Fiona resisted the urge to laugh as Lucille helped her up. "May I?" Lucille asked, motioning to the discarded cane.

"Of course."

Lucille passed Fiona the cane, and then to Fiona's surprise, Lucille placed her hand on either side of her face and then kissed her forehead softly.

"We should get to dinner." Fiona said, sighing.

She wasn't sure whether to be excited or concerned about Lucille's sudden surge of confidence, but now was not the time to dwell on it. They had a dinner to survive.

Lucille

*D*inner was mercilessly short as Mother complained of a headache, probably caused by the fact that the napkins were folded into vulgar swan shapes. Mother had said she was going to rest. Lucille wondered if this meant she was stealing linens or writing to her sisters. *Really it did not matter,* Lucille thought, just happy to be in the quiet warmth of Fiona's parlor.

"You must listen; this accounting system is complicated; this is a part of your lessons," Fiona said, pinching Lucille in the ribs. Fiona was sitting at her big oak desk with the ledger book open to last month's sums, and Lucille was alternating between leaning over her shoulder and twirling around the room.

"What if I don't care to listen?" Lucille cocked one eyebrow up, and a smirk danced across her lips. She walked about the room, half galloping, waving her around like a ballerina. She danced her way back towards the desk and then sat on the edge, knocking over Fiona's cup of pencils.

"Oh, I'm so sorry, that was an accident," Lucille said, rushing to gather them up as they rolled across the desk. "I'm sorry." She said, apologizing again.

"Luce, stop it," Fiona said, gently wrapping a hand around Lucille's neck and pulling her forward. Then Fiona kissed her softly, feeling Lucille's moans vibrate against her palm. Fiona trapped Lucille's bottom lip between her pointed teeth. Fiona rarely did this, but when she did, Lucille loved it.

Lucille pulled back. "I really am sorry."

"I don't care about the pencils." Fiona said playfully, "You are terribly irksome."

"Am I?" She smirked. "Your behavior seems to say otherwise."

Alma walked in and cleared her throat.

"We are retiring for the evening," Alma said, wrinkling her nose.

"Wonderful," Fiona said,

"Will you not escort me?" Alma said, nodding towards Lucille.

Lucille hopped off the desk and took a step forward, but Fiona reached forward and caught her hand.

"Are you in need of assistance finding your room?" Fiona said with a smirk.

"Well, certainly," Alma said.

Fiona made a flicking motion, and Alma flew out into the hallway. Fiona wiggled her fingers, and the pocket door slid closed.

"Lady Fondant!" Lucille exclaimed, swatting at Fiona's shoulder.

"I was assisting our guest." Fiona hooked her arm around Lucille's waist and pulled her closer.

Lucille closed her eyes and sighed deeply, "Thank you." She murmured into Fiona's neck.

"Now, what is this Lady Fondant business?"

"Thank you, Fiona," Lucille said so softly Fiona barely heard it.

"You know she's going to be livid." Lucille added.

"Well, yes, but she treats you horridly regardless. Besides, she just wants you alone to insult you or extort money." Fiona said with a shrug.

"Yes," Lucille said. She sounded so defeated it made Fiona's heartache. "They've just been so horrid, and I want them not to be, but they are. When they're here, it's so hard to pretend they could even be anything else."

"I know," Fiona said, pulling her into another hug. "It'll be over soon; let us have tea, cuddle, and then get back to our records."

"Do you truly believe a cup of tea and a cuddle will solve this mess?"

"Certainly not, but it'll be nice," Fiona said; she wiggled her fingers, and the bell on the wall tugged itself.

The pocket door slid open. *Hmm,* Fiona thought to herself, that was oddly fast. She looked towards the door but didn't see Marty, Perry, or a gingerbread man.

"Fiona?" Lucille said in a hoarse whisper. "I did not see you open that."

"I did not," Fiona responded. Before they could move, Fiona heard a tapping noise and looked down. A small candelabra sat there on the floor. It hopped up and down excitedly.

"Yes?" Lucille said, scooping it up. It wiggled excitedly in her grasp.

"Put it on the table," Fiona said. "It's trying to tell us something."

"Oh, I'm sorry," Lucille said, putting the candelabra down gingerly.

"Stop apolo-" Fiona said, then stopped herself as the candelabra began to tap aggressively.

"Your parents aren't poor..." Fiona listened for a moment. "Quite the opposite." The candelabra tapped more. "They just don't care for you, and your mother and father argue constantly."

"Pfft." Lucille sighed. "Well, I knew everything except for them not being poor...well, they certainly aren't wealthy."

The candelabra tapped aggressively, thumping against the wood table, and Fiona was convinced it would leave a dent. "No, they are quite wealthy. And apparently, they stole more of our silver." Fiona said, trying not to roll her eyes.

"Does all the furniture listen?" Lucille said, her eyes growing wide.

"Hmm?" Fiona said. "No, not all the furniture is enchanted."

"Oh good," Lucille said, visibly relaxing.

"Why?" Fiona asked.

"No reason," Lucille said quickly. "Thank you, candlestick. Why don't you go find Perry and get yourself a good polish and lit with good beeswax candles."

"Yes," Fiona said, giving the decor a gentle pat. "No more tallow rushlights for you."

And with that, the little candelabra was off.

"Fiona!" Lucille said as if suddenly realizing. "You put tallow rushlights in their room?"

"Mhmm," Fiona answered, personally, she couldn't stand the smelly candles but she thought it was fitting for Lucille's parents' stinking attitudes. "They'd probably have stolen the amber lights if they could get their hands on them for long enough."

Lucille nodded. "You are probably correct, Fiona."

"Say that again."

"Mhm?"

"Repeat what you said."

"You are probably correct…" Lucille said slowly, "You are probably correct, Fiona." She said, repeating herself.

"Wow, that is probably the most arousing thing you have ever said to me," Fiona said.

"Is that a challenge?" Lucille asked, winking.

Fiona

*L*ucille rolled over lazily to her back in her sleep and Fiona took the opportunity to kiss her brow.

"Mhm." Lucille grumbled.

"Are you asleep?" Fiona said, kissing her earlobe.

"Yes, soundly." Lucille said, eyes still closed.

"Would you like to have breakfast before the eels wake up?" Fiona asked, jokingly referring to Lucille's parents.

"They won't be up." Lucille said, finally sitting up.

"You're really confident." Fiona said, pulling Lucille against her.

"Perry set their timepieces back." Lucille said with a shrug. "Everyone was tired of them."

Fiona could not help but laugh. They took their time dressing and then made their way towards the dining room.

"Really, Luce, you must stop," Fiona said; she could taste the peach juice on lips as she kissed her. Fiona reached around her to take a swig of her champagne. The breakfast table was so full, she hardly had a place to sit the glass down so kept it in her hand.

"Do you mean that?" Lucille said, pulling back slightly. She knocked into the glass, and the bubbly liquid went sloshing onto both of them.

"Ah," Fiona said, putting the glass down on a plate of biscuits and blotting them both. "I'm amazed you've not had a single glass, and you're incredibly festive."

"Do you mean that?" Lucille asked again, this time whispering conspiratorially.

"Yes, you're in great spirits," Fiona said, rubbing her hand up and down Lucille's back. She pushed some of the dishes back towards the center of the table since Lucille seemed to have no care for how far she was leaning back into the table.

"I meant did you want me to stop," Lucille said, pouting.

"Not wholeheartedly, but if you don't stop, I'll lose my control and absolutely devour you. I'm certain you taste amazing." Fiona said, kissing her again.

Lucille twisted in Fiona's lap and then tilted her head so her bare neck was exposed and pulled down the neckline of her dress slightly and wiggled. "Feed away my Vampira."

"I've told you I'm not a vampire, and that's not what I-" Fiona could not help but stifle a laugh.

"What?" Lucille said innocently. She swatted Fiona's shoulder. "Tell me."

Fiona held up an orange ice. It had melted slightly in its orange skin bowl, so the texture was soft.

"Here, eat this," Fiona said, putting it to Lucille's lips.

"But you haven't explained," Lucille said, pouting again.

"I'm explaining now; it's a lesson," Fiona said, then more firmly. "Eat this."

"Alright." Her face was a mixture of bemused and confused. "Where's the spoon."

"You don't need a spoon; I'll hold it," Fiona said.

As Lucille began to work at the contents of the orange, swirling her tongue and slurping, Fiona snaked her hand up under her skirt. She had only made it to Lucille's inner thigh when the realization dawned on Lucille.

"Ooooh," Lucille said. She twisted around to face Fiona, cream dribbling down her chin. "Could you and I-"

Fiona nodded and kissed her, not caring that cream was running down her hand from the orange ice or that Lucille and her face were horribly sticky.

The door to the dining room began to slide open. Fiona held up her hand to stop it in its tracks, and Lucille slid off her lap, back into her seat. Lucille quickly dabbed at her face with a napkin. Fiona released the door, and it went slamming open so hard it bounced slightly before staying open.

"Your pocket door was stuck!" Alma said dramatically. Lucille's mother always seemed to be in a constant state of agitation.

"Oh? I haven't been having any issues." Fiona said evenly. "I'll have Marty look at it."

"You two look as if you've been eating from a pig trough!" Alma said.

Fiona glanced over at Lucille, she had wiped her face, but her makeup was smeared, and some of the drips of cream had already dried down. For her part, Fiona could feel the semi-wet champagne stains from her spilled glass, and her face was wet with cream.

"Oh well," Lucille said, standing up quickly. "We were done anyway. Besides, we have a lesson to get to."

Fiona pushed away from the table and began guiding Lucille towards the door on the opposite side of the room Alma had entered. It wasn't the fastest way to the kitchens, but it would put them close to her bedroom.

"You'll just leave us to eat alone?" Alma called behind them.

Lucille

$\mathcal{L}$ucille woke up to being shaken by Marty. It took a few moments to process that she was in Fiona's bed. What time was it? What was happening?

"Miss Waters!" Marty said excitedly.

"Is there a fire?" Lucille said groggily, trying to gather her wits.

"No, ma'am. My apologies; let us go downstairs." He spun around and then found her wrapper on the back of the chair and held it open for her. "Quickly, quickly." He said, shaking the garment.

It took a moment for her to register that his voice was filled with excitement. Lucille took the stairs two at a time and was moving so quickly that she nearly ran into Fiona who was on the landing, standing legs wide apart. Her hand was outstretched, and she was making shooing motions with her hands. Lucille watched as her parent's bags flew out of the open door.

"Morning, my wonderful whisk. Did I wake you?" Fiona said, looking over her shoulder.

"Uh, no, what are you doing?" Lucille said.

Before Lucille could answer her father peeked his head around the door frame. "Lucilla! Tell this mad woman to stop-"

Fiona cut him off by holding her hand out, and he flew back.

"Is there anything you would like to say?" Fiona asked, turning around and embracing her.

"No," Lucille said, shaking her head.

"Alright," Fiona said and raised her hand.

"Wait," Lucille said.

"Yes?" Fiona said, dropping her hand.

"Did you get your silverware?" Lucille asked.

Fiona nodded and then pointed to the forayer. Lucille took a few steps down the stairs and realized the floor was littered with silverware.

"Oh, then continue," Lucille said.

With a subtle flick of her wrist, Fiona slammed the door closed.

"How did you get them to give your silverware back?"

"I shook them," Fiona said with a laugh.

"Let us have breakfast, and you can tell me all about it." Lucille said.

"That sounds wonderful, I need to get the letter from my desk. The head confectioner has written to discuss the spring menu test."

Lucille noticed Fiona was breathless and dark bags circled her eyes. "I'll fetch it for you."

"I can do-" Fiona said, but her sentence was swallowed by a yawn.

"Please?" Lucille said.

"If you don't mind." Fiona acquiesced.

Fiona's desk was as messy as usual. The local newspaper, recipes in progress, and receipts were spread across the desk. There were only two folded sealed letters; one bore the wax seal of The Pebble and Fig. The other had a singular B intertwined in a styled oyster shell. Lucille picked up the letter Fiona requested and left the other where it was. She was certain it was from Bree. *Did she write often? Did Fiona answer? Would Bree be visiting? Had she sent her the new locket?* Lucille wondered, panicking slightly.

They ate and discussed the spring menu until Lucille couldn't focus for the thoughts of Bree that kept intruding.

"I have a few notes to write on a painting I plan to create," Lucille said, nibbling on the scone she had taken. "Then I must braid my hair, I imagine it will take several hours."

"After your notes, come to my room and do your hair there," Fiona said, stifling a yawn. "I'll be refreshed by then."

"I don't wish to intrude," Lucille said.

"You could never," Fiona said.

When Marty and Perry entered with more information on the spring menu test, Lucille took the opportunity to take her plate of food and hurry to her room. She sighed and tried to focus on her painting, she removed the notebook pendant from her neck, and when she went to slide it off her chain, it slipped through her fingers and clattered to the floor. She picked up the sheets of paper and then the front and back pieces. Lucille hadn't realized the back was engraved. She held it up to the window light. It read, "I would gladly give you every flower I find in this world and the next. Regards, F."

Lucille pondered this. She had chosen the word "would" and not "will." She had also signed it with "regards" and not "love.' She wondered if any of this mattered.

Part Four

Sugar, Spice, and Unsolicited Advice

Fiona

Now that Alma and Simon were gone, Fiona felt as if she could finally breathe. She watched from her bed as Lucille braided her hair. The linen shirt Lucille had borrowed rode up, teasing a further glimpse of her dimpled skin and revealing a constellation of moles on her left thigh. Even without seeing them, Fiona knew Lucille's full hips were adorned with curling stretch marks that trailed down her thighs like a beautiful poem written in cursive. She had memorized each and every line.

"You're staring at me," Lucille said, adding another gold cuff to her braid.

"Mhmm," Fiona said.

"What?" Lucille asked. "Out with it."

Fiona watched as Lucille tried in vain to tug down the shirt again.

"Don't do that," Fiona said. "I love seeing your thighs and your long legs. I'm enjoying you."

"You don't think I'm terribly tall? No one thought me tall at school," Lucille said nervously.

"Why do you say this? Never have you missed an opportunity to remind me of my short stature. What changed?"

Lucille shrugged. "You're perfect."

"As are you," Fiona said. "Now, we must turn our attention to important matters. The spring menu items will arrive in two days' time." Fiona said, pouring over the letter, which was four sheets long.

"I wager I could put my dessert in with the lot, and you would not be able to discern who made it," Lucille said mischievously.

"You're confident. What would you wager?" Fiona said, raising a brow appraisingly.

"Anything," Lucille said boldly.

"Truly?" Fiona said, looking up from her notes on which desserts would be arriving.

"I'll make you a deal; if you cannot discern who made the treat, then you must marry me." Lucille

"Is this a proposal?" Fiona said, laughing. Lucille's skills had improved greatly, but the Fondant family only employed the best of the best.

"Fiona!" Lucille said, swatting her arm.

"When I win, I want a huge portrait in oil," Fiona said, careful to pick something that Lucille could afford but was difficult, so she felt like it was a fair trade. The thought of actually marrying Lucille made her excited and scared all at once. Then the reality of the situation rose in her throat like an aftertaste: Lucille could never be happily married to her.

Fiona motioned her over and pulled her up onto the bed; she held out a sheet. "You have to make one of these so your dish fits in."

Lucille looked at her for a moment, expecting her to kiss her, but instead, she pressed her forehead into Fiona's and stared deeply into her eyes. "I'll win," Lucille said, her breath warm against Fiona's lips.

"Oh, I forgot to tell you. News of the nutty sweet treats has arrived!"

Lucille clapped excitedly. "How are they doing?"

"They're flying off the trays!"

"That is wonderful!" Lucille said cheerfully. She climbed off of Fiona's lap.

"Where are you going? Shouldn't we celebrate?" Fiona said.

Lucille laughed, "I have a competition to win." She picked up the menu that showed which desserts would be coming. "I'll be taking those."

"You'll have to study later; we still have a great deal of work to do with the spring menus."

"Oh," Lucille said; Fiona could see her mood sobering.

"What else is there to do?"

"We must create a theme for the upcoming season and a new lead dessert."

"I imagine the nutty treats aren't as elegant as we'd like."

"No, we must make something more elevated to be served at balls and such," Fiona said, then she rattled off the past featured desserts over the last few seasons.

"To the library?" Lucille suggested. "That is where all the best research begins."

Fiona watched Lucille pull on a simple white dress, and then she put on a velvet overdress, buttoning it closed right under her bust. Lucille smoothed the skirt. "How does it look?" Lucille asked.

"Magnificent," Fiona said.

As they made their way down the hall, a faded door with chipping paint materialized. Perhaps it was an older library, Fiona thought, opening it and stepping inside.

Lucille

*F*iona adjusted her jacket as if to check if it still fit, tugging on the front and smoothing down the lapels. Then as if thinking better of it, she tossed it on the back of a chair. The chair itself was simple, with an upholstered seat and back that was framed by delicate scrollwork. Much like the rest of the room, it was a bit worn but neat. The raw honeycomb print wallpaper was faded, and the furniture had small shiny rub spots and small nicks.

"What room is this?" Lucille asked; a book lay open on the small sideboard. At the top of the page, in blocky letters, it said 'A History of Herbal Flavors.' The text was small and faded, but it seemed to be a cookbook of some sort.

"Hell, if I know," Fiona said.

Lucille looked about; it was actually quite similar to Fiona's parlor. But it was dominated by yellows, golds, and light wood instead of rich dark greens and mahogany tones. "Perhaps this is better than a library. A good turn of fortune"

Fiona swiped a hand over her face but didn't respond. Her skin glistened with a slight dew, and Lucille wondered if she would be able to taste the salt on her skin if she were to kiss it.

"I honestly haven't a clue about how to arrange the spring menu," Fiona said finally. She said it like it was a confession.

"There is the matter of that," Lucille said flatly. She knew the young fashionable set would be descending upon the city any day now like a swarm of debaucherous locusts ready to devour every trendy, luxurious thing they could locate. What she did not know was the logistics of arranging the new menu or deciding what flavors would be most successful.

"Balance," Fiona said so softly; Lucille wondered if she had been meant to hear it all. Then she continued louder. "Our offerings must be fresh but not overly scandalous or strange."

"Sorry, I'm not making much sense," Fiona said.

"I'm sorry," Fiona said again, walking over to her.

No matter how many times Fiona's rough, strong hands touched her face, Lucille's body responded as if it was the very first time. *Would it always be like this?* It didn't matter; it was not as if she and Fiona were going to be forever; the feeling would probably be here for as long as they were together. Fiona cupped Lucille's chin in her hand and said something Lucille could not comprehend, but she nodded along. She tried to appear relaxed as if her entire body wasn't tense, trying in vain to contain the fast, erratic pitter-patter of her heart, which sounded more like hail hitting the skylight than an organ.

"And we'll solve this little mystery," Fiona said, kissing her forehead.

"Is this your uncle's study?" Lucille said helpfully.

"This certainly isn't my uncle's study," Fiona said, releasing Lucille's face.

"Aw, hmm." Lucille let out a mewling whine.

Fiona smirked. She still looked tired, dark half circles shadowing her eyes, and her eyes were puffy, but for a moment, she looked like her mischievous self.

"Was the stoic Miss Waters enjoying my caress?" Fiona asked. She said it in a joking manner, but she looked hopeful.

"I-" Lucille thought about lying but thought better of it. "Yes, I did."

Fiona looked visibly relieved.

"Your aunt," Lucille said stupidly as the thought flitted through her mind.

"Excuse me?" Fiona said.

"Your great aunt, your grandfather's sister. I noticed in her portrait she posed with a honey dipper and bees."

"I don't believe I've ever noticed," Fiona said. "I only met her once as a child."

"Did your family speak of her?" Lucille said, looking around the room.

"No, she was a wonderful confectioner. We occasionally use her honey cake recipe for religious events. It's topped with pomegranate seeds. We'll have to make it sometime." Fiona said, clearly getting distracted.

Lucille sat at the small desk and began to look through the drawers until she found a journal that was very similar to the ones she and Fiona carried around. A confectioner's book was an odd mixture of journal and cookbook.

"Ah," Lucille said, thumbing through the book. "This bar may be just the item."

Fiona leaned over her and began to read over her shoulder, so close to her ear, Lucille could feel the warm breath of her words. "Pistachio, saffron, honey, walnut, coconut, cinnamon."

"I don't understand." Fiona said, "This seems to be a recipe for cookie dough. But perhaps a cake or...a layered pastry?"

"I believe you're meant to layer the filling between the thinned dough, and when baked, it is a cookie-like consistency." Lucille turned the notebook to the side. "I believed she planned the decor to be simple, perhaps just the chopped nuts."

"That won't do," Fiona said, leaning back and pinching her nose bridge.

"We'll do dried flowers. Edible, of course." Lucille said quickly. "It'll look lovely."

Lucille stood up and hugged her, rubbing her back in small circles. "You're being so dramatic dear; we have weeks to get the featured item perfect. Besides, you'll want all the fashionable set to arrive and be settled before you release it."

"You'll help me?" Fiona asked softly.

"Of course," Lucille said, murmuring into Fiona's hair.

Lucille spent the next several hours testing various parts of the recipe, tweaking them before combining all of the steps. Fiona focused on deciding a tentative arrangement for the staple confections and projecting how many new additions they should aim for.

Lucille's first attempt at a crunchy herbal dessert was less than perfect in fact it was rather disastrous.

Fiona took a bite of the crispy baked good. Lucille cringed as she watched Fiona nearly choke. "I believe you've succeeded in making a birdseed cracker. We might have a good run selling this to the king. I hear his sailors are tired of hardtack." Fiona said. Lucille could tell she meant it as a joke, but it was tinged with annoyance.

"This is only the base," Lucille said, but she was not hopeful. They had thought the combination of chia, pumpkin, sunflower, and sesame seeds and a blend of pepper and garlic would create the perfect salty, crispy base for their dessert. Instead, it was overly dry, puckeringly salty, and it crumbled when they tried to cut it into discs and squares.

Lucille waited for Fiona to criticize her or call her foolish, but instead, she felt pulled into Fiona's strong arms. Lucille sank into her, closing her eyes and allowing Fiona's hands to rub up and down her back to soothe her.

"I made you candied orange slices." Fiona said, pulling away.

"How did you find time to do that?" Lucille said shocked.

"While you were napping." Fiona motioned to a covered dish.

Lucille groaned, she hadn't realized that her nap between batches had been that long. She raised the lid of the dish Fiona had brought to reveal several shiny slices of oranges, each dipped in chocolate and sprinkled with salt. She took a bite. "Mmmmhm." She moaned. "This is celestial, if only these could be the spring dish." Unfortunately, they both knew that the already common treat would not do, even if it was a warm weather staple.

Fiona chuckled. "I don't believe I elicit such noises from you unless I'm feeding you."

"I believe Perry would beg to differ. He says we interrupt his beauty sleep."

"Well, he can move further down the hall."

"He did." Lucille said, covering her face in mock shame.

"It is not my fault, it's a once in a lifetime opportunity to spend time with an incomparable." Fiona said with a playful smile.

"That's it!" Lucille exclaimed. "We should call this dessert the Peerless."

"Perhaps I would successfully complete it before naming it," Fiona said, "Also that's an odd name for a dessert."

"Says the woman who makes cheesecake with no cheese." Lucille said, rolling her eyes.

"Besides, it'll be wonderful when people speak of it. Even if they don't care for it, they'll call it peerless. A man is a nonpareil, a woman is an incomparable, and our confection is a peerless. It fits perfectly. It will be the best dessert" Lucille sighed. "Once we come up with something, if we come up with something..." Her confidence faltered.

"We will. I imagine this will be the best season yet." Fiona said, pulling her back into another tight hug.

Lucille sat for a moment and thought of all the sweets she enjoyed, macaroons, of course, vamazelli cake, mango with lime, chili, and salt, and candied oranges. Perhaps a crunchy, salty-sweet bar of some sort would be just the ticket, somewhere between a confection and a heartier treat. She gave Fiona a few vague adjectives of the cookie crust she was imagining and Fiona grunted in response; she could make a perfect cookie in a dead sleep. With that taken care of, Lucille set to working on the mixture. Lucille broke the thin noodles up, toasted them in butter, and then she mixed in her assorted seeds, Fiona's signature spice blend, and then she cooked it in warm milk.

"Have you finished the cookie crust?" Lucille asked.

"Yes?" Fiona said as she pointed to the dish in front of her.

Lucille let the mixture thicken and cool a bit. Then she pressed the mixture into the cookie shell.

"Now we let it set up," Lucille said, looking at the sad green and brown mixture. Once it had set, they cut it into squares. It was sweet with a nice crunch. The flavors mingled well; Lucille especially enjoyed the nuttiness.

"I don't mean to be overly critical, but while these taste delightful, they won't be particularly eye-catching," Fiona said softly. Lucille noticed she was reaching for another piece.

"No, it's alright," Lucille said. "I understand."

"Well, what if we were to drizzle the top with syrup and sprinkle crumbled pastry and flowers for garnish," Fiona said.

"That might do it, and cut them into diamonds," Lucille said excitedly.

"Peerless," Fiona said.

"Alright," Lucille said. "Let's do it once more. With detailed notes."

"Ugh, you sound as I do." Fiona said.

Lucille dropped her voice. "If I sounded like you, I would have said, 'We'll do it once more, making it as perfect as your smile.' Or something like that." She said, laughing.

When they finished remaking the dessert, Lucille took a step back to admire their handywork. The top of the dessert was adorned with a mosaic of dried flowers, woven into a lace-like drizzle. She was happy with the addition of the florals; the vibrant colors burst against the tapestry of golden noodles and toasted nuts.

Lucille gingerly picked up a diamond-shaped piece and held it out to Fiona, who simply shook her head and said "No, you."

Please let this be perfection, Lucille silently prayed. She took a careful bite, chewing very slowly, giving herself time to experience the myriad of flavors. The Peerless was slightly rough on her fingertips and it had some heft to it. Its density reminded her of fudge. The initial crunch released a harmonious blend of bold, nutty undertones, subtle sweetness, and the slightest hint of saltiness. As she chewed, the dessert crumbled and then melted in her mouth.

"Ah," Lucille said, covering her mouth with her hand. "The Ton will love this."

Fiona clapped her hands and her shoulders dropped in relief. Lucille watched as Fiona took a bite and then nodded, mouth still full as she spoke. "Yes. This. This is it!" Fiona said, her words garbled but still bringing a smile to Lucille's face.

"It may be the best, sweetest thing I've ever tasted." Lucille said.

Fiona reached out to take Lucille's hand, the contact sending shivers down her spine. "You are the sweetest thing I've ever tasted," she said softly,

Lucille bit her bottom, a soft smile spreading across her face as she leaned in closer. "And you," she whispered, "are the raspberry filling in my sponge, the sugar in my tea."

"And the milk," Fiona said teasingly.

"Yes, and the milk." Lucille giggled.

Now that the bulk of the spring recipe stress was done, Lucille could turn her attention to winning her wager with Fiona. She made her way downstairs and the door that appeared in front of Lucille was familiar; it led to Fiona's favorite kitchen. She had chosen to make festooned apples. Several of the confectioners were submitting it for tasting. Lucille's first inclination was to make macaroons, but they were simple yet risky. Next, she considered making a plateau or centerpiece, but she wasn't sure what the latest fashion was; she also didn't know how to make the sugar temples or hedges that would be required to make a halfway decent garden. Her painting skills with the food dye were not to the skill that she dared to make a sugar sculpture card of the Fondant family crest. Festooned apples could be very elegant, she thought to herself.

"Moderate oven." She muttered to herself as she gathered the ingredients. If she'd had more time, she would have made the jam fresh, but instead, she chose a grape jam from the pantry. Fiona would have been able to tell her if this variety would complement orange marmalade. Everything else was easily sourced; flour, cinnamon, sugar, water, butter, salt, a bit of animal fat…what was she forgetting?

She spun around the kitchen. Apples!

Lucille carefully cored the apples, leaving a bit of extra flesh at the bottom. She consulted her recipe again. First was making the sauce, then after filling the apples, one must simply make the dough, wrap them and bake them. After a great internal debate, she decided to add minced meat. She did all the steps with trembling hands.

When she pulled the apples from the oven, she was pleasantly surprised. Nearly all turned out. The pastry had browned to warm gold, and the pleats were still defined. They looked like little parcels. She drizzled on a bit of the reserved sauce and a sprinkle of currants.

Lucille nervously surveyed the dining room table which was filled from end to end with various confections. Marty and Perry had set all of the dishes on mirrors and placed delicate sugar paste sculptures of farm animals in between the dishes. Fiona stopped at each one, took a bite, occasionally two, consulted her list, and wrote a note.

"How does this system work?" Lucille whispered to Marty.

"Lady Fiona is presented the dishes with numbers that correspond with the name of the confectioner. She is not told of their identity, of course," Marty whispered back. "Any that don't pass the inspection are noted. Exceptional ones are also noted. Dishes that are technically well made but are deemed impractical or unsophisticated are removed from the spring menu."

Lucille nodded. Fiona took a bite of several pastel macaroons. She wrinkled her nose and placed it down. The macaroons on the platter beside it, Fiona did not even bother to eat. Instead, she flipped it over, and even from her vantage point at the end of the table, Lucille could see it was burnt to a crisp. Fiona kept her face neutral, but Lucille noticed she made a smile at a lemon custard and took three bites of a pound cake adorned with flowers. Fiona frowned at both the rhubarb fool and the pastel whipt syllabub. Lucille tried not to get excited as Fiona approached the festooned apples. Four other confectioners had made festooned apples. Lucille's looked nearly identical, and to her disappointment, Fiona didn't make a discernable facial expression.

"I am done," Fiona said finally. "Invite everyone to partake in these; most of these are edible."

Marty nodded. He took the notes from Fiona's hand excitedly.

"Alright, which is yours." Fiona said with a wry smile.

"No, you must tell me," Lucille said, coming to stand beside her. "The currant cake?"

"No!" Lucille said, beaming with pride.

"Please, not the macaroons," Fiona said in mock horror.

"You insult me!" Lucille said.

"Tell me," Fiona said.

"The festooned apples."

"I am quite impressed. Truly I did not know." Fiona said, the realization slowly dawning on her face.

"Are you not excited?" Lucille said quietly.

"I am, I just…I'm very proud…" Fiona was speaking very slowly.

"We have come to assist you all with the desserts!" Perry said happily. The visiting attendants and servants, both gingerbread and human, cheered behind him.

"Yes, everyone come in." Lucille forced a smile on her face. "If you'll excuse me, I am having a headache."

Marty frowned. "Care for tea, miss or-"

"No," Lucille said, practically racing to the exit. "Thank you, I need rest." She said, calling over her shoulder.

Fiona

Fiona ignored the pain in her knees and hobbled up the stairs as quickly as she could manage.

She turned to the handle of Lucille's door, but it would not open.

"Lucille!" Fiona yelled. "Open this, I will not argue with a door."

"We are not arguing!" Lucille said. Fiona could not make out the rest of what Lucille was saying, but it did not seem pleasant.

Fiona thought for a moment. *I have to bait her into opening the door.* "You never argue; you just take out whatever the world doles out." She said loudly, enunciating slowly. She didn't believe this, but hopefully, it was enough to get a response.

"Would you like me to argue?" Lucille said, and the door flew open so fast that Fiona was shocked it was still on the hinges. "You gave me your word!" Lucille said angrily.

"It was a playful wager, Lucille. I will keep my word. I'll provide for you." Fiona said, stepping into the room. All of the gifts she'd given Lucille were laid out in neat piles.

"Are you leaving?" Fiona said sadly. "In truth, it is probably for the best."

"I can hardly make sense of anything. What is make-believe and what is true." Lucille said so quietly that Fiona was uncertain if she was meant to hear.

"I cannot provide what you need in the emotional sense, but I have more than enough financial means to-" Fiona said, her throat raw. She felt guilty, selfish, and sad all at once.

Lucile angrily turned her back and began to fold a shawl. "Cannot or will not?"

"Let us not argue semantics. It will just make us both bitter." Fiona said simply.

"Is it because of your fiancé? Is she more present than the former? Are you still in love with her?" Lucille said she didn't give Fiona a moment to answer before she said. "Is that what she wrote to you?"

Fiona scoffed. *Had Lucille been snooping around?* Fiona thought better than to ask; there wasn't anything she was hiding from Lucille.

"No," Fiona said firmly. Then she thought better of it. "I believe she wrote to me because of the gossip rag, I did not read the letter; I burned it."

"I saw the closet full of dresses, drawers full of jewels. Were those hers?" Lucille asked. Fiona could tell she was on the verge of tears.

"No. Those are for my wife. I told you I am not engaged." Fiona sighed.

"A wife and a fiancé? I'm hopelessly lost now." Lucille said. She bawled up the shawl and threw it down.

"When I marry, my wife will get all the things I've accumulated for her over the years. It is a custom, a bride gift."

"I see," Lucille said, shaking her head.

"I wish you could be her, but it is not-"

"You've spent the last few months convincing me of my value, my desirability. But I did not realize it was charity…" Lucille said. "A transaction."

"It was not. You're all the things I told you that you are and more." Fiona said, taking a step towards her.

"Then?" Lucille pressed.

"I don't wish for a wife who is galavanting across the world for her art. I need a partner." Fiona said quietly.

Lucille rolled her eyes. "Oh, as if that's all you're worried about. Respect me enough not to lie to my face like a coward. You know I would be accommodating and manage my artistic ambitions."

"I know. I know you would." Fiona said, her voice still soft.

"Do you doubt me?" Lucille asked.

"No. And that is why we cannot marry. You do not love yourself as much as I love you." Fiona said finally.

"I see. You profess your love but are exceedingly cruel." Lucille spat out.

"Listen-"

"It concerns me that you are incapable of compromise," Lucille said angrily.

"That-"

"No!" Lucille said, putting her hand up. "If you had ever truly wanted me by your side, your initial thought would not be to push me away."

Lucille motioned to the door. "Please excuse yourself, Lady Fondant. I don't wish to keep your company at the moment."

"Wait," Fiona said. "You made several strong arguments."

"Is this a test?" Lucille said, sitting down on the bed and sighing.

"No," Fiona said.

"I feel as though you've lured me onto thin ice and are about to skitter away, leaving cracks in your wake, allowing me to plunge into the depths," Lucille said.

"Now, who is speaking in metaphor?" Fiona said.

"I've been in poor company," Lucille said slowly. Fiona realized after a moment that Lucille was joking, a tentative mean joke, but a joke nonetheless.

Fiona stood there for a moment, every muscle in her body taut. She willed her jaw to unclench but could not force her body to release its tension. Fiona ignored her aching joints, although the emotional turmoil was currently causing her more pain.

"What do you want, Fiona?" Lucille said exasperatedly. "Why are you still standing here?"

She called me Fiona, that is an improvement, Fiona thought as she almost smiled, but this was not the time. The first flippant remark to come to mind was that it was her house, but she didn't want that to be misinterpreted.

"I want you to always be the portrait in my locket, I want you beside me in my kitchens, I want you in the evenings making a mess of my parlor and-" Fiona said simply.

"I don't make a mess."

"Luce, let me finish before I start gagging on my admission that I've been foolish," Fiona said.

"Hm," Was all Lucille said with a curt nod.

"I am not certain where to start; I could hire artists to teach you, you could take trips…we could adjust," Fiona said, partially apologizing, partially musing.

"You could start by apologizing," Lucille said.

"I apologize. I was simply scared." Fiona said lamely.

"Speaking of lockets. Did Bree send you the new locket?"

"What?"

"I said-"

Fiona held up her hand. "No, I heard you. I didn't get a new locket. And I told you that I've had no correspondence with her."

Lucille groaned. "But you did, I saw it."

"No, let me explain. I added your miniature to my grandfather's locket and added it to my watch chain. That is all." Fiona explained as she pulled the chain out of her pocket. "If you open it fully, you'll see your portrait."

Lucille would not look, so Fiona sighed and jammed the chain back into her pocket.

"Hmph. I would like to rest now," Lucille said, lying on the bed, fully clothed, stiff as a board, hands clasped over her stomach.

"Alright," Fiona said.

"Fiona?" Lucille asked.

"Yes?" Fiona asked, hope to rise in her chest.

"Can you close the door?" Lucille said, rolling over.

"Yes, of course," Fiona said, closing the door tightly behind her.

*L*ucille fell into a restless sleep. She opened her eyes, and for a moment, she thought she saw a gold orb floating above her. It was most certainly Fiona; for a moment, she considered calling her name, but she thought better of it, and when she reached for it, it disappeared. She blinked a few times and sat up. Her fire was out, and she was terribly cold. Lucille laid back down, pulling the covers over her head, too tired to get up and restart the fire. The morning sunlight came through in what seemed like a moment. She cursed herself for not drawing the bed or the window curtains. Lucille rolled over trying to block the light but her face touched something cold and hard. It was Fiona's watch chain, true to her word, Lucille's self-portrait, now encased by a tarnished locket dangled beside the other charms. She could see her own familiar eye in the small cutout and when she opened it, it was her doppelganger painted in oil looking back at her. "We've been foolish," she muttered to the tiny likeness. Lucille dressed and made her way to the first kitchen that appeared in front of her. Inside, Fiona was sculpting what appeared to be a sugarpaste fish.

"I believe this is yours." Lucille said, tossing the chain on the table casually.

"Did you sleep well?" Fiona asked, putting her stylus down. She eyed the chain but made no move to take it.

"No," Lucille answered truthfully.

"Nor did I, but I realized something," Fiona said solemnly.

"What is that?" Lucille said, sitting beside her and beginning to shape a sugarpaste bunny.

"I fear I am in love with you," Fiona said in the same somber tone.

"Have a ginger chew," Lucille said, pinching out too-long ear shapes.

"Is that not the remedy for nausea?" Fiona said.

"Heartburn, lovesickness, nausea, ginger is a cure-all," Lucille said, peering down at the bunny that was beginning to take form. "The proportions of the head to the body are off. Perhaps I should have used a mold."

"Is that it?" Fiona asked. "Ginger is your remedy?"

"I believe they have benefits for energy as well."

"Not what I meant, Lucille."

"What would you like me to say?"

"What do you think?" Fiona said softly.

"My apologies. I rarely do that; ask me again tomorrow." Lucille stood up and began to search the shelves for the bunny mold.

"Lucille, be serious," Fiona said, coming up behind her, putting a hand on either side of her waist.

"I love you too." Lucille felt herself spin around so fast she stumbled; she took a step, trying to catch her balance. Fiona's arms wrapped around her, clutching and supporting her as she steadied herself. She'd only regained her composure when she felt Fiona's mouth come crashing down on hers. Lucille let herself sink into Fiona, lost in the smell and taste of her until she felt something graze the top of her head. She looked up, and the pendant of the candelabra tickled her nose.

Lucille looked down. Far below them was the table littered with sugarpaste and tools. She had been so lost in their kiss that she hadn't felt her feet lift off the ground.

"Fiona, we're floating," Lucille squealed, grabbing at Fiona's biceps.

"There's nothing to weigh us down," Fiona said, kissing her again.

A Note From the Author

Dearest Reader,

I want to express my heartfelt gratitude to you for reading Sweet Nothings and Other Confections. I sincerely hope that it provided you with moments of joy, laughter, and perhaps even a new perspective on chronic illness and anxiety.

If you enjoyed the book and feel compelled to spread the word, I would be incredibly grateful if you could take a moment to leave a review. Your thoughts and feedback will not only support me as a newer author but will also help other readers discover the book and embark on their own adventures within its pages. Additionally, if you believe that this story could resonate with someone else in your life, I encourage you to share it with them.

If you'd like to stay connected with me and be among the first to know about my future releases, I invite you to sign up for my newsletter (https://tr.ee/GrkTkWcgic). Through my newsletter, I'll share exclusive content, behind-the-scenes insights, and updates on upcoming projects. It's a wonderful way to remain part of my reading community. If newsletters aren't your thing, you can follow me on TikTok or Instagram @authorsualsullivan.

Once again, thank you from the bottom of my heart for reading and for giving my book a chance. Your support means everything to me!

Happy Reading!

-Sula

Acknowledgements

I would like to take a moment to thank my incredible village, who, without their unwavering support, this novel would not have been completed. I would also like to express my gratitude to my parents and sisters. It also took a dedicated team of professionals to see this project to completion. Thank you to Chey, editor extraordinaire, Alenna Rucoba, the talented artist who brought the cover to life, and Andrew, whose formatting complimented the text amazingly.

Made in the USA
Middletown, DE
16 June 2023